I0699652

I Scream! We All Scream!

A Small Town's Post-Pandemic Orgasmic Tale

KT Nalla

Contents

Dedication

For J.G.D.K.

Tu es ma raison d'être

Chapter One

The morning seemed more foggy than rainy as the weather transitioned from rain to snow. The last bit of sun had shown on New Year's Day which was over two weeks prior. The dampness and darkness only deepened the sense of the gloom Emma felt as she made breakfast for her three-year-old son Artie, short for Arthur Michael, and two-year-old J.J., short for James Joseph. Both sons had been named after their maternal and paternal grandfathers, respectively. Emma stood in front of the kitchen sink, savoring her single maternity-permitted dose of caffeine in the form of her morning black coffee with a touch of oat milk. She hadn't yet revealed her pregnancy to her husband, Craig, after confirming via an at-home test the prior week. There was enough stress in the house right now, and she would need to find the right time to deliver the news of the impending "surprise." Her previous pregnancies had been relatively easy, but this time the stress of family life and the activity level of the boys was draining both her energy and enthusiasm for a third child.

Emma stared out into the dreariness of the morning, lost between the urgency of this day's potentially life-changing news and the drone of the hideous women of The View splathering on about some irrelevant hate-filled topic playing on the television in the next room.

"Seriously, was it a cash stipend at the door or on-the-spot lobotomies that brought the overly enthusiastic audience of women into that geriatric shit show every weekday?"

Her trance was immediately broken by the sound of breaking glass and Artie's scream.

"Look Mom, J.J. just tossed his fuckin' bowl of Cheerios across the room."

As she scrambled to address the mess, she stopped fast as her brain processed her young son's scream.

"Arthur Michael, what did you just say?" As soon as she said it, she regretted asking him for a repeat performance.

"I said he tossed his fuc...."

"STOP RIGHT THERE! Where did you learn that awful word?

We don't use words like that in our house!" "I learned it from you, Mom."

"What do you mean you learned it from me?"

"I heard you yelling at Dad last night. You said he had better get a fuckin' job soon or else—what's a soonerelse?"

Emma sat down at the kitchen table next to J.J.'s highchair. As she dropped her face into her hands from the weight of the morning events, she began to weep.

Chapter Two

Craig Mayfield walked proudly out of St. Gerard's Hospital delivery ward to inform his parents, in-laws, and young son, Artie, that a new Mayfield boy had just been born. James Joseph, named for Grandpa Jim, entered the world at eight pounds, eight ounces at precisely 8:00 p.m. Both Emma and J.J. were doing fine, and everyone would be able to visit within the hour after they were moved up to the postpartum floor.

Walking back into the labor room, Craig couldn't help but feel the weight of his testicles expand in his designer boxer briefs as he pondered his current life position and the past and future trajectory of his career and family life. At age 32, he had sired two male heirs and had recently been named a junior partner in the real estate development firm of Douglas, Ingram, Collins, Kravitz, and Stein. After Ned Kravitz and Wally Stein were added as partners ten years earlier, the firm moved away from the use of a corporate acronym in favor of a full partner enunciation by the receptionist and on letterhead. Competitors in the rough and tumble world of real estate development still referred to the firm and its partners as DICKS.

In anticipation of the new child and the promise of junior partnership, Craig had convinced Emma that it was the perfect time to expand their humble brick bungalow into a more suitable home for the up-and-coming Mayfields. Craig hired the most prominent architectural firm in Clanford to design the sprawling new home. No expense or creature comfort was spared as the home evolved. Construction began, and the home was finished, furnished, and decorated in a little over a year—just in time for the arrival of the new baby.

Craig had spent almost a full year on the first international project the firm had ever undertaken. Based in Taipei, the mixed use residential/commercial building would be a capstone for the senior partners of the firm as they promised to transition the next generation into the more lucrative partnership spots. Craig introduced the partners to the idea of the Taipei project after one of his college buddies of Taiwanese descent told Craig of the huge success his uncle was having by investing in Taipei commercial real estate. Because of the scope of the project and being the firm's first international investment, the partnership capital of the firm was leveraged well beyond the range used in domestic projects by almost four-fold. It was a big bet, but one Craig and his mentors felt was a "sure thing."

As Craig spent more time overseas, Emma resigned from her marketing position with a local residential real estate company to be a stay-at-home mom. With just a single income now, Craig continued to assure Emma that the Taipei project bonus would eliminate their very large new mortgage and car loan as well as build a nice savings balance and college fund for the boys. In addition, there would be enough excess funds to apply for membership in the very exclusive (and expensive) Butternut Club, THE golf and tennis club in Clanford.

Chapter Three

What Could Go Wrong?

Craig, Emma, and the two boys settled into a comfortable routine in the newly built home. Craig continued to travel for weeks, sometimes months, on end, and Emma toughed out the single-parent life with an infant and toddler. Emma was happy with how life was moving forward but had a continual worry about the amount of debt the couple had taken on to build and furnish the home. She looked forward to the Taipei project closing so she could breathe a little easier financially. Emma had grown up in one of the only modest neighborhoods in Clanford. Her parents were both grammar school teachers, and she was an only child. She was unaccustomed to both extravagance and debt. Craig was not a local. He grew up in the small town of Cairo, Illinois, at the confluence of the Ohio and Mississippi Rivers. His dad was a barge mechanic and his mom was a nurse's aide.

Craig was also an only child who was a less-than-stellar athlete. Instead of sporting pursuits, he focused on his grade point to ensure an easy and permanent exit from the disintegrating town of Cairo.

They met freshman year at The University of Illinois. Emma was studying marketing and working part time in the dormitory snack bar. Craig was studying finance and accounting, and he also was working part-time as a bar back in a local pub. Emma was quieter and more reserved and focused on her studies to retain an academic scholarship. Craig was smart but tended to focus on the social benefits of college life. He pledged Phi Gamma Delta his freshman year and rose to social chair his senior year.

When Emma returned to Clanford after college, Craig followed. Although he had initially pushed to move to Chicago for better opportunities, Clanford, Illinois' zip code was ranked second nationally for highest net worth per capita. Clanford would be the place for Craig to make his mark and build his career. He quickly found an associate position in real estate development, and Emma found an interesting marketing job in residential real estate. They had a quick engagement period of just six months and were married on the same date that they graduated a year earlier.

Chapter Four

Clanford, Illinois

The Ford Brothers were notorious bootleggers who plied their trade via a network of stills spread throughout the Kettle Moraine region of Southeast Wisconsin. Selling into the growing city of Milwaukee and the farm towns dotting the Wisconsin landscape, Buford "Nick" Ford and James "Pappy" Ford were becoming wealthy from their illicit business endeavors. Nick and Pappy were ten and twelve years old, respectively, when they were orphaned by the death of their mother. They were both the progeny of drunk liaisons their bootlegging mother had while conducting business. With no family to help or support them, they fired up the still the day after they buried their mother in an unmarked grave by Holy Hill.

Even though they were young and unschooled, they had a fierce business sense. The profits from the single still that their mother ran were reinvested into the business to build an increasingly large infrastructure. After just five years, they were running a total of twenty-five stills, producing ten gallons of shine per day each and employing over thirty runners. As teenagers they were running an enterprise that if legal, would have been in Wisconsin's top 50 income companies. They were brutally frugal, saving all profits that weren't being reinvested into the business. By age 18 and 20, they had become a serious threat to the taverns and breweries in Milwaukee. They had also become a major threat to the wedded bliss of many farmers. Flush with cash and youthful good looks, they charmed themselves into the beds of many frustrated farm wives in afternoon trysts as their farmer husbands tended work in the fields. Both of their nicknames were the result of these high-risk activities. Buford was caught dog-style in the milking barn with one Mary Lou Byers. Upon making his second exit, he was confronted by a gun-toting, one-eyed, bespectacled Clyde Byers, who was 20 years Mary Lou's senior. Aiming to kill as he raised his gun against the naked Buford, he missed the chest and shot off half of his penis instead. After running home naked and bandaging his bloodied unit, he claimed to his brother James, "wern't nothin' but a nick." His original endowment had allowed him to continue his social activities after convalescing, even with half splattered on the milking parlor walls.

Unlike Buford, James had chiseled good looks with a prominent cheekbone and an upturned nose. A face any aristocrat in Europe at the time would have killed for. James was much more discreet than Buford in his sexual pursuits. He brought perfumes and flowers to woo his prospects and told each of the many women he bedded that he had a true love for them. It was the local midwife who was also in James' rotation who nicknamed him "Pappy" after noticing the increasing number of newborns in the community with high cheekbones and upturned noses.

Although their sexual escapades were causing an increasing risk of personal harm, it was their business success that was truly putting their lives at risk. By 1860, there were more than fifty breweries in and around Milwaukee. Many owned attached taverns and sold to the local independent barkeeps. The increasing flow of Ford moonshine was cutting into the profits of the legal alcohol trade, and they decided to act. A consortium of the brewers met to discuss a solution. In the backroom of a bar, they decided to hire a posse of newly emigrated German twenty-somethings hungry for work and cash. They were dispatched to the Kettle Moraine to find and destroy the stills. They were deputized by the Milwaukee sheriff and told they could shoot to kill anyone getting in their way.

Word of the impending onslaught reached Nick and Pappy, and being the astute numbers guys they were, realized thirty against two was not a winning hand. They removed the boxes of cash profits they had accumulated from safekeeping, hitched their two strongest workhorses to their buckboard, and with only the clothes on their backs, two shotguns, and fifty gallons of shine, they headed south to the great state of Illinois never to return. The cash they carried to their new adventure was over $200,000 (approximatcly $10.0 million in today's dollars).

Once they crossed the Illinois border, they headed east toward Lake Michigan. After spending three nights sleeping under the wagon, they found an east-west road that they figured would bring them close to a large town. Along the road, they encountered a small way-stop tavern. It was run by a Scottish woman named Molly MacIntyre, whose husband had died on the voyage from Scotland to New York fifteen years prior. She was a tough but likable woman who loved her drink. Weighing more than Nick andPappy together, she took no bullshit from the men who traveled through looking for a stiff drink and a hot meal.

The Fords stayed with Molly for a week and in return for a bath and place to sleep, unloaded about ten gallons of shine as payment. In the evenings, Molly regaled stories of being raised in the highlands of Scotland with her large clan that numbered in the hundreds. The clan were sheep herders who were known for the highest quality wool in the highlands. They owned and controlled large treks of land and numerous towns. Both Nick and Pappy were enthralled by the thought of the large clan and the control of the finest wool products and towns. After saying goodbye to Molly and traveling eastbound, they decided that they were going to start a clan and build a reputable family and business legacy.

After two more days of travel, they entered the town of Waukegan, which was incorporated just a year earlier in 1859. It was a small town with a post office, trading post, and sheriff. There was also a land surveyor who doubled as an agent for land purchases in the area. The Fords met with the surveyor to inquire about possible large tracts of land in the area for sale. The Fords were thinking about farming as a new and reputable career. The surveyor was originally from Chicago and had been a quick study in how to swindle potential buyers on worthless land.

There was a large tract of 5,000 acres that was being sold by the estate of one of the original settlers in the area whose family now resided in Chicago. The land was about thirty miles west of Waukegan and was a combination of some forested as well as marsh land. It wasn't tillable because of the shallow water table and the dryer area was mostly wooded with hardwoods. Instead of taking them to the actual land available for sale, the land agent took the Ford brothers to see a rolling piece of property that they would envision as prime farmland. They fell hard for the land and immediately agreed to sign a purchase agreement. The land agent quoted a price of $10 per acre when the going price for prime farmland was less than half that price per acre, and the value of the actual property was a fraction of it. The Fords told him they would retrieve the $50,000 and set a date the following week to close. They met in the land agent's office and after turning over the cash, were handed the deed as well as the survey for the worthless property. The agent excused himself from the meeting, and by the time Nick and James figured out the swindle by evaluating the survey, he was long gone with their money.

The Fords were now the proud owners of 5,000 acres of pretty worthless property a day's ride from Waukegan. They spent the next several weeks staking out the property to understand exactly what they had bought. More than once, their wagon became stuck in the marshy land on the west end of the property and the forest on the east end of the property was so thick it was difficult to navigate, even on foot. They agreed that they needed to formally establish their new land as property of the Ford Clan and thereby named the property "ClanFord."

Over the next ten years, the brothers both sought out and found wives to begin the process of building the clan. Pappy again proved very prodigious, fathering eleven children, including one set of twins. Over that same period, Nick's "nick" proved problematic in allowing the regular flow of white gold needed to seal the deal for future generations. Given the available resources on their property, the brothers decided to build a sawmill and begin a lumber operation. They handled small orders for nearby neighbors and inbound Waukegan residents looking to build new homes and barns. The business was steady but mostly covered day-to-day expenses.

Everything changed on the night of October 8, 1871. Igniting that evening and burning for the next three days, the Great Chicago Fire consumed three square miles of the city, destroying 17,000 buildings and killing more than 300 Chicagoans. It would take over two weeks for word of the fire to reach the Ford brothers, but both immediately understood the opportunity that the fire would have for their business.

They rode into Waukegan and posted immediate job opportunities at the Ford Sawmill, paying double the going wage for laborers at the time. They bought up every available wagon and workhorse from businesses and farmers in the area. They felled trees and cut lumber eighteen hours a day throughout the winter, using the moonshine profits to fund their workers' labor, housing, and meals. Within six months they had cleared five hundred acres of hardwood and had fifty acres of finished inventory ready to ship to Chicago. James, being the more articulate and business-savvy of the two, took a passenger ferry from Waukegan to Chicago as soon as the ice was off the lake. He met with business leaders, construction companies, and city officials, offering the product at hefty prices, promising quick and dependable delivery. He also hired out three river barges before he received one order. It wasn't long before the orders began to materialize, and the product was being shipped down Lake Michigan in three days' time. Word of the labor opportunities at the mill became known in Chicago, where thousands of men had become jobless from the fire. They arrived by the hundreds, and the Fords offered jobs, meals, and tent lodging for everyone who was able-bodied. The pace of production required a second and then a third mill to meet the continually growing demand. Women were recruited to manage the growing need for food, clothing, and other necessities and formed a trading post right on the property. As the trading post flourished, other businesses serving the growing work force also began to appear and grow as well. Several saloons, a restaurant, and a whorehouse followed. Wages were recycled from the workers to the businesses and back to the Fords via rent and partial ownership of the new businesses. Within two years of the fire the Fords had once again built one of the most successful and profitable enterprises in the state, this time all legal. Clanford was quickly becoming the second largest town in Illinois behind Chicago. Because they were so cash-flush, the Fords began to buy up prime land in Chicago that had been devastated by the fire for pennies on the dollar, much of it on the lakefront. They then partnered with developers, requiring them to use only Ford Sawmill products. It was the equivalent of triple dipping.

Much of the marshland in Clanford was filled with debris from the fire, shipped up on the return voyages of the barges. Specific areas of the town were segregated for housing development as well as retail stores. New schools were built, and a convent and convent school were built for an order of nuns who had descended on the town to try and bring about a religious revival. They were called the Sisters of the Blessed Humility and originally had opened a home for unwed mothers, a major issue in the fast-growing and bawdy community. All the while, the demand for lumber seemed almost insatiable. Within five years of the fire, over seventy-five percent of the forested land had been cleared, making room for even more development. The Ford brothers were now multi-millionaires, focusing their efforts and finances on creating a more flourishing and respectable town. They each built massive mansions in the town center and began constructing a railroad to connect with Chicago. Workers in the sawmill were encouraged to buy shares in the development company that was building homes and businesses and buying up land that was adjacent to the original 5,000 acres. These development shares doubled and even tripled in value in a year's time, making many of the original workers wealthy in their own right. The whole area had become an immense wealth-creation machine for the happy residents of Clanford.

Over the ensuing hundred years, Clanford continued to grow, modernize, and innovate. Descendants of the original Fords, as well as descendants of the early settlers and development company investors, enjoyed the generational wealth and ease of living that their ancestors had created for them. The Butternut Country Club, opened in 1921, was the pinnacle for Clanford Society climbers. The club, named for the grove of butternut trees it was built on, had an 18-hole golf course, tennis, paddle, and pickleball courts, an Olympic size competition swimming and diving pool, and a children's pool and waterslide complex. Formal, informal, and poolside dining options were afforded the lucky membership. So coveted was a spot at the club that the waiting list for even social membership stretched years. It was the place to see and be seen. The Butternut Club Women's Auxiliary set the tone and pace for Clanford High Society inside and outside the club. Membership in the Auxiliary was often passed down from mother to daughter. It was scientifically proven that the Women's Auxiliary membership's shit really did not stink. FACT!

When Emma and Craig set down roots as a married couple, Clanford was a medium-sized but prosperous family and small business friendly town. With a population of just over 100,000, the main industry in town was wealth management, serving the generational wealth of the descendants of the original settlers. All the large banks had a presence in town, with modest signage on office fronts but lavish and often gaudy interior reception and conference rooms. In addition to the large "outside" firms, there were several Clanford-centric family office wealth managers who had built businesses combining personal wealth and outside money. These firms had a long history within the town and were seen as the most exclusive money managers. The firm topping the list of these exclusive managers was Ford, Ford, Unger, Clipper and King, second generation Fords, and early development company investors Unger, Clipper and King. The per capita wealth under management in Clanford rivaled Zurich, Switzerland.

Small business thrived in Clanford. Although luxury products were available in the designer boutiques along Michigan Avenue in Chicago ninety minutes away, the locals preferred the long-established small retailers that had rights to many of the same high-end brands, in addition to exclusive limited lines that were produced specifically for them. The pinnacle of haute couture in Clanford was found at Twink's High Fashion, run military style by owner Twink Buston-Ford, a descendant of the original Ford family.

Education trusts that were originally established by Nick and Pappy had created a public school system in Clanford that was the envy of the nation. The school district's reputation brought award-winning teachers into the area, and students' achievement scores across all grade levels were consistently off the charts. The trust endowment was so large that the school system took no money from either the state or federal education departments.

The most prestigious school in Clanford was the Clanford Academy Day School. Historically called the SBH Convent School (originally and currently run by the Sisters of the Blessed Humility catholic order), the name was changed in 1980 to reflect its growing prominence as an advanced center for learning. In addition to the "day students," the school maintained its original charter of ministering to young, unwed mothers with a boarding dormitory still housed in the original building from the early days of Clanford. The unwed mothers attended daily classes with the rest of the student population but stayed in the dormitory until their babies were born. Many of the infants were placed in loving homes through the order's adoption program so the young women could continue to pursue a top-notch education. Although the young mothers-to-be were considered part of the mainstream student population, the day schoolers often referred to them (using the historical SBH acronym) as "Sistas with Bad Habits" and "Sistas with Busted Hymens" Interestingly, the demographics of the "overnighters" was well diversified across racial, economic, and educational backgrounds. Although many had come from the Chicago area via the SBH convent on the south side, there was an equal number of young women from the most prominent families in Clanford. The unwed mother ministry was well known for lifting many young women out of poverty and providing them with life-changing opportunities via the coveted education they received. Over the years, many of the SBH "Sistas" had risen to prominent positions in the corporate, legal, and medical fields, one becoming a Supreme Court Justice.

Medical care in Clanford was one of the many bragging rights of the town. The Clanford Medical Society was equally as financially endowed as the school system and was the governing body of the medical facilities in town. The hospital system included a heart center, cancer research center, and world-renowned rehabilitation center. Patients traveled from around the world to visit Clanford's hospitals for care.

The known wealth of Clanford citizens brought in the best top chefs and restauranteurs, the high-end car and yacht dealerships, prestigious travel companies, and the highest of highest jewelers. Everything one "needed" was available within the community.

Life in Clanford was very special, and the very special people of Clanford reveled in their daily lives. The sign at the entry to town read, "Welcome to Clanford, Where There is Never an Unhappy Day." And so stood Clanford on the eve of what would soon be known as the COVID-19 Pandemic of 2020.

Chapter Five

What the Fuck?

Craig was rushing to the Taipei airport to catch the last flight of the day back to Chicago when he received a panicked call from Emma.

"Craig, are you still going to make it home today?"

"That's what I'm shooting for. Fucking dickhead driver had car trouble, and I had to flag down a cab to get me here in time. Should be pulling up to departures in about ten minutes."

"Craig, I'm scared..."

"Emma, what's the problem? Are the boys okay?"

"Yes, the boys are fine—it's the news stories on this weird disease that is spreading all over the world. They are talking about shutting down the country to stop its spread."

"Emma, what are you talking about? I have been tied up 24/7 for the last three days trying to finalize negotiations on this deal. Let me check my news feed."

Emma continued, "It's some type of respiratory flu that is killing people quickly. Said it may have started in China. Are you feeling okay? Have you been around anyone sick over the past few days?"

"I'm feeling fine and no, I haven't noticed anyone sick at the law firm where we were meeting."

"Okay, just get home as soon as you can. I really am scared."

After fourteen hours in the air, Craig's flight landed uneventfully at O'Hare International. It was what happened after the landing that began a slow panic in Craig. After the flight reached the gate, a ramp attendant in a full hazmat suit entered the plane. Craig was sitting in first class and could see him as he crossed into the aircraft. He picked up the intercom phone and began a muffled but very serious announcement on exiting procedures into the airport. Everyone needed to present their passports to him before they could exit. Chinese nationals would line up against one wall of the exit passage, and all others, including U.S. citizens, would line up against the opposing wall. Everyone would be checked with a handheld thermometer for any sign of an elevated temperature. All Chinese nationals would be subjected to a nasal swab.

After passing the temperature test, Craig proceeded through immigration and customs. The scene continued to be surreal. All employees were dressed in hazmat suits, including gloves and full-face gear. After retrieving his bag and exiting the international concourse, he noticed the complete lack of passengers or awaiting families. The airport was completely empty, and he quickly realized it had been closed to any outgoing flights. The driver he had pre-hired for the 90-minute drive to Clanford was ghosting him so he had to bribe a city taxi $500 to take him home.

On the drive to Clanford, he voraciously scanned his phone for updated news on the health scare. President Trump had called for a complete shutdown of the country to "slow the spread" of this mysterious disease. Some people claimed it was chemical warfare created in a Chinese lab and released into the biosphere. Others claimed it was a virus that "jumped species" from animals to humans in a Chinese meat market. It was so confusing and unnerving.

Craig immediately began to worry about the Taipei development deal. They were within days of finalizing the financing to close the deal and receive the bulk of the firm's earnest money back into its accounts. His bonus and his partnership were on the line with the success of this deal. Was it possible that this could derail the deal and allow the Singapore bank to back away from its funding commitment? He had read Mac (Material Adverse Change) clauses hundreds of times before but always considered them boilerplate language. Could a world health scare really be a Mac? Could he lose his funding that quickly? Could the construction company then keep the earnest money? His head was spinning, and he began to feel nauseous. No reason to go there yet. Stay Cool. Stay focused. Reach out to Mr. Chen in Taipei overnight when it will be the beginning of his business day in Taiwan. He tried to close his eyes and relax, but the effort was futile.

Emma met him at the door wearing a face mask and gloves and holding a container of Clorox disinfectant wipes. She asked Craig to put all his clothes in the bag, wipe off the luggage with the wipes, and shower in the basement before coming upstairs to see the boys. She would fill him in on all that was happening after he showered.

Craig couldn't believe what was happening. As he took a long hot shower, concern for the deal continued to bring thoughts of financial catastrophe. No deal, no bonus. No bonus, no mortgage relief, let alone payoff. No mortgage relief, no keeping the new house...Where did it end??

Even worse, if the deal cratered, he knew in his heart that not only would his partnership offer be at risk, but his actual job would also be at risk. Everything was crashing down around him. Mental fatigue was setting in, and he became weak in his knees. He quickly finished showering and put on the clean sweats Emma had laid on the basement guest room bed. Now was NOT the time to bring any of this up. Emma did not need to be worried about this yet. He needed time to understand the whole picture and devise a plan for each potential outcome. This is what Craig excelled at, creative problem-solving. This was his hallmark at work. Give him the facts and he could figure out a solution. He just needed all the facts as soon as possible.

Emma had dinner ready. She and the boys had baked and decorated a "Welcome Home Dad" cake. The baking activity helped keep both her mind and the boys occupied. Emma didn't need to have Craig lay out all of the horrible potential financial ramifications of the pandemic. She had already thought through all of the worst-case scenarios on her own. She better than Craig understood the monthly finances and monthly cash burn. Her frugal upbringing had made her keenly aware of the price of everything. Even before they built the new house, she had watched every penny and clipped coupons for groceries. Craig, technically, did not receive a salary. He was given a monthly draw against the annual firm profits that were set aside for non-partners at the end of the year. The size of each non-partner draw was designed to cover reasonable living expenses while keeping the employees hungry to work hard and boost firm profitability. Before the new house, Emma had been able to structure a budget that covered all expenses, left money for entertainment, and secretly squirreled away several hundred dollars per month into a rainy-day fund. When they took on the new mortgage, Craig had also taken a home equity loan that he was using each month to pay the incremental amount of the mortgage. This was intended to be very temporary until the deal closed and the large bonus was received. Luckily, they owned Emma's five-year-old minivan outright, but there was a monthly payment due on Craig's BMW 700 series (he had to look and act like a baller in his industry). Emma thought that if they sold the house quickly, they might be able to recoup some equity. Just like Craig, she was coming up with escape options for the worst-case scenarios.

After dinner, Craig helped Emma get the boys to bed and clean the kitchen. He cracked a Corona Light and poured Emma a glass of Sauvignon Blanc. They sat in the sprawling new family room and awkwardly tried to make sense of what was happening while at the same time appearing in complete control of their respective emotions. Craig feigned confidence that the Taipei deal would remain on track and close shortly. Even if he couldn't travel back for closing, he was sure that they could sign the documents electronically. He just needed everyone, everywhere, to stay calm and let this whole pandemic thing roll through over the next two, max three weeks. Emma shared that her close friend Kathleen, who was an ER nurse at St. Gerard's, felt that all of the hype was unwarranted. This, in fact, was an outright lie. Emma had spoken to Kathleen's husband, who said that she was required to stay at the hospital because the place was under siege. Kathleen was working constant shifts, taking turns with the other nurses and doctors, getting a few hours of sleep in the resident on- call rooms. St. Gerard's was asking all Clanford that only the most vulnerable and sickest patients be brought in. The mortalities were quickly rising but the mayor and hospital president had agreed to keep numbers under wraps.

Emma and Craig went to sleep that night both believing that they had convinced the other that there was really nothing to get worried about. All the while, they both knew that they were in for some very scary times ahead.

Chapter Six

The Shit Show Arrives!

The unfolding of events came fast and hard. Emma took control of the domestic side as she focused on getting the house supplied with food and toiletries for the long haul. Grocery store shortages of basic necessities, as well as disinfectant wipes and sprays, set off a panic in the town. Her moms' text group was useful at first in finding availability for many items at the various retail stores but soon turned full Hunger Games when misinformation was being posted to keep many of the moms off the scent of new deliveries.

Emma was determined to fund all of the non-mortgage monthly needs out of her rainy-day fund, which had grown to almost $15,000 by the time the pandemic started. Nothing was wasted. Food was stretched for as many meals as possible. Alcohol was limited to one twelve-pack of Corona Lights and two bottles of Kim Crawford per week. Mentally, she knew that these would be the first two items jettisoned off the grocery list if things continued to tighten. She started a children's clothing exchange group with women from her church to pass clothing between families as sizes changed. Even though local restaurants were struggling with the mandatory closures, she could not worry about their livelihoods when her own family's was at risk. Every day, she was in battle mode. Her first focus was on keeping the boys happy, safe, and engaged. No small task, given the northern Illinois weather in March and April was mostly cold and rainy. She counted the days until summer, hoping that by then, the world would right itself, and if not, at least she could be outside with the boys most days.

Craig was almost completely absent from home for the first three weeks of the lockdown. Because of mandatory office closures, the DICKS team had set up a war room in Wally Stein's home which was a 20,000-square-foot monument to himself and his third wife, "Bunny." Although Bunny was long on breast tissue and short on cranial neurons, as well as twenty-five years Wally's junior, she was a great hostess, providing the team with ample eats and even more ample eye candy. She had an interesting habit of always bending at the waist when she inadvertently dropped something around the team, revealing an ample caboose that JLo would have coveted. Even with many, many square feet of boudoir separation in the house, Bunny could be heard late at night squealing and giggling as Wally cried out More, More, Oh God, STOP! During this time of corporate and personal peril, the "WUNNY" (think BRANGELINA) nocturnal escapades allowed the rest of the team a slight smile as they slipped off into another night of fitful sleep.

All eyes were on Craig to fix the Taipei problem and quickly get the cash back into the firm. Although the partners had voted unanimously to approve the Taipei venture, it quickly became Craig's problem to solve, so much so that the deal was now being referred to as "Craig's deal" as opposed to the original deal name of "Project Slant" (Old man Douglas, the most senior and least self-aware partner gave it the original name).

The first blow came within days. The Singapore bank that had agreed to finance the construction of the building, rescinded their financing offer based on, wait for it, a Material Adverse Change, just as Craig had feared. Craig had their lawyers doing research to see if the Taiwanese laws could protect them against the pulled financing. Unfortunately, the laws in Asia were more lender than investor- friendly.

The challenge now was to ease the fears of the Taiwanese investors and construction company that the DICKS had partnered with to complete the project. Under the terms of the partnership agreement, the DICKS' $40 million of capital was placed as the first loss to attract the remaining $110 million of equity capital to secure what was supposed to be $850 million of financing to cover the $1.0 billion construction completion cost. The first loss capital was used to secure the "dirt" to build on and give a non-refundable deposit to the construction company to purchase initial construction materials and secure sub-contractors. Under the terms of the partnership, once construction began, 90% of the DICKS' capital was going to be purchased by an additional investor for 50% of their ownership, leaving them with only $4.0 million of capital left in the deal and still retaining 13% of the completed building's value. As structured, the deal provided considerable upside for the DICKS but held the possibility of almost a complete wipeout on the downside.

Craig pleaded with Mr. Chen to facilitate a conference call with the remaining Taiwanese investors, the construction company as well as the prospective buyout investors for the DICKS' capital. He wanted to assure them that with a little bit of time, the markets would settle, and they could re-engage with the existing bank or find another bank eager to partner with them on such a fantastic deal. Mr. Chen, it soon became apparent, had some personal upside in seeing the deal unwind. He was the brother-in-law of the construction company owner, who contractually had the first right of the first loss capital to secure his "upfront expenses." A certified invoice was prepared by the construction company itemizing exactly $40 million of upfront expenses in materials and sub-contractor commitments essentially wiping out all of theDICKS capital. The construction company was one of the largest in the region and had the market heft to cancel any materials or sub-contracts without penalty. Essentially, by tanking the deal, they received a no-risk windfall of $40 million whereby Mr. Chen received a complimentary 15% finder's fee.

THE DICKS WERE FUCKED! The $40 million they had pledged to the deal was more than 80% of the firm's retained capital. The five capital partners of the firm had most of their net worth held in the business. The $10 million of capital left meant that each partner's shares had dropped in value to only $2 million each. In the town of Clanford they had quickly been demoted from wealthy to also-rans. As news spread of the firm's demise, Bunny hightailed her tight ass out of Wally's house and took up with the younger and supposedly more endowed (financially, of course) owner of the Clanford Motorcycle Shop. Local gossip claimed that in learning to ride a motorcycle, she spread her legs almost as much daily as she did when courting old Wally. Poor Wally put the Casa d'Bunny on the market for half of what he had invested in building it and still had no buyers ever materialize. He was found dead months later when his former housekeeper came looking for her final paycheck. The coroner ruled his death accidental by asphyxiation. He choked while eating an order of Hasenpfeffer in bed.

Chapter Seven

Craig returned home after three weeks with no job, no partnership, no bonus, and no possible prospects of gainful employment anytime soon. Emma had prepared herself for the worst one week into his absence. Ever the optimist, she met Craig at the door and first comforted him but quickly shifted the conversation to what the next "adventure" for the family would be. Craig smugly replied, "Most likely bankruptcy."

Emma would have none of it. She couldn't allow a moping husband to ruin the "COVID feng shui" she had created in her home. Lysol wipes always faced north, while diaper wipes were eastern bearing. Only pure vegetable-induced stools could linger in the diaper pail. Most importantly, there were two children to keep busy and happy. Craig would have to figure it out.

The first weeks of lockdown found Emma and Craig living pretty separate lives. The Mayfield Manse, with over 6500 square feet of "smart modern," still was not large enough for the family of four and the added inhabitants of worry, fear, and anxiety. Emma did the best she could, attending to the rituals of daily life. Luckily, Emma had convinced her mother just weeks prior to the pandemic to invest in an iPhone so she could share pictures of the boys with her and show her how to create photo albums on her phone. Since her father was a lifelong diabetic and her mother was asthmatic, she demanded that they stay quarantined in their home, even from their only child and grandchildren. Given the physical distance, Emma walked her mother through the process of FaceTiming which began a daily ritual of morning, afternoon, and bedtime virtual visits. Seeing and talking to her parents allowed Emma to regain some semblance of normalcy. Even though the topics remained fairly constant each day, she watched the clock anticipating each new visit.

Craig, on the other hand, was struggling to adapt to his new reality. Although he had a history as a partier, he also was always a hard and conscientious worker. He took pride in his work and, more importantly, in his success. Although the new home had a dedicated gym space in the walkout basement, the gym equipment had never been ordered in lieu of family room furnishings. He had already specked out the latest Techno gym package of weight and cardio training equipment. Just needed that bonus check to get it in the queue. Now, as he perused the internet for new and used gym equipment, he realized that demand and supply had moved the fitness equipment even farther out of their budget.

"What the fuck! These goddam used Peloton bikes are trading at double the retail price, given new orders are taking 18 months. Even simple rowers are almost $1,000!"

He tried running in the neighborhood, but it seemed it was only placing more emphasis on the fact that he wasn't working. He decided that physical fitness would have to wait. He needed to focus on his job search.

The job prospects were growing thinner by the day. Everyone was now working "remotely." WTF? He searched LinkedIn hourly, and nothing showed up for any kind of real estate finance position. He would even consider an analyst role if it could get him back in the saddle. Having his DICKS experience on his resume was not helping very much. The whole market knew about the busted deal and the meltdown of the firm. Other members of the team had been scapegoating him in real estate development chatrooms. He was the fall guy. All the other DICKS needed to find jobs too, and one less man in the pack would be helpful to them. He tried staying up to speed on the markets by incessantly watching CNBC, but the state of the world only deepened his depression. His days were long and oppressive, with no reasonable end in sight.

Craig took to staying up late at night and sleeping well past eleven in the morning. This schedule allowed him only limited time in front of Emma. He had a hard time facing her, given how much he had taken. Their modest but comfortable first home, the security of a balanced family budget, and the closeness of a marriage built on shared goals. He saw only failure when he looked in the mirror each morning and struggled to keep himself together.

His sleep-inducing drug of choice each night as he watched the wall-mounted television in his office, was a twelve-pack of Corona Extra and a box of Little Debbie Swiss Cream Rolls. Even though Emma had severely restricted the weekly alcohol purchases in the new budget, Craig had found a loophole.

One Saturday morning when he had taken Emma's minivan for gas, he had inadvertently pulled out his corporate credit card to insert in the gas pump. It wasn't until after the sale was approved and the gas was flowing that he realized his mistake. "Hmmmm, that was interesting," he thought. He knew that the firm was officially shut down, but also remembered that Mary Swanson the controller, was still working to close all loose ends. Could she have possibly overlooked the credit cards? In reality, Mary was no fool. She was devastated by the firm's demise and, in her role as unofficial overseer, had planned to extract as much revenge as possible. Before the partners had the chance to extract what cash was still in the accounts, she paid off the corporate credit card balance. The corporate cards were structured as one single account with sub-accounts for each of the employees' given expense account privileges. Once paid off, she reasoned that she had 60 days to run up as many expenses as possible before the bank would cut the cards off for non-payment. They could then get in line with the other unsecured creditors of the firm. She wasted no time. The first purchases were new furnishings for her home. She spared no expense on new furniture, appliances, and carpets. She wasn't concerned that this would raise eyebrows with the card company because she had overseen refurnishing the offices the prior year. Plenty of furniture and rugs had been put on the card. Even if delivery might be delayed, she didn't mind waiting. Next was the purchase of gift cards on each of the major airlines in amounts totaling over $100,000. Again, she wasn't concerned about fraud alerts because the monthly travel bills were always close to six figures. She planned to double dip on this over the course of the two months. She charged weekly groceries and spent hours on Amazon buying as much as she could. Who would question Amazon or groceries when the whole country was stockpiling food and binging on Amazon products? To add insult to injury, she also cashed out the credit card reward miles on a two-week cruise for her family of four planned twelve months forward.

Curious as to whether the card charge was a fluke, Craig walked across the parking lot from the gas station into the Piggly Wiggly grocery store. There, he picked up a Sports Illustrated magazine, two Snicker bars, and a 20-ounce bottle of Diet Dr. Pepper. He decided to use the self-checkout line so that if the card was declined, he would simply leave the small bag of groceries on the bagging shelf and walk out the doors. After scanning the four products, he inserted the card in the payment slot and held his breath. Sale approved! BINGO! He felt like Macauley Culkin's character in Home Alone II when his dad's credit card is accepted at the Plaza Hotel. "It worked!" He now had a source of cash for which he didn't have to account. Fuck his old firm. Let them try and come after him.

And so it began. Each night after bathing the boys and getting them to bed, Emma retreated to the master bedroom to read in bed while Craig retired to his office to begin his nightly television binge. Emma was usually asleep by 9:00 o'clock, 9:30 at the latest. Once he confirmed her slumber, Craig would slip out the back door of his office and drive to the "Pig," local slang for the Piggly Wiggly. There, he would buy an ice-cold twelve-pack of Corona and add a value pack of Little Debbie's, which held eight individually wrapped two-packs of the deliciously chocolate Swiss rolls. Deep into the night, he drank and ate until all liquids and solids were consumed.

Well buzzed and slightly hyperglycemic, he would clean up all evidence of his gluttony, quietly deposit his empty bottles across several neighbors' recycling containers, return home and stumble up into bed. He drifted off to sleep into a recurring dream of closing the Taipei deal and winning his firm's Deal of the Year award. Emma beamed with pride as he accepted the award. He beamed with self-pride. This night, like all previous nights, reality had once again been banished to the clutches of cerveza fria.

Even though he became addicted to and greatly anticipated this nightly reality-numbing tradition, it was not without pain the following mornings. A pounding headache accompanied the fog of nausea moving through him as Emma reminded him, quite loudly, that the morning was just about history and his ass had better get to job hunting post haste. In addition to her persistent attacks on his laziness, she added insult to injury when she commented one morning that he was becoming a fat ass. This probably stung the most since Craig had always been proud of his athletic physique in spite of the fact that he was never an athlete. The cycle of this nightly ritual and the resultant morning berating had increased the level of stress in the Mayfield home to an almost unbearable level. Craig had no intention of giving up his nightly pleasure but needed to figure out how to get Emma off his back. Then he remembered it. Mr. Chen's man-up pills.

Chapter Eight

MAN-UP! ORIGIN

As the deal team lead for Project Slant, Craig was responsible for not only helping to structure the transaction but also to keep the interested investors close at hand and fully engaged. In addition, he needed to negotiate with the prospective funding sources and construction companies. Since this was the firm's first international investment, Craig also had to deal with the physical distance, the time change difference, and the cultural differences between business practices in Taiwan and the United States. This is where his introduction to Mr. Chen became invaluable.

Mr. Chen was a forty-something Taiwanese National who had grown up in both Taipei and San Francisco. Craig was introduced to Mr. Chen by his college roommate's uncle. Once the introduction was made, the uncle fell quickly out of the picture. According to Mr. Chen, his father was a lumber broker, and his mother was an obstetrician. Craig was only introduced to him as "Mr. Chen" and never was able to learn a first name. Interestingly, when he googled the surname and Taipei, thousands of Chens appeared with similar likenesses, but none that perfectly matched his new partner. Mr. Chen was an enigma but, apparently, a well-connected one.

Craig remembered the first physical meeting of the two men. Mr. Chen told Craig to meet him in the bar at the Mandarin Oriental Hotel on

Dunhua North Road in Taipei. Craig would recognize him among the many Taiwanese men in the bar by the bright blue sports coat he would be wearing. So very cloak and dagger. When Craig entered the bar, even in the low light of early evening, his eye was immediately drawn to the electric blue jacket Chen was wearing sitting at a small table in the back. As Craig approached him, he jumped up and came toward him with an open hand and a wide smile. He aggressively grabbed Craig's right hand and shook it strongly.

"Mr. Mayfield, so nice to meet you."

"Please call me Craig. It is a pleasure to meet you as well, Mr. Chen. What should I call you?"

"Mr. Chen, of course."

Craig had done considerable homework on the Taipei luxury residential market as well as the growing demand for commercial retail spaces. The commercial real estate market in Taiwan was growing at double digits, with even more explosive growth in the Xinyi district of the city. Mixed-use luxury apartments with ground- level retail space were a sure bet if Craig could attract additional equity investors as well as make connections into the commercial construction network of the city. Craig could have just as easily been doing business on the moon, given how foreign the whole process was to him.

Mr. Chen laid out the ground rules for making introductions into his network. Mr. Chen would attend all meetings. He would allow Craig to present the investment/construction opportunity to each of the interested parties. Mr. Chen would then confer with the meeting participants and only allow Craig to answer their questions through him. Every one of the meetings began with Mr. Chen giving what Craig assumed was the background and highlights of the proposed opportunity, always in their native Mandarin. Craig usually sat across the table from at least four meeting attendees who were stone-faced and usually chain-smoking. Smoking indoors! During his entire lifetime, Craig had never seen anyone smoke indoors. Smokers were usually relegated to some small area outside of office buildings where they huddled daily, indifferent to weather or side eyes from the more enlightened office workers. Craig had zero idea of what they were thinking because they had no facial expressions whatsoever. At the end of the meeting they typically rose from their chairs and exited without any pleasantries. They are certainly a tough crowd and acted very differently from participants in U.S. meetings where the ice was typically broken ahead of meetings with topics ranging from the latest sporting events to recently played golf courses.

In Taipei, Mr. Chen had complete control of everything. This gave Craig an immense amount of anxiety because he was used to having control of his projects and, thereby, his destiny. Although Craig knew the interested parties spoke and read English (his PowerPoint presentations were in English), he was annoyed that all conversations between them and Mr. Chen were always in Mandarin. What was Mr. Chen hiding? What promises was he making to these people that Craig might have to live with but had no knowledge of? Were they scheming to complete the deal and box Craig and the DICKS out or structure something that left them without the value they were anticipating? These questions were constantly swirling in

Craig's head. Each day he steeled himself against these thoughts to push on and make the deal happen. The success of this deal would be life-changing for Craig and Emma, and Craig never lost sight of that fact.

Weeks of meetings turned into months. Craig often woke in the morning not knowing exactly where he was or what his schedule for the day would be. Everything blended together: time, meetings, hotels, and meals. It took a double espresso upon rising for Craig to snap back into reality and get his bearings. The time differential made it tough to have regular calls with Emma, especially when Craig was attending "mandatory" evenings of dining and drinking with prospective investors. It was a long slog, but Craig kept the ultimate prize in his sights.

The more time Craig spent with Mr. Chen, the more peculiar Chen became in Craig's mind. He would go silent for several days at a time, leaving Craig with postponed meetings and more dead time in the hotel room and gym. Then, out of nowhere, he would reappear, literally at Craig's hotel room and hurry him off to an unplanned but very important meeting. When Craig asked for updates on converting interest to commitments from all these meetings, Mr. Chen would reply that everything was "on track." What the fuck did "on track" mean? More than once, Craig wanted to tell Chen to go fuck himself, pack his bag and get the fuck out of this ass-backward deal. How could someone do business like this? This was an alternative universe for Craig, who was used to having meetings, making presentations, engaging in due diligence dialogue, and hearing back in a reasonable timeframe if the investors were in or out. One of the hardest parts of this whole process was trying to manage his expectations and figure out what Mr. Chen was up to.

The DICKS $40 million capital commitment to the project was sufficient to start garnering real interest from other equity investors in the deal, almost all of them local. Slowly, the painstaking process began to bear fruit. After three months of meetings, Mr. Chen called Craig and said he had a "fishy on the line." "Fishy?? Really? WTF? Be it a fishy or a fish, Craig was excited to get more details immediately. He and Mr. Chen met for lunch at a local cafe next to the Mandarin Oriental. Over plates of hot spicy beef noodles, Chen laid out what his first investor looked like. It was a local insurance company looking to diversify into the luxury real estate market. Historically, they were strip mall investors. They had plenty of available cash and would consider an investment of up to $50 million on terms very close to those outlined in Craig's presentation and term sheet. Craig couldn't believe it. $50 million was almost half of the $110 in equity they needed to close the equity book and move on to engaging a bank to finance the remainder and a construction company to commit.

Mr. Chen proceeded to outline some of the "stips" (stipulations) that the investor wanted to clarify. First, the construction needed to be completed in 36 months from the time they broke ground. Craig knew from experience that this was very possible, at least his U.S. experience told him so, and thought to himself that this was not an unreasonable ask. Second, the investment funds would be escrowed and disbursed only after the initial $40 million from the DICKS had been utilized. Again, not too tough of a give. Third, the insurance company would have an approval right on who the other $60 million of equity investment came from. Craig wasn't crazy about this but figured they could make it work one way or the other. He wasn't going to lose such a large potential investment over a deal point he felt confident he could manage when the time came. Fourth, and just as important, the investment team wanted to spend some serious time with Craig to get to know him as a person and potential partner in the deal. No brainer! Craig's role as social chair for the FIJI's at Illinois had prepared him well for this challenge. Language barrier be damned! Craig was born to party and would draw on his many, many, many invaluable college experiences to seal the deal.

Mr. Chen laid out the details for the first evening of getting to know each other. The investor deal team consisted of four men ranging in age from twenty-five to forty-three. When Craig was first introduced, he could hardly tell each of them apart, let alone try and figure out who was the senior versus junior members of the team. They all spoke English but with varying degrees of proficiency. Craig would realize later that the level of their language proficiency was inversely proportional to the amount of alcohol they consumed. The evening was to start with dinner at Lin Dong Fang, one of the top restaurants in the city. When Craig heard the name, he chuckled to himself, thinking that the words "dong" and "fang" should never be placed anywhere in proximity to each other, let alone the real things. OUCH! Even though the usual wait list for reservations was weeks, if not months, somehow Mr. Chen's connections managed a table in the main dining room where diners coveted the prime "to be seen" spots. Dinner was multi-coursed, with the appropriate wine pairings complementing each dish. As each new course was delivered, Mr. Chen conferred with the sommelier, in Mandarin of course, which made Craig cringe at the thought of the impending tab. Dinner consisted of three hours of casual conversations as Craig strained to keep the dialogue moving. He also strained to understand what they were saying as the very expensive wine flowed. Dinner ended, and Craig paid the bill, intentionally not looking at the final amount. That he would deal with later, they had a fishy on the line, actually four fishies and he intended to land them all.

The evening progressed to the nightlife district. Specifically, his new partners were interested in a particular dance club that was also considered one of the hottest spots in the city. A dance club? Craig began to feel like a broken record, WTF! Were these four nerds going to get up and dance or what? He began to feel very, very uncomfortable but kept the all-important end game front and center in his mind. When they arrived at Taboo (Jesus!), Mr. Chen instructed Craig to slip the bouncer a couple of "Benjamins" (Benjamins?? Benjamins??) to expedite their entry into the darkened club. In a scene right out of The Godfather, Craig folded three $100 bills horizontally and gently stuffed them into the breast pocket of the bouncer's bedazzled, taboo black and purple sports jacket, lifted his sunglasses (which he put on to add to his "American player" persona) and winked at the moonlighting sumo wrestler as he led the group in. Craig had a flashback to the frat house "butler," Mr. P., who kept the place in working order and as clean as was humanly possible given the juvenilesque residents. His famous line to the frat boys, as they showered and primped ahead of their Saturday night escapades, was always, "If youse wants to be impotant, youse gots to look impotant!" Craig was certainly both feeling and looking "impotant" as he dove into the Taipei dance club scene with reckless abandon.

***

Craig couldn't identify the light buzzing sound that was recurring in his brain as he began to regain consciousness. The buzzing would run a few minutes, then stop. Run a few minutes, stop. He couldn't quite grasp the source of the sound or whether it was real or part of a disjointed dream. Finally, he was able to begin lifting his eyelids as his head pivoted sideways on his pillow. It hurt to move. It hurt to think about moving. He closed his eyes and waited and waited for a generous death to arrive. Unfortunately, death did not come, but the incessant buzzing began again. It sounded like his phone, but a very muffled phone ring. With the next series of buzzing, Craig regained some sense of feeling in his lower extremities. The phone was somehow wedged between the cheeks of his ass. Wowowooo! How did that get there? He tried to turn over and reach down to remove the phonoloscopy, but his entire body was disengaged from his brain. As it buzzed again, he began to laugh quietly and thought of all of the jokes he could talk about to his buddies in the firm at some later date. In the meantime, he needed to figure out who was trying to reach him so desperately. As he began the process of retrieving the phone, he became worried. Had he taken a shit after he showered for the night out with the Taipei dancing crew? Usually, that was his morning, not evening ritual, but he had no sense of what day, let alone what time it was. The blackout curtains in the hotel room disguised any clues as to the time of day or night.

He was finally able to kick the sheets off the bed and began to maneuver his hand toward the phone, which was buzzing again. He quickly realized he was stark naked with no recollection of how he came to such a state. Usually, he slept topless in a pair of loose-fitting sweats. He grasped the phone, held it up to his nose, and thankfully realized it was clean but still a little moist from bed sweat. He didn't move quickly enough to answer the latest attempt but was shocked to see his screen read 86 missed calls.

"86 missed calls, HOLY SHIT!"

As he began to scroll down his recent call log, he saw that the missed calls were from a combination of his office, his wife Emma, and most recently from Mr. Chen. As he was scrolling down further, he jumped as the phone began to ring again in his hand. It was Emma. When he picked up, she screamed.

"CRAIG—WHERE THE FUCK HAVE YOU BEEN? WE'VE BEEN TRYING TO REACH YOU FOR THREE DAYS!"

"Three days, what are you talking about? It's Saturday morning, isn't it?"

"SATURDAY? IT'S ELEVEN P.M. YOUR TIME ON MONDAY!"

"Emma, slow down," Craig begged. "I need to get a grasp of what is going on here."

As he sat up in bed, he saw that the clothes he had worn to the club were sitting on the dresser across the room: pants, socks, boxers, and shirt, all perfectly folded and symmetrically arranged.

"CRAIG, ANSWER ME! WHERE HAVE YOU BEEN? I'VE BEEN SICK WITH WORRY! EVEN THE GUYS FROM YOUR OFFICE WEREN'T SURE OF YOUR WHEREABOUTS SINCE YOU HAVE MOVED HOTELS SEVERAL TIMES OVER YOUR STAY."

"Emma, I just woke up. I've been in bed since Saturday night or Sunday morning whenever I returned from my night out with our investors' team. I have no idea what happened. I'm trying to remember where I was last with those guys. I do recall a dance club, but only vaguely.I don't even remember how I got back to my hotel."

Craig purposely left out the parts about being naked in bed with his clothing neatly folded. He would have to figure all of that out when his memory returned.

"Craig, you need to get this deal done and get home. This isn't healthy for any of us. I know how important it is for us, but I'm becoming worried about your safety. Please take a break and come home," she pleaded.

"Baby, let me get my bearings here and figure out what happened. Maybe I was slipped some kind of knockout drug. I'm fine now. Let me check my emails and voicemails and call you back in the morning tomorrow. I love you! Hugs and kisses to the boys."

"I love you too! Please be safe. We all need you on this end." Craig laid his head back on his pillow.

"Holy fuck, what the hell happened?" he said out loud to no one.

He tried desperately to remember what had happened over the previous seventy-two hours. He closed his eyes and rubbed his temples. His head was pounding. He needed some Advil right away. The Keurig coffee machine sat on the small wet bar in the room. The first step: coffee. He stood up quickly and immediately fell back onto the bed.

"Whoa! What the fuck?"

Could his leg muscles have atrophied that quickly? He tried again slowly, and though he was wobbly, he soon realized the reason for his lack of strength. Without a light to confirm his suspicions, he breathed in the strong scent of vomit. Not a small whiff but a large punch in the face smell. He slowly moved toward the bathroom and switched on the light. The sudden optic shock made him wince. When he refocused his eyes, he was confronted with what he would later compare to a crime scene. Sprayed across the bathroom cabinetry, toilet, shower glass, and floor was a reddish-orange coating of pure digestive retaliation. The volume was incomprehensible. The coverage was consistent with that of an application by a spray paint gun. How could there be so much? How did it project in so many directions? He envisioned a temporary possession like the girl in the movie Exorcist, with his head spinning 360 as he expelled an even more dangerous form of "evil spirit" than Satan himself.

"HOLY FUCK!"

He suddenly had the urge to piss. As he tried to maneuver toward the toilet, he realized the coating of personal shame on the bathroom interior was completely dry. He stood in front of the toilet to relieve himself and began to concoct a story to tell the hotel maid when she came to freshen the room. There wasn't enough perfume in France to freshen this room. That would be tomorrow's problem.

He finished and returned to the bedroom. He slipped on his boxers and noticed a long white piece of paper sitting next to his clothing, also neatly folded. It was a restaurant receipt from a place called Taboo.

"Ohhhhh, Taboo!"

He unfolded the long receipt and gasped as he saw the total at the bottom. $26,850.00 which included a generous $10,000.00 tip.

'HOLY FUCK!!! I AM TOTALLY FUCKED!!!" he screamed.

Screaming was not a good idea. He immediately began to dry heave and quickly returned to the bed. He laid flatly and breathed deeply, desperately trying to get the nausea to pass. In a few minutes, he regained a more stomach-stable condition. As he laid on the bed he began to reconstruct the events of his evening out.

Taboo was that creepy dance club that the insurance investment team insisted on visiting after dinner. The place was dark, and the music was a combination of U.S. cover dance songs and some K-Pop shit that had the dance floor mostly covered with girl couples dancing. A scantily dressed waitress approached the table with a light-up menu offering exorbitantly priced libations. For the first time since he had met these guys, he saw something other than the usual dull, lifeless expressions on their faces. As the waitress began to engage with them, they immediately became extremely animated and talkative. They were close to giggling when they exchanged conversation, in Mandarin of course. She wrote down their order and then turned to Craig and Mr. Chen for their drink of choice.

Surprisingly, she spoke perfect English when she made several "bottle" suggestions to Craig. He deferred to Mr. Chen, who ordered what sounded like expensive champagne.

The drinks rolled in, and the party began. Bottle after bottle arrived at the table, and the drinking prowess of this team immediately became apparent. They may have been amateur investors, but there was nothing amateurish about their drinking; they were clearly professionals on this front. Craig felt compelled to keep pace and quickly lost track of his intake and surroundings. After the liquid confidence took hold, the deal team jumped onto the dance floor, gyrating first toward each other and then toward some younger girls (professionals) who became enamored (yeah, right) with their dance moves. One by one, each retired to a back room with their newfound friends for what was advertised as a foot massage for their tired dancing feet. Craig was still lucid enough when he began to realize he would be paying for all these foot massages. He was silently hoping to himself that they were charging by the length of their" feet," given their Asian heritage. Another bottle arrived for Craig and Chen, which was the second to the last thing he remembered. The last was his buddy Sumo Sam, the bouncer, lifting him into the back of a black car for a ride to who knew where.

Suddenly, there was a loud pounding on the door.

"Open the door right now."

"Go the fuck away!" yelled Craig. "Craig, it's me, Mr. Chen. Open up."

What the fuck does he want? Craig jumped up and put on his pants. On the way to let him in, he quickly closed the bathroom door, silently praying Chen wouldn't ask to use the can.

"Where have you been, Craig?" demanded Chen. "I've been trying to reach you for days."

"I've been here, trying to recover from the shit show you orchestrated with the investor group. Seriously, what the fuck was that all about? Those guys went from boring nerds to party animals, and I just saw the final bill!"

"That was the final step of the investment process, Craig. You show them a good time, and they commit the cash. They really don't give a shit about the deal; they just look for some partying to help make their boring-as-shit lives a little happy."

Craig got it. They just wanted a fishy tickle to approve the deal.

"Does that mean they are committed?"

"You bet they are! Get dressed, we need to go celebrate!"

The thought of the $50 million commitment provided an immediate boost to Craig's vitality, and he put on his shirt and shoes and grabbed his wallet. $50 million fucking dollars! Suddenly, Craig realized Mr. Chen had opened the bathroom door and was about to walk in.

"Don't go in there," he screamed.

"Why? I need to take a leak. What the..."

Craig lurched for the door to shut it before Chen could seethe condition of the bathroom, but it was too late.

"Holy shit, Craig, that is one serious blowout! I would love to be a fly on the wall when the housekeepers walk in here. Hahahahaha!!"

"Don't laugh! This is all your fault! You ordered the boatload of booze that put me in a three-day coma! I could have died!"

"Craig, man up!"

"What the fuck do you mean, man up? Give me a fucking break!"

Craig immediately regretted using the f-word in front of Mr. Chen. He was all about respect and this was the most disrespectful thing Craig thought he could be saying to him.

"Craig, man-up is one of the best-kept secrets we have in Taiwan. It's a locally produced traditional drug we use to keep us from getting a hangover after a wild night out. Only men can use it, it is not safe for women. Women go CRAZY when they take it. We don't even tell women about it. Every guy around here knows what "man-up" is. I have some in my briefcase in the car. I will give you some when we head out."

Over a bottle of champagne (for Chen) and San Pellegrino (for Craig), Mr. Chen outlined for Craig the next steps for finishing the equity raise as well as securing the bank financing. He also discussed the process to finalize the beauty contest for choosing the builder. Several builders had already expressed a strong interest in the development project, but secretly, Mr. Chen had already chosen the building contractor owned by his brother-in-law.

Regarding the remaining equity and debt, Mr. Chen would follow a similar process as he had for the first investor. Craig should be prepared, once investors get close to committing, to entertain them in a similar fashion to the insurance company team. It was money as well as brain cells worth expending to get the deal to the finish line. Mr. Chen assured Craig there would not be a repeat of his multi-day misery post-entertainment. He would secure an ample supply of Man- Up for his new friend and partner.

After their short celebration, Mr. Chen handed Craig two unmarked prescription-type bottles filled with tiny blue pills the size of a baby aspirin. Craig estimated there were easily three to four hundred pills in each bottle. He instructed Craig that although small, the pills were very, very potent. After a heavy night of partying, he should make sure to take one while he still had enough of his faculties to open the bottle and pop one in his mouth. Man-Up proved invaluable in helping Craig navigate the subsequent two months while he nailed down the final capital needed to begin the construction process.

Chapter Nine

Twenty Months in Lockdown

As November of 2021 opened, the Mayfields, like the rest of the world, had now endured almost twenty months of lockdown. Although Artie had turned three in August, no three-year-old preschool was available to ease the daily child-rearing grind. Emma had successfully stretched her rainy-day fund past the initial goal of one year to almost eighteen months. Early on in his unemployment, Craig reluctantly agreed to sell his BMW and netted almost $5,000 after repaying the loan from the sale. As expected, the DICKS corporate card was cut off after about three months, so this car windfall was kept secret to fund his drinking. Hell, if he had to give up his car, he should at least be able to keep his beer. Craig and Emma both liquidated their 401k plans to pay the monthly mortgage. This covered the first fifteen months, and once those funds were exhausted, they began drawing on the home equity line to stay current. Each day, they became deeper in debt as they covered just the bare necessities of living.

Craig was actively job searching throughout this time. With the man-up solution in hand, he could continue his nightly drinking pursuits and start fresh the next morning. During the lockdown, a new concept called "remote work" became the norm, and office buildings remained shuttered. Investment in new commercial real estate deals was essentially dead, with zero hope of a resurgence any time soon. Craig had widened his search in financial services beyond his background in real estate. His U of I credentials were viewed very strongly, especially in the Midwest. He was currently focusing on Chicago financial firms and would rather deal with a three-hour round-trip commute each day than even consider the thought of moving. Most of the jobs he found in his search were for entry-level or low-level analysts paying less than $100,000 per year. He initially ignored those openings in the hope of a more senior role. As time passed, he realized he could no longer be so selective. With his 34th birthday a week away, he swallowed his pride and applied for a financial associate role at a hedge fund located in Lake Forest, thirty minutes north of Chicago and less than an hour from Clanford. Within hours, he received a positive response back requesting an interview in mid-January since the role was budgeted for 2022. He accepted the invitation with a mix of emotions.

It had been tradition since they were married to spend a weekend in Chicago to celebrate their birthdays, Craig's in November and Emma's in May. They typically alternated between the Four Seasons and the Peninsula hotels. Both were in the Gold Coast area with walking access to shopping and restaurants on the Magnificent Mile and River North. They usually spent two nights and rotated between the top sushi and steak houses that Chicago was famous for. Craig loved the bar at Maple and Ash but felt the steaks were better at Gibson's. Emma was a sushi lover and looked forward to Omakase at Momotaro. The weekends typically included a couples massage and long walks along the city's River Walk and Millennium Park. Emma also loved the changing exhibits at the Art Institute.

Emma called these weekends their "re-connectors." Both had demanding jobs, pre and post-children. Emma especially looked forward to these get aways to pull Craig away from his constant business engagement. There was a no phones rule except for calls from Emma's mom when she had the children for these weekends.

Of all the things that had changed and been lost because of the previous two years of events, Emma longed mostly for one of their "re-connectors." She could not believe how the stress of life had pulled her and Craig apart rather than moved them closer together. She knew she was just as much at fault as Craig. Emma was determined to reverse the flow and get them both to refocus on each other and their relationship. She would start with a plan for Craig's upcoming birthday.

Craig awoke to age 34 with his two sons bringing him Dunkin' Donuts coffee and chocolate long johns in bed. They squealed with laughter as Craig feigned sleep and then grabbed them both as they approached his side of the bed. Emma followed the boys into the room and started a chorus of "Happy Birthday to You."

She smiled at Craig and sweetly mouthed, "Happy Birthday, Honey."

Wow! Craig hadn't heard Emma call him honey forever. He smiled back with a thank you. Although it was early November, the day was unseasonably warm, so the family of four took bikes to the local park for a few hours of play pre-afternoon naps. As the boys played on the playground equipment, Emma snuggled up to Craig on the park bench, putting her arm across his chest and placing her head on his shoulder.

"I love you, Craig. I want us to be like we used to be. I want US back."

"I love you, baby. I want that, too. These last two years have been hell. I'm sorry if I've disappointed you. I feel that this interview in January will be a game-changer. Once I'm working again, we can get our finances back in order and start looking forward to the future again."

Emma squeezed Craig tightly and whispered, "That's my dream."

After a dinner splurge of filets, baked potatoes, Caesar salad, and a bottle of cabernet, Emma hurried the boys through their evening routine of baths, books, and bedtime kisses. She knew the extra hours of outside playtime would send them off to dreamland, especially quickly this evening. Craig was finishing the last of the dishes when Emma came up from behind, wrapped her arms around him, and said, "Meet you in the shower in five minutes."

The long-dormant section of his hypothalamus, controlling his unit, immediately began to fire wildly. The front portion of his oversized sweatpants expanded horizontally as Craig ran upstairs to the master bathroom jumping three steps per stride as he vaulted the long staircase. The new master bath had a shower the size of his previous living room and was outfitted with all of the most current spa attachments, including multiple sprayers and two shower heads. Craig fired them all up and awaited Emma's entrance.

The oversized sweats that Craig wore daily had become his security blanket after Emma had called him a fat ass the year before. Craig couldn't argue that he had gained weight (nightly Coronas and Little Debbie cakes) but felt her attack was overly aggressive. The next day, he went on Amazon and ordered a three-pack of Russell Basic Essentials sweatpants and sweatshirts in XXL, all black. He figured he could hide his "fat ass" from her with this new wardrobe. Historically, Craig wore a large in all his athletic wear. The sweats had become his togs of choice for almost 18 months.

The first thing Emma noticed when she entered the steamy shower was Craig's physique.

"Holy Shit,Craig, you have a six-pack! When the hell did that happen?"

"Are you complaining?"

"God, no. I just can't believe your body. You look fantastic. How did you lose all that weight, and when did you find the time to weight train? Your ass is as tight as a drum! Bring that over here now!!"

The passion started in the shower and promptly moved to the overpriced mattress and boxspring set. Craig finished quickly, but Emma didn't care. She was thrilled to be cuddled closely with Craig feeling, for the first time in a long time, completely loved.

As she laid in Craig's arms, Emma started to question this new body revelation.

"Craig, I need to understand your new fitness routine. I just can't believe I've been so clueless about your weight loss and muscle toning."

"Emma, it's a long story."

Before he could continue, Emma interrupted. As she thought through everything, the pieces just didn't make sense to her.

"Craig, I have a confession to make. I have been aware of what you do every night in your office. The beer, the Little Debbies, everything. That's why I don't understand how you could have lost all that weight and toned up so much."

"Wait, how could you possibly know about that? You fall asleep every night by nine."

"Craig, you aren't exactly a quiet drunk. You barrel out of your office with clinking bottles around 1 am and then you drop, not quietly place, them into the neighbor's recycling. Everyone in the neighborhood is aware of your escapades. Some have even called with their concern."

"Wait, what? You've known all along? Why didn't you say something?"

"Because I knew you were struggling and felt like you were functioning fine each day once I told you to get your act together. I just figured you would stop when you got back to work. The only thing I haven't figured out is how you have paid for all that beer."

"Like I said, it's a long story, both the weight loss and the money."

"Don't feel like you must explain yourself, Craig. It can be just your business."

"No, Emma, I need to set the record straight, for both of our sakes."

Craig then proceeded to outline, in detail, what he had been up to each night since he had lost his job in June of 2020. He told her about the corporate card for the first several months and then the equity from the sale of his car. He knew that both were wrong and unfair to Emma. He then explained the use of the "man-up" pills from Mr. Chen and how he was introduced to them after one particularly long and hard night of partying with some of the Taipei investors. After numerous beratings from Emma about his slow mornings and dreary attitude, he found the bottle of pills and began taking them. In addition to tamping down any effects from the overdose of alcohol and sugar each night, the pills began to change his overall physique. He began to lose weight without losing muscle mass. In fact, he thought he was gaining muscle mass from the pills without any weight training. He further explained that the pills were some local concoctions that the men in Taipei took religiously after drinking binges. They weren't a commercial product but rather just some home-grown remedy.

Emma took it all in, and although she had reason to be mad, she really wasn't. They finally talked openly about what was going on, and she felt that this would help them heal the lack of communication in their marriage. The bonus for her was the hot husband she was now lying next to in bed.

When Craig, moved to get out of bed for a drink of water, Emma enthusiastically pulled him back into her arms.

"Ready for round two?" "Duh!"

Craig laid back and enjoyed his double bonus birthday present. Thirty-five was starting out as a very good year for Craig Mayfield.

Chapter Ten

OPENING UP

Craig returned from the interview in Lake Forest even more discouraged than before. Although he hit it off right away with all the guys he met, his final meeting with one of the partners was not as convincing as the rest of the team. Craig was clearly a smart and qualified candidate. The problem was that he was probably over-qualified. The partner explained the amount of time and resources his firm invested in new employees getting them up to speed on the policies and procedures specific to their investment philosophies. They were a busy shop, and taking time out to train anew guy who might leave for a more challenging role as the market opened up did not make sense to him.

Craig countered that he was with his previous firm for over ten years before its collapse. He had been approached numerous times over the years for jobs with quicker role and responsibility ascension and more money but had stayed loyal to his former partners. He looked at this job opportunity as an entry into one of the top hedge funds in the country and was willing to do his time in a more junior but important position. He was in full charm mode but to no avail. He would be "kept apprised" of any future openings.

The drive home in the minivan was torturous. He had high hopes for a celebratory dinner with Emma where they would map out the steps toward gaining financial security. He knew Emma was nervous when he left. She had been acting particularly strange the last several days, but he chalked it up to the stress of him and the interview. Now, he would have to deliver the disappointing news while trying to stay upbeat about future openings. The world did seem to be opening up, so he tried to convince himself that a new job was right around the corner.

Emma knew when he entered the house that he would not be delivering the news she had hoped for. She felt bad for him because he was trying hard to ease her concerns and stay positive. Things had been better between the two of them since his birthday "party." Unfortunately, he had lapses of drinking and, in her current state, had screamed at him two nights prior that he better get the "fucking job." She later apologized and blamed it on her period. She was trying hard to move forward. That was the only way she could process things now, especially since she was two months pregnant.

Earlier in the day, Emma had visited her mom with the boys. While she was there, Twink, the proprietor of Twink's High Fashion and a longtime friend of her mom, had stopped by. Twink was also close friends with the woman mayor of the town, Colleen Fray. Over dinner the previous fall, Colleen had intimated to Twink that she was planning an announcement on February 1st that she would be canceling the COVID lockdown in Clanford, allowing local businesses to reopen and office workers to return to their mothballed desks. Even though the fat ass governor of Illinois was still not willing to let the kids back in school, let alone get workers back in their offices, she would call eminent domain and let him try and shut them back down. He was currently trying to make excuses for why his wife and daughter were frolicking at his horse estate in Florida while he was telling all Illinoisans to stay put in their homes. What hypocrisy!

After receiving the news from Colleen, Twink made quiet trips to Paris, Milan, and New York to order the latest fashions for the spring and summer markets. She knew the women of Clanford would be dying to get their hands on anything other than leisure wear, and she stocked the store accordingly. She was planning to open promptly on February 1st after the mayor's announcement. She was currently looking to find some part-time help in the store, given that one of her previous long-term salespersons had died sadly from COVID. The work would be mostly weekends, and she would pay a base hourly rate plus a generous commission. Emma jumped at the opportunity, asking Twink if she could have the position. Her mother chimed in that she would help with the boys when needed. Twink would be happy to have Emma join her business. Even though she knew that Craig's new job would help alleviate the immediate financial issues, having a second income could add some cushion to the situation. Emma was thrilled at the prospect of working, especially at a shop that was held in such high esteem in the community as Twink's.

Over a somewhat subdued dinner after the boys had gone to bed, Emma began filling Craig in on her two very important pieces of information. First, she broke the news of her pregnancy. She waited for all the reasons this was not a good time, etc. but they never came. Instead, Craig reached over and held her hand and smiled.

"That is the greatest news I've heard in a long time. How have you been feeling? To be honest, I thought something was up with how you've been a little erratic lately."

"Craig, we can't really afford a new baby right now. We are barely subsisting as it is. The state health insurance we are on now might not even cover the OB practice I went to with my previous pregnancies."

"I'm assuming you are about eight weeks. Birthday baby, right?" "That would be correct!"

"Emma, I really don't want you stressing about this. I am going to figure out a path forward for us. You concentrate on staying healthy, and I will take care of the rest. Have you told your mother yet?"

"Not yet. I took the boys over to see her this afternoon, but Twink showed up at her house and I didn't have the opportunity to tell her before we had to leave. I will tell Mom and Dad tomorrow, and we should also call your parents. Craig, that brings me to the second thing I need to bring you up to speed on."

"I'm all ears."

"This afternoon at my mom's, Twink told her and me about the mayor's plan to open up Clanford on February 1st. All businesses, office buildings, and schools."

"That's great news! It's about time. What about the governor? Isn't he still telling everyone to shelter in place?"

"Same thing my mom asked Twink. Apparently, Mayor Fray doesn't care that much about what he wants. She says she runs the city, and she has an obligation to do what's best for her citizens, especially the school-aged kids. She's tired of the bullshit politics and how the Chicago Teachers Union has Governor "silver spoon" by the balls all the time. My mom was thrilled too that she and my dad would be back in the classroom soon."

"Wow, Mayor Fray is one serious badass!"

Emma continued. "Okay, topic number two. Twink is opening her clothing store immediately on February 1st. Colleen Fray told her about her plans to open the city after the holidays last fall, so Twink went on an inventory-buying spree over the last four months. Also,...Twink hired me today as a part-time salesperson..."

Emma waited for the protest. Craig paused for a moment and then replied, "Emma, do you think you will be up to it with your pregnancy and all? Is it worth your time to be a salesperson? How much can you possibly make?"

"First, both my pregnancies so far have been uneventful, as you know. If I found I was getting too tired or anything that might compromise the baby, I would obviously quit immediately. Second, the pay is $15 per hour, CASH, plus a 15% commission on all sales. You know how expensive the shit Twink sells in her store is. She has dresses that cost $5,000! It could add up to some nice money quickly, and we could slow down on the borrowing. Third, it will give me a chance to reconnect with some women other than the moms I see at the park. It will be good for me, and it will be good for our family. I'm actually very excited about starting next week."

Craig had mixed emotions about this.

"Okay, I want you to be happy, and I know we can use the money. I just feel like it's one more strike against me as a husband who can't provide for his family."

"Craig, we just went through a fucking pandemic. People died, businesses closed, and the world was literally on fire. You should never, ever feel that you are letting us down. I have complete confidence that you will be working very soon in a job that you love." Craig smiled back at her.

"Oh, and by the way, I think Twink is a little concerned about my existing wardrobe. She told me to meet her at 7:30 a.m. at the store on the 1st before the grand re-opening at 10 a.m. She said we would have a little "dress-up" party so she could provide me with some outfits for work. Apparently, all for free! It will become a "surprise party" pretty quickly when I tell her that I am pregnant!"

Craig laughed out loud at Emma's joke.

Unbeknownst to both Emma and Craig, Twink's "drop-in" at her mom's that afternoon had been a highly orchestrated "coincidence" by the two old friends. Emma's mom had confided in Twink about the family's financial plight. Twink, being the magnanimous friend that she was, was more than happy to provide Emma with a job to help her out.

Unbeknownst to everyone involved, this small act of kindness was about to set in motion the string of events that would change the people of Clanford forever.

Chapter Eleven

Twink

Upon meeting any new acquaintance, Twink Buston-Ford would introduce herself as a direct descendant of James Ford "thrice" removed. Most would silently wonder what the hell thrice meant. And, even more importantly, what the hell was she removed from? Just as curious was why she was referencing some guy named James Ford even though, unbeknownst to these inquisitors, he was the founder of most of their wealthy feasts. Twink's last name was hyphenated to reflect the combination of her mother's and father's surnames.

Her given name was Estelle, which she hated from the moment she could utter it. Twink was the product of a short liaison between her father, Harold Ford, and her mother, Sister Mary Buston, a novice at the SBH convent. The other nuns jokingly called her sister Mary "Bustin' Out" behind her back because of the profound rack she tried to conceal under her habit. This was an obvious play on her last name, Buston. One of her fellow novitiates was an English teacher in a previous life and hated superfluous words, so she shortened the nickname to Sister Mary Tits. One other went further and baptized her SMT.

As a direct grandson of Pappy Ford, Harold was a wealthy individual from the moment he was conceived. Unlike many of his cousins, Harold was an outdoors, man's man kind of guy. When he (barely) finished high school, he already knew college was not in the cards. Despite his considerable trust fund, he decided to start a handyman business to keep himself busy and feel the satisfaction of having a real job.

One of his first clients was the SBH convent. Since they had no men in employ at the convent, Harold was the go-to- guy to do repairs, small painting jobs, etc. Harold loved being on the SBH campus because of the beauty of the old buildings and their setting on the heavily wooded landscape.

During one particular assignment, Harold came into contact with one of the novitiates when he inadvertently took a wrong passageway into the convent laundry. Harold had been moving some old furniture out of the basement so some foundation work could be completed. It was a hot and humid summer day, and he was sweating profusely. The coolness of the basement passages was a welcome reprieve from the steamy day. Harold had removed his shirt as he walked through the basement alleyways, wiping his brow with one of its sleeves. When he entered the laundry, shirtless, Sister Mary Tits was busy loading bed linens into the commercial-sized washer. Although the basement was cold and dry, the laundry room was hotter than the temperature above ground. Sister Mary had removed her outer habit and was dressed only in a thin slip and a bulging, double-underwired bra to cool herself off. Sister Mary couldn't help but stare at the muscular and hairy physique of the shirtless Harold. Harold couldn't take his eyes off her imposing breasts, and he was known for being a breast guy. Before they knew what hit them, carnal knowledge had overtaken them both, and they were soon atop the wooden folding table casting sacrilege about without caution. SMT was on all fours as Harold taught her a thing or two about the ABM position (anything but missionary). They both rolled off the table with badly splintered knees and even more badly splintered souls. Harold quickly hiked his trousers back up, put on his shirt, slapped SMT on the ass, and left. As he exited, Harold thought to himself that at least he wouldn't have to confess an impure thought to the good father in confession. This had been a truly impulsive impure act.

Five months later, Harold was summoned to The Mother Superior's office, where he thought the topic was going to be an expansion of his responsibilities. It was not. Rather, it was a discussion about the expansion of Sister Mary Buston's waistline. Standing next to the convent general was SMT in her full glory. Even with the loose-fitting habit, Harold could see her extended belly was almost now parallel with her abundant chest. SMT winked at Harold when Mother Superior's head was buried in some papers on her desk.

"Mr. Ford," Mother Superior started in. "We seem to have a situation here with our dear Sister Mary Buston."

Harold steeled himself against any hint of laughter. If she meant pregnant when she said situation, then they were on the same page. Harold slowly looked over to SMT and gave her a wink back.

"After thoughtful consideration of this "situation," she continued, "We have decided to send Sister Mary to our convent in Chicago, where upon childbirth, she will deliver the newborn to a loving and qualified adoptive family."

"Excuse my French, Mother Superior, but no fucking way is my baby going to be given up to some Chicago candy-ass family. He is a Ford, and he will have access to all the benefits of being a Ford."

"I beg your pardon, Mr. Ford, and no, I will not pardon your French. This child is a bastard child, conceived in the ugliest possible influence of Satan himself's depravity."

"Actually, Mother Superior, it was conceived because your little sister here has an incredible rack, and I'm known as a tit guy. For your information, she was just as into me as I was into her, no pun intended."

"MR. FORD! Enough of your sacrilege. This matter is settled. The baby will be born and given up for adoption. You will have no further responsibility for your vulgar actions beyond today. Good day, Mr. Ford."

As Mother Superior began to leave the room, signaling it was the end of this meeting, Harold grabbed her by the arm. She was stunned by his aggressive behavior.

"You listen here, Mother Superior, for over one hundred years, this convent has been able to grow and flourish because of the benevolence of the Ford family. Your successful mission of education and single-mother care is the result of my extended family's generosity. I have the means to care for and raise this child, and that is what I intend to do. If you try and stop that, you can count on a total reversal of the convent's fortunes. That is not a threat. That is a promise."

Mother Superior was stunned but quickly understood his power to severely impact the convent's mission. She pulled herself away from him and quietly said, "As you wish, Mr. Ford. We will make sure you are notified of the birth of your child, and you will be given sole custody of the newborn."

SMT had zero interest in any rights to the child. She was originally relegated to the role of a wet nurse after the birth of the baby but eventually left the convent to join a motorcycle gang from New Jersey. Neither Mother Superior nor Harold ever heard another word from her, but Harold had burned into his memory the sound of her large breasts slapping up against each other during their brief but passionate encounter on the laundry room folding table.

Upon her birth, Twink was named Estelle for Harold's long- deceased mother. He immediately nicknamed her Twink because of the twinkle in her eye he couldn't help but notice when the SBH nuns handed the baby over to him. He was just twenty years old and a new father, and he loved every minute of it.

Harold quickly closed Harold's Handy Man and visited his wealth advisor to get a better understanding of what he was worth. He was amazed when he was given the number and knew right then he was going to provide his beautiful Twink with all the finest things and adventures.

As soon as she was able to walk, he began traveling to different parts of the United States, the finest resorts as well as historical venues so he could provide a hands-on education along with exposure to a more genteel way of life. The two of them celebrated her third birthday at Disneyland in California. They were an inseparable duo.

When Twink turned eight, Harold believed it was time to show her (and himself) the major cities of Europe. They flew to New York and boarded the QE II for the weeks-long voyage to England. They had first-class accommodations replete with their own butler. For the week prior to the voyage, Harold had hired a New York personal dresser for Twink so that she would be appropriately outfitted for the four-month trip. Twink marveled at the colors and textures of all the fancy dresses, coats, and daily wardrobe. She held pieces of the trousseau to her face, taking in the feel of the fabric and the nuance of color against her pale skin. From that moment on, she was hooked on fine couture.

Throughout their visits to London, Edinburgh, Paris, Lisbon, Barcelona, Seville, Rome, Milan, Venice, Munich, Zurich, and Vienna, not to mention the many side trips, Twink was mesmerized by the outfits the ladies were wearing. Since she and Harold were staying in the finest of hotels, she was exposed to the full spectrum of day and evening wear. She especially loved the boutiques in Paris and Milan. Even though they did not cater to young women of her age, she still insisted on dragging Harold in so she could experience the gracious process of outfitting grande dames. Twink had decided at the young age of eight that her life calling would be in fashion, specifically dressing the most sophisticated women.

Over the next ten years, life for Twink was picture perfect. She attended the SBH Convent School, lived in a beautiful home that Harold had built after she was born, had a doting governess, Maria, whom she loved dearly, and continued to travel on school breaks and her summer holidays. In her early teen years, Harold had decided to rent an oceanfront home on the island of Nantucket each summer. Twink loved the ocean and the proximity of daily jaunts via a private jet, of course, to New York, Boston, and Newport. Twink had several close girlfriends who would join her for parts of the summer. She made plans to attend the Fashion Institute of Technology in New York to launch her career in fashion design.

It was a Monday afternoon, Maria's usual day off, two weeks ahead of high school graduation that Twink's life changed forever. When she entered the front door of her home after school, things seemed strangely different. Harold, without fail throughout her school years, would greet her at the door with a big smile and hearty hug and inquire about her day. She honestly could not remember a day that he had ever missed. The house was eerily quiet. Harold was not there. She walked to the side window to survey the driveway and saw Harold's car parked in its usual spot.

She called out, "Dad, are you here?"

There was no response. She called louder, and still no response. Maybe he had fallen asleep and couldn't hear her. He never took naps, but maybe he was a bit under the weather. She tried to stay positive, but her whole body began to shake as she climbed the stairs to the second floor. She started in his bedroom and found it completely spotless, with the bed made as usual. As she rounded past his small dressing area next to his bathroom, she noticed a light from under the door.

She called again. "Dad, are you in there? Is everything okay?" Silence.

Twink began to shake violently, and tears overwhelmed her vision. In her gut she knew he was in there but felt incapable of moving her body forward. She then thought that maybe he needed her help, so she pushed the bathroom door open and found him. He was lying on his back in his pajama bottoms, his face was blue but serene. When she knelt to try and wake him, he was cold to the touch. Twink collapsed over his body and began to weep. How could this happen? He wasn't even forty years old. He was fit and happy and always listened to her about his food choices. WHY? WHY? WHY? She held him so hard she began to lose feeling in her arms. She had lost the only man she had ever loved. She had lost her protector and joke maker, her teacher and best friend. Without a mother, Twink quickly realized she was an orphan. What a horrible and treacherous word" orphan" really was.

Because Harold was not under a doctor's care at the time of his death, the coroner was required to do an autopsy to determine his cause of death. The outcome of the autopsy showed that Harold had died suddenly, caused by a large rupture in his aortic valve, usually known as an aortic aneurysm. The coroner told Twink that the tear was of such a size that her dad was most likely dead before he hit the bathroom floor. Twink took little comfort in this news.

After the quiet family funeral, Twink attended graduation. Not because she wanted to but because Maria had convinced her that her father was looking forward to her accomplishment of being named valedictorian of her class. She had been working on a speech for weeks but knew she could not deliver it in front of her classmates now. She asked her favorite English teacher, Ms. Baker, to be her proxy. The whole class gave her a standing ovation, but any sense of accomplishment was lost in her overwhelming grief.

The following summer was not spent in Nantucket. Although Harold had rented the home as usual and it was already paid for, Twink could not bear the thought of being there without her father. She reluctantly spent too much time with her father's attorneys and wealth advisors. His will and estate plan were very cut and dry. Twink was the sole heir to his fortune. She would never have to work a day in her life. Just the income from the trusts alone could support a lifestyle tenfold of what she was used to. The money didn't matter to her. She was terribly lonely and had a recurring dream at night of her father returning to the house and the two of them living life like it used to be. On the mornings after those dreams, she would find her pillowcase wet from tears.

In late August, Twink tearfully bid farewell to Maria and headed off to the next chapter of her life in New York. F.I.T., as it was called, offered her the chance to refocus her attention toward her dream of becoming a famous fashion designer. Twink was snap-smart and determined. She was also six feet two inches tall and beautifully slim with broad shoulders. Her presence in the classroom immediately drew the attention of some of the up-and-coming New York designers who worked with the students at F.I.T. She received multiple requests to model the fashions these designers created at meetings with boutique owners spread around the city. She became the most sought-after student in her class for these modified runway events.

Unfortunately, Twink could not fully embrace the experience that she had dreamed of for years. She found New York life suffocating.

She was so melancholy at times that she couldn't make it to class. Her freshman advisor approached her halfway into the semester. There were concerns from her professors about her absences and from the designers she had ghosted for modeling appointments. Twink confided in her about her father's death and her daily struggles. Her advisor told her she was most likely suffering from depression and suggested she return home for some counseling. Twink would not lose her spot in the class. She could return to school the next semester. Her advisor then told her she thought Twink was one of the most gifted students she had met at the school and assured her when the time was right, Twink could look forward to a successful career in design.

After three months at home and numerous failed attempts at finding a psychologist to help her, Twink decided she was going to live in Paris. She checked into the Ritz in Place Vendome and started looking for an apartment to rent. Even though money was no object, she wanted an age-appropriate pied a terre close to the Champs- Elysées. Twink figured her apartment needed to be close to many of the boutiques and upstart designers. She perused the local papers while sitting in the bar at the Hotel Georges V., her favorite in Paris. She also started a new habit, one that never ever crossed her mind: smoking. Paris was not only the City of Light, but it was also the city of lighters. Almost everyone she met or observed was a chainsmoker. Gitanes became her nouveau vice of choice, and she embraced it enthusiastically.

Once she secured her walk-up on Rue Madeleine, she began her new life as a femme de Paris. Her daily ritual was to stop at the cafes along the street for a strong coffee and half a pack of Gitanes. She became addicted to the strong European coffee. She loved to people-watch and found Paris even more beautiful and interesting than the visit with her dad. As always, she was focusing on the clothing the women were wearing. Afterward, she would make her way through the many famous and not-so-famous designer boutiques. Her beauty and stature immediately caught the attention of the boutique proprietors, and she was made immediate offers to both work as a saleswoman and model the apparel both in-store and during trunk shows.

Twink had arrived roughly one month prior to the acclaimed Paris Fashion Week, typically the end of February through the beginning of March. All the famous designers were hosting lavish parties and dinners as they were set to release their latest fashion lines. Twink quickly found herself in the inner circle with multiple invitations to these sought after events. One evening while having a drink at the very packed George V bar, she was approached by an upstart British designer by the name of Alexander McQueen. He had seen her the previous night at the Chanel party at the Louvre (THE hottest ticket that year). He, like most who first saw her, was completely "gobsmacked" (his words) with her beauty and poise. Over numerous dirty martinis (no food, of course), he offered her a job in his small boutique and asked her to be his primary model. Being more drunk than she had ever been, she accepted.

Twink enjoyed the attention and the opportunity to work with a visionary in the constantly evolving world of fashion. She began to make both women and men friends, most attached to the industry in some way. Slowly, she opened herself up to dating. She mostly dated men she had met through acquaintances. Sometimes, she would accept invitations from men she met at the cafes or bars. Although she tried very hard to really engage in a relationship, the available candidates just didn't measure up. Unfortunately, for all of them, the unit of measurement was her father. Although her father had an unimpressive school record, she always considered him the smartest man she had ever known. When they visited Washington, D.C., and Williamsburg, he was able to reduce the gravity of these historic places to understandable and relatable stories. She only knew her dad as kind and always a gentleman to every woman with whom he came in contact. He was naturally witty and quick to extract giggles from her, even in her moodier days as a teenager. He was the gold standard that these potential par amours needed to emulate. None came close.

When she closed in on the end of her first-year lease, Twink decided she was going to leave Paris and return to Clanford. Going back to New York was completely out of the picture. As much as she loved Paris, she couldn't help but feel like a true fish out of water. She had made great friends and even greater contacts in the industry, but she continued to mourn the death of her father and needed the familiarity of her home and hometown to try and move forward. During her long morning cafe visits, Twink had spent time developing, in her mind, a business plan for opening a high fashion boutique in Clanford. She knew Clanford women had money, regular high society events to attend, and the overwhelming desire to one-up their friends. She spent her last month in Paris filling a shipping container with French antique armoires, chairs, tables, and dressers to occupy her new boutique on the other side of the Atlantic. She added the finest French fabrics and wallpapers to the mix. Twink even purchased an eighteenth-century marble fireplace from a chateau in the Loire Valley. All these pieces would be repurposed to create a fabulously beautiful haute couture experience for the wealthy women of Clanford. No longer would they have to travel to Chicago or New York for their wardrobes. Twink would bring the finest European and American fashions to them.

In the spring of the following year, Twink opened her eponymous boutique, Twink's High Fashion, in a large storefront on Main Street. She put her name on the business as a tribute to her father's nickname for her. For the decades that followed, Twink's was the center of fashion for all Clanford. Twice yearly, she traveled to Paris, Milan, and New York to secure the most popular designers' latest lines. Many created specific wardrobe pieces just for her boutique.

Twink was an ever-present fixture in the store, overseeing the flow of women and fabric with a sharp eye and even sharper tongue. She never held back in either her praise for a particular fit or her disdain for a fashion failure. Her most often heard admonishment was, "Don't even think about trying that on, darling." No customer ever questioned her judgment or openly argued with Twink. Doing so would mean immediate and permanent banishment from her boutique. Twink spent her entire day with a Virginia Slim cigarette in one hand and a double-strength cup of Néscafe instant coffee in the other. Ashtrays throughout the store overflowed with red lipstick-ringed cigarette butts. Her signature bright red lipstick always matched her long, finely shaped, and polished fingernails. When indoor smoking was banned in most businesses during the 1990s, she set a worktable up next to a window on the alley side of her shop and held her cigaretted talons out the window.

On the eve of the post-pandemic opening, Twink was well into her six-ties, still wealthy beyond measure, lionized in the world of haute couture, and excited about what the next chapter of renewal in Clanford would mean for her and her beloved fellow citizens

Chapter Twelve

The Grand Re-Openings

Twink wasn't the only Clanford insider who was made aware of the town's impending re-opening. Ashley "Fluffy" Williams, the ascendant president of the Butternut Country Club Women's Auxiliary Board, was also in the know. Ashley was the daughter of Marguerite Ford Smythe, the previous long-term Auxiliary President, Ford family descendant, and all-around rich bitch who had taken emeritus status the year that COVID hit. Rumor had it that Ashley received her sobriquet at birth when Marguerite, upon holding her for the first time, said to the governess to whom she quickly passed the infant back, that this baby looks "fluffy." Fluffy was Marguerite's code name for fat. Much to Marguerite and her daughter's dismay, fluffiness was hardcoded in Ashley's DNA.

Fluffy grew up in the lap of luxury and Clanford high society. At sixteen, she was "presented" to the Chicago Cardinal at the annual presentation ball fundraiser for Chicago Catholic Charities. Although her mother was Episcopalian, her father was a staunch Catholic and insisted Fluffy be raised in his church. Since the governess was raising Fluffy, Marguerite didn't really care. In fact, one child was all she had the "energy" for, and Fluffy was raised as an only child. She loved tennis and was half decent at golf. She spent the first eighteen years of her life between her parent's estate and the country club.

Upon graduation from the Clanford Academy Day School, she set her sights on Southern Methodist University, also known as SMU, but never to be confused with SMT. She arrived freshman year with a full wardrobe and a Mercedes S Class convertible, white on white, of course. On-campus parking was not available to freshmen then, so she immediately demanded her father buy a home in nearby Highland Park so she could garage the car. During her four years on campus, neither she nor anyone else had ever entered the large house.

Fluffy was a fun spirit and made friends immediately. Having a car as a freshman also expanded the group of willing party companions. She partied hard and was known to drink many of the frat boys who pursued her under the table. She was also a "fun spirit" when it came to sex. Although just a freshman, her reputation for bedding all class levels of boys on campus created a fraternity network name for their hook-ups, "fluffer-nutter." It was used much like the phrase, getting laid by the frat-ties. A way too common answer to the question "Any luck on Saturday night?" was "fluffer-nutter." That said it all.

Fluffy did not have the look of the usual female SMU co-ed. She was only five foot two inches tall, had brown hair (not the usual blond), and weighed in at one hundred and sixty pounds. Despite her fluffy stature, many of the wealthy life partner search crowd on campus were aware of her background and means. There was no lack of wealthy students at SMU, especially the legacy crowd of the oil patch families. Although that was some very real wealth, most of it paled in comparison the Ford-Smythe trusts, and those in the know knew it. A young man in search of a partner to elevate him into such a lifestyle might look past the physical attributes and focus more on the fun spirit of this available young woman.

Fluffy enjoyed the attention but knew deep down what most of these guys were after. She played it well. Fraternity formal dance invitations poured in, and she was very selective of whose she might accept. During one such dance in her senior year, she met C.J. Williams IV. C.J. (Charles John), was a quiet guy, also a bit fluffy, who was studying petroleum engineering. C.J.'s great-grandfather was a wildcatter in Oklahoma in the late 1890s who quickly figured out that there was going to be a great need for moving this oil around the quickly expanding United States. He started one of the first pipeline companies that moved oil south, eventually settling in Texas. The subsequent Williams generations built the privately held company into one of the largest in the country. C.J., like Fluffy, was a country club rat who was also raised in privilege. In spite of that (as well as his scratch golf handicap), he was a genuinely kind and gentle soul, and Fluffy fell hard.

After graduation, C.J. and Fluffy journeyed back to Clanford so that C.J. could properly ask Fluffy's father for her hand in marriage. Although Marguerite was less than impressed with the man, she quickly understood his family's legacy and became a fan. Her father was initially less inclined to give his blessing. During their meeting, C.J. revealed that his family were Southern Baptists. He was deeply involved in his church and had invited Fluffy to join him for the extended services each week. Fluffy became quite enthusiastic with the preaching, the music, and, most importantly, the emotion that was generated in the congregation. C.J. was upfront with Fluffy's father that he and his daughter would live a faith-based life as members of the Baptist, not the Catholic Church. This was a huge blow to Fluffy's dad (her mother couldn't care less), but he saw true happiness in his daughter's eyes. Some church was better than no church. He gave C.J. the answer he had anxiously and nervously awaited: Yes!

Fluffy and C.J.'s wedding would be the high point of the following summer's social season, held (where else) at the Butternut Country Club.

***

With the early heads up from Mayor Fray, Fluffy had immediately alerted the management team at Butternut to anticipate a re-opening in early May with the annual Women's Auxiliary Spring Luncheon. The spring luncheon was the official start of the summer social season. This year, it was especially important because plans were being made for the club's centennial celebration which had been postponed with the COVID lock-outs. All members of the Auxiliary were expected to attend. The first part of the luncheon was a short housekeeping meeting. Board members were re-nominated (death was usually the only reason to give up this coveted spot), the summer calendar was ratified, and any new Auxiliary applications for membership were voted on. This vote was a mere formality because the board members painstakingly vetted any potential membership requests before they were even nominated and presented for approval.

Immediately after the holidays, the process of restoring operations at the club began in earnest. The club manager, William Wells, was in charge of overseeing a return to the grand and seamless operations that had laid dormant during the previous two-year lockdown. The staff was re-hired, the supply chain relationships were re-established, and the hard work of cleaning and revitalizing the physical campus began. This latter part was no small task. The club's main building, excluding the golf locker rooms, pool facilities, pro shop, and racquet center, was over 100,000 square feet of highly ornate and detailed hardwood paneling, trim and moldings, marble fireplaces, flooring, chandeliers, and furniture.

The Butternut Club was built on 150 acres of the highest elevation property in Clanford so that the privileged membership could both literally and figuratively look down upon the less fortunate Clanford citizens. The main clubhouse was placed at the precise spot of maximum elevation. In addition to the large stand of Butternut trees for which the club was named, there were also smaller stands of mature walnut, white oak, and mahogany. As the trees were cleared to establish the golf course and club footprint, the resulting hardwood lumber was preserved by local craftsmen for use in the club's interior.

The main clubhouse was truly a grand architectural gem. Designed in the Tutor revival style, the exterior was a combination of local fieldstone, Chicago-manufactured brick, large local timber, stucco, and a slate-tiled roof. The finished building resembled an English manor home high atop a rolling estate. The gated driveway from the public street to the covered entry was almost two miles long. When the club was built, butternut saplings had been planted on both sides of the winding brick driveway. Over the next fifty years, they matured into a deciduous canopy so thick and manicured as to protect drivers from inclement weather.

The interior was even more spectacular. Italian marble floors, polished to an almost mirrored finish, covered the grand foyer and all the hallways throughout both the first and second floors. Members were self-trained to walk slowly and intently across them to avoid a disastrous and embarrassing fall. The center foyer gave way to two sweeping and opposing staircases that met at the midpoint of the second floor, which was the entry point for the grand ballroom. The grand ballroom was a 30,000-square-foot tribute to eighteenth-century English manor life. The walls were paneled in red mahogany, with carved flourishes and molding. The ceiling was decorative plaster with rose medallions positioned at the center of each of the three main and six Auxiliary crystal and gold chandeliers. The room held one singular red and gold wool rug woven with the Butternut Crest in the center. Club history reveals that it took a total of fifty men to haul the two-ton rug up the stairs and into the ballroom, with one worker being badly injured when his leg was crushed between the rug end and the doorway. The far end of the ballroom was a wall of Palladian-style windows that overlooked the sweeping fairways of the golf course. This room was reserved for only the most formal of events, including the Women's Auxiliary lunch, the summer club cotillion, and the Christmas formal dinner dance.

The use for wedding receptions was restricted to direct club members and their families only.

On both sides of the main foyer on the first floor were multiple- paneled reading and small gathering rooms. Each of these rooms was considered a "library," and each was named for some of the original club families. Large ornate fireplaces, overstuffed furniture, and deep carpets were the common theme of these lounges. Historic paintings depicting English landscapes, still lifes, and unknown royal portraits graced the wood-paneled walls, all imported from London art brokers upon completion of the original club construction.

***

As she anticipated her inaugural year as Auxiliary Board President, the pinnacle of Clanford Society, Fluffy took on the role of taskmaster to ensure the club looked and ran to its highest level of perfection.She would open the club with grace, elegance, and full fanfare at the Auxiliary Luncheon, setting the stage for the centennial celebration in July. This was Fluffy's moment, and she embraced it mightily.

***

The line started forming outside of Twink's High Fashion well before 5 a.m., despite temperatures in the low twenties. By 7 a.m., the line stretched well down Main Street and was over one hundred women strong. Twink snuck in the alley door a little before 8 and, after seeing the long line, instructed Emma and the other two saleswomen to open up a little over two hours early by allowing ten women in the boutique at a time. A loud cheer arose amongst the "ladies in waiting" as the first group was ushered into the store. She also called her friend Maya at the Dunkin' Donuts store across the street from the boutique to request immediate delivery of boxed coffee to her freezing clients. The lucky women inside would have access to the fully stocked bar in addition to the Veuve Clicquot mimosas being served, a long-held tradition for Saturday morning appointments.

In anticipation of a very strong and pent-up demand by the Clanford social set, Twink had double ordered her inventory for the grand re-opening. As usual, most of her sought-after togs were available in European sizes 30, 32, and 34 (US equivalent sizes 0, 2, and 4), with a few specifically picked sizes 40 and 42 for the "mature" women clients.

The initial group frantically grabbed at the racks to secure their claim to the formal and informal dresses and casual wear that Twink deliberately ordered singularly to avoid any awkward encounters of her clients wearing horrors, the same outfit! They stood, arms piled high, giddy with excitement as they awaited their turn in the dressing room. Twink, with her ever-discerning and highly perceptive eye, immediately realized she had a huge problem on her hands as she sized up the initial group. With coats stripped off at the door, the happy customers were no longer her perpetually starved and bone-thin regular clientele. They were beefy. They had stomachs and butts, and some even revealed FUPAS and drippy Weenus'. Twink was shocked. This is the crowd who had regularly feigned digestion in favor of tight-fitting skirts and exposed knee joints. Malnutrition was the means to achieving the coveted Rose Kennedy mouth. What was going on??

Twink took a large slug of Néscafe and a long drag on her Virginia Slim before approaching the ladies in the dressing rooms.

"Darlings," she stated in a more robust and higher-pitched voice than usual. "Please come out of the dressing rooms and place your clothing on the counter." She directed the ladies waiting in line to do the same. The women immediately complied. She continued, "It appears that this long, unfortunate pandemic thing has robbed you all of your prior figures."

Twink was working hard at being diplomatic but had never really been too concerned with the occasional offense if it was what she felt was needed.

"Let me be more to the point. You are fat! You have forsaken the first rule of Clanford Society, faint before food, addled before ass, befuddled before baked goods. What has become of you all?"

Twink felt empowered to preach on this for two reasons. First, she was perpetually anorexic because of her usual diet of coffee and cigarettes. Second, her shop was filled to the brim with small-sized apparel that none of them in their current states could squeeze into.

"Before anyone deludes themselves into thinking the sizes that they have chosen to try on will actually fit, and before any damage is done to my precious inventory in an aborted attempt, I want each of you to walk in front of the full-length mirror and remind your brains of your current conditions."

Twink viewed this command as therapeutic, given that she knew for a fact that each and every woman in her store and those in line had avoided any full-length mirrors for months, if not years. The women complied, with many breaking out into disquieted sobs, reaching furtively for a mimosa to calm their nerves.

"Ladies, we have two months until the Women's Auxiliary Luncheon. Two months to get serious about yourselves and get your fat asses into shape. I'm confident you can all get your acts together and do what is needed."

Unfortunately, Twink didn't have the same level of confidence that her inventory would ever be moved out this season. She told Emma to allow the remaining women in line into the shop, but now in groups of just five. Twink instructed each to remove their coats and present themselves in front of her. Unlike the Roman emperor's thumbs up which meant immediate death to the gladiator, Twink's upward extended opposable digit spared the awaiting customers the shame of being told to get home and get skinny. The small fraction that received the positive signal was allowed to stay and purchase from Twink's vast inventory. By noon, Twink told the girls to close the shop for the day. She was crestfallen with the dire condition in which the pandemic lockdowns had left her precious clientele. She tallied up the meager sales for the day and paid Emma and the other girls a small fraction of the commission each was expecting from the enthusiastic client group. Twink told them she would reach out to them the next week about her plans for the shop going forward.

***

At dinner that night, Emma relayed the day's events to Craig in full detail. She was sad that the anticipated source of badly needed cash flow would not materialize as planned. Craig laughed as Emma described Twink's reaction to the expanding waistlines of the high society crowd. They both wondered out loud what it would be like to have so much money that your only problem was trying to keep your calorie count in check. They would love to be burdened with such problems!

Chapter Thirteen

A Plan is Hatched

The combination of worry and nausea kept Emma awake most of the night. When they heard the boys running downstairs around 7 a.m., Craig woke up and told Emma he would cover breakfast duty. As he exited the bed and made his way to the door shirtless, Emma spied his tight physique and toned chest. She laughed to herself as she remembered the whole episode of Craig's nightly drunken escapades and Little Debbie bingeing, as well as his dramatic weight loss from those crazy hangover pills.

"Wait—those pills..."she said out loud. "Where are those pills?" Again, she said to no one.

She made her way down to the kitchen where Craig was making chocolate chip pancakes for the boys, who were running around hitting each other with Nerf swords. The smell of the pancakes and the chaos brought on another wave of nausea. She made her way to the kitchen table and sat down.

"Craig, those pills, those goofy hangover pills, do you still have them?"

Craig was busy flipping the pancakes to avoid getting them too dark. He turned to Emma with a quizzical look on his face.

"The man-up pills, you mean?"

"Yes, the ones you took that burned all of that fat off of you— and there was so much fat..."

"Easy, easy, Em! That's a little aggressive."

"Craig, those pills were like a miracle drug. Look at you now.

You are really buff."

"I know, but it seems strange that they did that. They were supposed to just cure a hangover."

"Maybe it's a metabolism thing. Maybe they energize your fat-burning mechanism or something. No matter what, they worked."

"Okay, but why all of the interest in them now?"

"Craig, don't you see, those pills could solve the fat problem for all of Twink's customers. We give them the pills, they get skinny, they buy lots of clothes, and I rake in the commissions—winners all around!"

Craig turned his attention back to the pancakes, "Shit, I burned them again." He quickly scraped the pan clean and started his second attempt at breakfast. "Emma, give me a minute here. I need to get the boys settled with some food so we can talk about this."

Two fluffy stacks were placed on the table, and the boys started in on them with gusto. With the boys fully occupied, Craig turned his attention back to Emma's plan.

"Seems like an interesting idea but why give these rich broads anything for free? They can certainly pay for it and my guess is they would do so enthusiastically. Let me run upstairs and see how many I have left in my DOP kit."

Emma nibbled on a pancake, trying to quiet her nausea. Craig returned with a small prescription bottle in hand. He sat down, spilled them on the table, and began to count.

"Looks like there are a little over one hundred pills here. I never counted them when I got them, but there were probably a couple more hundred when I brought them home. How many do you think we need?"

Emma did some quick calculations in her head.

"Well, a little over one hundred women passed through Twink's shop last Saturday. Except for maybe five or six who could fit into Twink's inventory, everyone else could be a prospective buyer. So, let's say a solid one hundred to start. How many pills did you take to burn off your fat ass?"

"I said EASY on that. Well, I took one every night after downing a twelve-pack of Corona. So...thirty per month, five months...a total of about one hundred and fifty."

"Wait, you took a pill every night? What were you thinking? Did you ever think these might be bad for you if you were on them long- term? Jesus, Craig!"

"Mr. Chen told me to take one to prevent a hangover."

"So, you take a bottle of who knows what kind of pills from a shady guy in Taiwan who probably bought them in a back alley, and the thought never crossed your mind that this might be a problem??"

"Emma, you make it sound so sinister. This is like a homeopathic cure for these guys. Probably just a bunch of herbs and shit. One of those things handed down over the generations. It certainly kept me from getting any serious hangover, and the after-effect was a bonus."

"I can't speak to the hangover cure, but it really did make you lose all that weight. How should we think about this regarding Twink's gang?"

"I think what we do is get Twink to speak to five women and offer to give them each five pills to start with. Once they start dropping weight and believe me, they will, we'll have them hooked, and we'll figure out some outrageous price for their next purchase."

"Jesus, Craig, you sound like a drug dealer—get them hooked and then become their suppliers?"

"This isn't heroin, Emma. It's diet pills, and we have a willing and wealthy potential market."

"Okay, let me reach out to Twink and see what she says. Then we can go from there. How are we going to get more pills if this works?"

"I will call that asshole Chen and tell him to ship me some. He still owes me for tanking my deal and getting wealthy while doing it."

***

Emma called Twink to request a time to meet. She felt that this all needed to be discussed in person because of the wacky backstory she needed to relay ahead of any discussion on her proposal. Twink was intrigued by

Emma's claim that she may have a solution to the fat problem in Clanford and agreed to meet in her store at 2 p.m.

When Emma arrived, Twink was already in the boutique with the lights on and the door sign clearly dissuading any potential walk-ins— "Closed Until Further Notice." As usual, Twink was impeccably dressed, hair done with coffee and cigarette in hand. Twink approached Emma and offered her usual French bisé on both cheeks.

"Well darling, what is this secret plot you've concocted to rid Clanford Society of all this grotesque pandemic weight? I'm all ears!"

Emma started in with the background of Craig and his job loss, the nightly binges, and the weight gain. She continued about how she shamed him with her fat comments and jokes. Unbeknownst to Emma, Craig continued his drinking exploits but was taking some hangover pill that he was given while on one of his many trips to Taipei before the COVID lockdowns. Long story short, the pill burned all the fat right off Craig but didn't touch his underlying muscle structure. He was back to being his college weight with all his muscle tone intact. It was only after Emma saw the post-medication results that Craig fessed up to the pill routine.

Without emotion, Twink took a long drag on her Virginia Slim and held it briefly before releasing the smoky cloud upward toward the ceiling. This was followed by a strenuous sip of Néscafe. Twink set down the cup on the table and looked intently into Emma's eyes before speaking.

"Darling, if what you say is true, this could be the equivalent of finding the holy grail. If these pills really hold the key to perpetual slimness, you will become "la doyenne premiere" of all Clanford."

Emma watched her, half afraid to speak.

Twink continued, "Emma, this is much larger than I think you realize. The women of Clanford Society are some of the wealthiest in the country, if not the world. Their lives revolve around oneupmanship or, should I say, "oneupwomanship." Their oxygen is status, and their status is highly dependent on their personal presentation. They transact their daily lives in luncheons, teas, and philanthropic dinners and balls. They are on stage 24/7. My business model is built on their unslakable thirst for more and better couture. The events that unfolded last Saturday, right here in my boutique, have completely upended the normal flows of the social tides. I have been on the phone non-stop with the highest members of the social strata, talking them off the ledge. They are inconsolable in the realization of what they have allowed their figures to become. They are seeking out plastic surgeons and quick fad diet gimmicks to try and get the extra pounds off in time for the Auxiliary luncheon at Butternut. Several have asked me to have bespoke outfits created in Paris for them in larger sizes, just in case. Money is no object to them. Two women independently have offered me several hundred thousand dollars to escort them via private jet to Europe."

Emma remained silent but began to realize the opportunity at hand.

"Twink, Craig suggested that you contact five women who we can give five pills each as an introduction to the product. Once they see the results, we can figure out some high price to charge for the next round. As he says, once we have them hooked."

"I like Craig's style; he certainly has a good mind for business," Twink said as she took another long pull on her cigarette.

"But I don't think we give them away. I will reach out to Fluffy Williams and have her choose the other four guinea pigs. I will tell her this is top secret and that they will be given additional optionality only if they show meaningful weight loss from the first set of pills. We will charge each of them $1,000 per pill to start."

Emma gasped so loudly that Twink's reflexive reaction shook the long ash from her cigarette onto the expensive carpet.

"Emma, how many pills do you and Craig have right now?"

"Twink, that's the problem, Craig only has about one hundred at the house. We will need a much larger supply if this takes off."

"I agree. How does Craig go about getting more?"

"I'm not sure. These pills aren't sold in regular pharmacies in Taiwan. He bought them from some back-alley shaman in Taipei."

"Do you think he can get some more right away?"

"I will ask him. The problem is we really don't have the money to buy a ticket for him to travel back there and if it's sent via mail, they might not let a large bag of unmarked pills through customs."

"Emma, tell Craig to give me the travel information he needs right away. I will call my travel agent, Suzanne, and have her book a flight and hotel ASAP. We need to get a big supply in hand by the end of this week. Is Craig free to travel?"

"I'm sure he is. I will talk to him as soon as I get home. Do you really think that we can sell them for $1,000 a piece? I mean, this could be life-changing for us. We are in such a deep financial hole right now that this could bring us back to normal. Twink, how much of that will Craig and I get?"

"First, I am positive about the $1,000 price. That is scratch to these women. Second, darling, you and Craig will keep it all. I see this is a win, win, win for you, my boutique, and the queen bees of Clanford. Now run along and have Craig call me with the travel details."

Emma's head was spinning as she tried to calculate the potential income from this venture while navigating her way home in the minivan. One hundred pills at $1,000 per pill was $100,000! What if he brought back one thousand pills? She couldn't even do the math in her current state of hypoxia. "Take deep breaths, take deep breaths," she kept telling herself.

When she arrived home, Craig had the boys in the driveway shooting hoops on the Little Tykes basketball set. Emma jumped out of the car and ran to Craig. She was so flushed with excitement that she couldn't begin to tell Craig of Twink's idea.

Seeing her heightened state of excitement, Craig grabbed her by the shoulders, thinking she was having a medical emergency.

"Emma! Are you okay? Is the baby okay? What is going on...?"

Emma strained to regain her composure but finally was able to calm her shaking body.

"Craig, I spoke with Twink. She loves the idea of selling the man-up pills to the society ladies. She is going to reach out to one of the tippity top women at Butternut and have her choose four other women to start taking the pills. Twink said not to give them away for free. She said she is going to charge them $1,000 per pill!"

"Are you fucking kidding me?"

Artie chimed in, "Mom, Daddy just said fuckin', and you said that was a bad word."

Craig sheepishly looked over to Emma.

"Sorry about that. Hey, wait, how does Artie know about the f- word?"

"It's a long story," Emma continued. "Twink wants you to call her right away with the flight and hotel information for Taipei. She says you need to go back to get more pills as soon as possible."

"Wait, what??"

"Craig, you need to go and get more pills. Twink says these women will go crazy for them. We can start at $1,000 each but can possibly raise the price if things go well."

"Emma, slow down. We don't have the money for me to go to Toledo, let alone Taipei right now."

"Craig, I told Twink that. She is paying for everything. She said to go and get as many pills as you can bring back. We need to have a big supply as more and more women come looking for them. This could be our ticket out of debt, Craig, and allow us to get back on our feet. You need to do this for me and the boys."

Craig couldn't disagree with that argument. He immediately understood the potential of this new endeavor but was a bit uneasy about heading back to Taipei. He hadn't been there in over two years. The place held nothing but bad memories for him. He left the city in disgrace and vowed to never return. Now he was going to head back and try and navigate the back alley pharmaceutical world to secure a large supply of "man-up." What could possibly go wrong?

***

Within an hour of speaking to Twink, Craig received an email from Suzanne with his full itinerary. A black car would pick Craig up at 4 p.m. the next day to whisk him off to O'Hare for his 8 p.m. United flight to Taipei. He was pleasantly surprised to see that Twink had instructed Suzanne to book him in business class and secure a room at the Mandarin Oriental instead of the Hilton that Craig had requested. Twink certainly knew the art of fine travel. Deep down Craig was grateful for all the kindness that Twink had shown to Emma and his entire family.

During the fifteen-hour flight, Craig laid out in detail his plan to secure the pills as quickly as possible, disguise them as best he could in his carry-on as well as design a backup plan to abort everything if things got dicey.

After clearing customs and grabbing a cab to the city, Craig arrived at the Mandarin Oriental around 6 am. Thankfully, Suzanne had secured the room for the previous night so Craig could get in immediately upon arrival. He was too wired to sleep, so he took a quick shower and ordered a pot of coffee and the American Breakfast from the twenty-four-hour room service menu. While he was eating, he texted Mr.Chen, telling him he was in Taipei and needed to meet that morning if possible. Craig figured Chen had a regular supplier of the man-up pills, given he was the one who introduced him to them initially. Craig suggested a breakfast meeting at the hotel at 9 a.m. He figured a free meal would help Chen commit to meeting. He also clearly stated this was about a new venture he was pursuing so as not to put Mr. Chen on the defensive about the failed real estate transaction.

Chen responded almost immediately. His response was far from what Craig expected and immediately infuriated him. Mr. Chen declined the meeting "with regrets." Apparently, the windfall from the busted deal had allowed Chen to relocate to Bali, where he was currently pursuing his certification as a master diver.

"Master Diver, my ass!" Craig screamed to the bathroom mirror. "He's a master swindler is what he is."

The physical effects of the long flight and time zone change added to Craig's level of anger. He was doubly frustrated by Chen's unavailability to help him with securing the pills as well as the realization that Chen's new lifestyle was made possible by his now previous employer's earnest money capital. He screamed again and punched the wall, immediately realizing the error of this adolescent response. He could feel the blood flow into his knuckles, and the pain radiated all the way back to his wrist. What a stupid move.

After finally settling down and immersing his hand in the hotel ice bucket, he texted Chen back and asked him for the contact information for his "man-up" supplier. He made it sound like it was an afterthought and not the main reason for his visit. Chen gave him a name and a rough address, just a street and a landmark of a black-painted building with a street food vendor in front. Craig looked up the street name on Google Maps and realized that it extended at least several miles through a serpentine maze of named and unnamed passages. He could only imagine what this place looked like.

Craig then remembered that he had briefly conversed with his college roommate's uncle during the early stages of his real estate investment process. The uncle actually had made the introduction to Chen. He also remembered that the uncle became scarce when the investment started falling apart. He lit up his phone several times but, not surprisingly, was ghosted.

Craig needed a new plan. He looked again at the Google Maps and tried to look closely down the road via the street view option. It was a slow and painful process. He needed to find a black-painted building but also had to hope that when the view was recorded the street vendor had been there at the time. He reviewed the street for more than an hour and finally found what appeared to be three black-painted buildings. None of them, however, had a food vendor anywhere near them.

Before Craig left for his trip, Twink had sent over $9,000 in cash that she had withdrawn that morning from the bank. She chose the amount to avoid the risk of any reporting requirement for the large withdrawal. Craig had secured the money while he traveled in the zippered pockets of several Lululemon joggers in his carry-on bag. He had pulled the cash out and was now faced with the dilemma of carrying it inconspicuously into the seedy part of town. He called down to the concierge and asked him to send up a roll of white athletic tape. The concierge immediately dispatched a runner to pick up the requested item at the nearby pharmacy.

Within an hour, Craig was securing the stash of $100 bills to his calves and thighs as well as across his tight ABS. He pulled on his joggers and an oversized sweatshirt and headed down to the hotel lobby. He approached the concierge again and explained, through a tale of high fiction, how he needed to find a friend's elderly parent in the city but only had a building description, not a firm address. Could the concierge recommend a bi-lingual guide who could assist Craig in locating the building and be available for any translations, if needed, in order to find the right person? The concierge knew just the right person. He directed Craig to wait in the lobby bar, and he would send the guide over as soon as possible.

Craig sat uncomfortably up to the bar. The strap of cash against his stomach restricted his ability to completely bend at the waist. He ordered a bottle of Tsingtao and asked for some snacks to munch. The bartender obliged with a cold bottle, frosted glass, and bowl of pretzels. Craig reviewed the Google Maps again and decided he would relay a little more information to the guide to make sure he found the right location and supply of pills he needed.

After two beers, a middle-aged man appeared at Craig's side and introduced himself as Mr. Wu, the guide he had requested. Mr. Wu was dressed casually, well-groomed and spoke impeccable English. Craig awkwardly slid off the barstool and shook Mr. Wu.'s hand.

"It's very nice to meet you, Mr. Wu, and thank you for agreeing to help me on such short notice."

Mr. Wu gave as light bow and explained to Craig that this was a side job for him. He taught Mandarin at the American School to many of the expatriate families' children. He himself had spent the first fourteen years of his life in Washington, D.C., as the son of a diplomat. His family returned to Taipei with the change in the Taiwanese political environment. Wu confessed to Craig that he was still a Washington Nationals fan which gave them both the opportunity to share childhood memories of Major League Baseball fanship and visits to several of the famous ballparks.

Upon arrival at the hotel, Craig had exchanged $500 U.S. for local currency. He gave Mr. Wu the street name and building description that Chen had provided. He was a little more forthcoming with Wu, telling him he needed to secure some local homeopathic pills from a black-market pharmacy. Craig also showed him the Google Map screenshots of three buildings on the street that fit the description. Mr. Wu didn't react at all to Craig's request. He led Craig outside to the bell stand and had the parking attendant hail them a cab. As they entered the cab, Wu barked out orders to the cab driver, and they were off.

The ride through the streets of Taipei was somewhat harrowing as the cabbie gave no leeway to the many motorcycles and scooters that aggressively fought for space in the tight streets of the inner grid. As they made their way out of the more commercial area, the streets became narrower and the neighborhoods more imposing. Craig recognized the street name on the side of a building as they rounded a corner onto a long passage of brick buildings of varying heights and ages. The street became impassable via cab because of the large pedestrian presence. Craig and Wu got out, and after a few moments of Wu and the cabbie screaming at each other, a reasonable fare was agreed upon and they made their way into the throng of people. The air was filled with the aroma of spicy food as they passed numerous street food vendors.

Craig felt completely overwhelmed by the crowd and the less-than-friendly atmosphere of this area.

"Mr.Wu, is it safe for us to be here?"

Mr.Wu laughed, "Of course, this is just one version of the open markets in the many small business districts of the city."

As they made their way through the crowd, Craig suddenly felt the need to be completely transparent with Mr. Wu. He pulled him to the side of the street and told him that he was looking to buy a large supply of "man-up" pills, maybe as many as five or six thousand, and that he had a very large quantity of U.S. cash taped to his body under his sweatsuit.

Wu laughed hard.

"You seem like a pretty young guy to be needing so many boner pills."

"Wait, no! Not Viagra, man-up, the hangover pills."

Wu made a funny face at him.

"What do you mean, hangover pills?"

"That's what this guy Chen called them. He gave me a bottle of them so I could recover quickly from hard-drinking business dinners that I had with clients here several years ago. I've taken them. They work."

Wu drew quiet, and Craig could tell he was racking his brain to figure out what Craig was talking about.

"Mr. Wu, they are a very tiny round blue pill. They didn't have any markings on them. Mr. Chen told me that guys took them all the time. They were black market, made from some ancient recipe or some shit like that."

Mr. Wu had been raised in a higher social class than the crowd pressing up hard against them in the street. He had never heard of such a thing but agreed to help Craig find a pharmacy on the street they were attempting to navigate and inquire with them.

As they rounded one particular curve in the street, they both spotted the black-painted building directly in front of them at the same time.

In tandem, they both shouted, "There it is!"

They quickly crossed the street. The building looked to have a clothing retailer in the storefront and apartments on the floors above. There was a gangway to the left of the building leading down a long flight of stairs. Wu pointed, and they both walked down the cement and brick passageway. At the bottom was a wooden door with a sign hanging by a nail.

"The sign reads walk-in, Craig. I will go first."

They pushed open the door and entered a small room with a glass counter filled with what looked like hundreds of different pharmaceuticals as well as other sundry items. A taller man and shorter woman appeared from behind a black curtain that blocked the view of a high level of activity that seemed to be going on in the back room.

Wu addressed them both in Mandarin and began describing the large number of pills that Craig was looking to purchase.

Immediately, both the woman and man began laughing out loud and pointing to Craig.

"What the fuck are they laughing at?" Craig demanded.

Wu was laughing too and spoke, "They want to know why you need so many boner pills."

The couple continued to laugh as the man started waving his hand in the universal sign language for jerking off.

"Tell them my boner is fine! I don't need help with that. I want hangover pills!!"

Wu was now laughing as hard as the couple, and Craig became indignant.

"Why can't you explain about the man-up pills? Have they never heard of them?"

Wu caught his breath but had tears still streaming down his cheeks.

"Man-up is an American expression that does not translate well here. Mr. Chen must have either made that name up himself or heard it from some other Westernized guys."

"Okay, so do they have the pills regardless of the name?"

"They told me about the local name for them, but they don't make them here. They gave me the name and address of another supplier that is also on this street that can make large quantities of pills. It's about a ten-minute walk. We must ask for a guy named Chia-hao that's how they know that we are good to be let into the operation."

The second spot, which was one of the buildings Craig had identified in Google Maps, was even more sketchy than the first. This time, the entry was down two flights of stairs that were badly lit. The door had a small slot with a sliding metal cover. After knocking, two eyes appeared in the slot on the other end. Mr. Wu invoked the name he was given, and the door was opened, and they were quickly ushered in. The size of the room was much larger than the building footprint it was under. It seemed like it stretched at least half of a city block. In neatly lined rows, women sat on low stools next to pill manufacturing machines, feeding powder into large, paddled chutes that fed the mixture into the pressing compartments. At the other end, perfectly shaped pills by the hundreds were shot into a metal bucket. A second set of women took the finished pills and fed them into a machine that sorted them into even rows for the final step of blister packing them.

Craig was amazed at the size of the operation and the efficiency of the workers. There was no speaking between any of the women. The only sound one heard was the constant thumping of the pill- creating process. Craig estimated in his mind that there were over two hundred machines in operation.

Wu quickly approached the man who seemed to be in charge. Again, in fluent Mandarin, he explained what Craig was looking to purchase. The man looked at Craig for along time and then re- engaged with Wu in conversation.

Mr. Wu approached Craig and said, "He wants to know how many you need."

Craig replied, "It depends on how much he charges, but I'd like to buy around five thousand, maybe more."

Wu relayed the response. Once again, the man looked at Craig very suspiciously. Mr. Wu explained that Craig had American dollars and would be paying in cash.

The man again spoke to Wu, and Wu relayed the message to Craig, "He wants $5 per pill, and you have to buy a minimum of two thousand."

"That's too much," Craig answered. "I can't pay that much. I need at least five thousand and I have $8,500 in cash on me right now."

Mr. Wu thought for a minute before speaking. He didn't want to offend the man, nor did he want to put himself and Craig in any danger. Mr. Wu did know, however, that many wealthy Taiwanese and Chinese were always looking for ways to launder local currency into hard currencies like the U.S. dollar. Many used the casinos in Las Vegas to do that. He again began conversing with the facility owner. This time, Craig noticed the man slightly nodding his head as Wu spoke to him. He spoke back to Wu but in a measured tone, which Craig took as a good sign.

"He has agreed to make you five thousand pills. It will take him two days, but you must pay upfront the $8,500."

"Whoa, how do I know he won't just take my money and refuse to open the door when we return?"

Mr. Wu smiled as he spoke to Craig so as not to divulge Craig's insult to the owner's reputation. He relayed to Craig that this man had agreed to his terms and that he himself believed the man was conducting business fairly.

Craig told Mr. Wu to relay that he agreed to these terms and then put his hand out to shake on the deal. The owner relayed to Mr. Wu that he wanted to see the cash before shaking hands. Once again, Craig became the object of the owner's and several of the women worker's laughter when he took off his shirt and sweats, revealing the packs of hundred-dollar bills strapped to his body. He winced as the tape pulled out his body hair, as he removed the cash for counting. A mirrored wall across the room disclosed to Craig why they were laughing at him. It seems Craig didn't think that he might have to hand over the cash in front of anyone when he put on his joggers that morning. As the laughter in the room increased, Craig's reflection revealed to himself and the hundreds of workers that he was completely naked except for the patchwork of taped-on dollars on his legs and stomach. He quickly grabbed for the joggers at his ankles and pulled them up as quickly as he could. Unfortunately, they got stuck on the stacks taped to his calves, and as he pulled harder, he lost his balance and fell to the floor, hitting the back of his head on the concrete floor. The roar of laughter now drowned out the sound of the machinery. Even Mr. Wu was crying with laughter as he tried to help Craig up from the floor.

"What the FUCK?" Craig screamed as he finally got the dollars off and his pants righted. "What is so fucking funny? Look, I'm bleeding!" Craig held out his hand, showing blood from the wound on the back of his head. A large goose egg was already forming. The crowd only laughed louder. "What is so funny?"

He knew damn well what was so funny, but he was angry from embarrassment and pain. As he was regaining his composure and holding a towel to his head, Mr. Wu and the owner were verifying the $8,500 in cash on the counter. The owner's whole body was shaking as he continued to laugh while counting.

Craig stayed quiet and watched. Suddenly, he had another thought. He turned to Mr. Wu and asked him to inquire if they could dye the pills hot pink instead of blue. Craig thought they might be an easier sell to the women. Wu obliged and inquired about a possible change in color. Without looking up from his counting, the owner shook his head in agreement.

Finally, the count was confirmed, and the owner approached Craig with a smile still moving across his face. He held out his hand to shake on the deal and told Mr. Wu that they should return in two days for the finished product. Just as he was turning to leave, the owner held out a bottle of pills and told Wu that they were for his head. He continued to laugh as Craig and Mr. Wu exited up the stairs.

***

Back at the hotel, Craig treated Mr. Wu to beers and American burgers at the lobby bar. He paid him the equivalent of $200 U.S. and asked him if he could come back in two days to accompany him back to the pill supplier. Mr. Wu agreed, thanked Craig, and left the bar. It was now almost seven o'clock, and Craig was tired from the day's events and sore from the hand punch and head wound. He ordered one more beer and then retired to his room. Since it was only 5 a.m. in Clanford, he would wait at least an hour before he called Emma to relay his first full day in Taipei.

Emma was already up and showered when Craig called her at 6:30 a.m. She was glad to hear his voice and tried to keep from laughing out loud as Craig relayed the day's events.

"Boner pills, really? They actually called them boner pills?"

"Yes, they did, crazy ass people!"

"Craig, what are you going to do for the next two days while you wait for the pills? Do you think there is any risk that they just took the money?"

"I plan to take a twenty-four-hour nap and try and expunge any memory of today from my brain. I'm not too worried about losing the money. Mr. Wu, my new buddy, thinks they will deliver."

"Craig, do you realize what this can mean for us? If we sell all those pills, we will get $5million! $5 million!!!"

"Emma, don't count that money yet. We have a ton of work to do to get these sold, and we have no idea if Twink's claim that these women will pay $1,000 per pill is realistic."

"Craig, I know, but for the first time in a long time, I feel like we are on a good path forward. I love you, baby, and I miss you. Be safe and get home soon."

"I love you too, Emma. I will be home on Friday."

As Craig drifted off to sleep, he couldn't help but count the $5 million that they would realize from this scheme. All the dreams he had for himself and his family before the pandemic were re-emerging in his brain. He slept soundly for the first time in a long time.

Thursday morning, Craig met Mr. Wu in front of the hotel, and once again, they navigated the streets of Taipei with an aggressive cab driver. They descended the two flights of stairs and were shown into the pill production room upon uttering the password through the metal door slot. The owner smiled as they entered, and a good number of the women working that morning looked up and smiled as well. Craig tried to ignore them as he offered his hand to the owner. Mr. Wu and the owner exchanged some pleasantries in Mandarin.

They moved together toward the counter where the owner produced a cardboard box holding fifty blister sleeves holding one hundred pills each. Craig smiled, thinking of the huge margin he would be making on the sale of these pills. All the humiliation was worth it. He even felt a little proud that he had negotiated such a good deal. He chuckled to himself, imagining how angry the owner would be if he knew the sales price per pill in Clanford.

Craig and Mr. Wu thanked the owner again and left with the pills. Craig immediately realized that he had a new problem to solve. How would he get this large quantity of pills through security and customs both in Taipei and Chicago? The blister packs had foil on the backside of them which would surely show up on the x-ray machine and draw the attention of security. If he emptied them from the blister packs, they would still show up in the x-ray. As he passed a shop on the street on the way to find a cab, Craig saw something that gave him an idea of how he could get them through security. He asked Mr. Wu to wait outside while he went into the shop to make a purchase.

***

Craig repeatedly wiped the sweat from his face as the cab drove him to the airport on Friday morning. It wasn't the heat of the day that caused his profuse sweat. Rather, he was nervous about his ability to get his pills through security and customs. When he exited the cab, he went into the restroom to splash water on his face and dry off as much as possible. He didn't want to draw attention by looking nervous and perspiring.

The customs segment went fine, and he advanced to the security checkpoint. He made sure he put his phone and watch through the X-ray belt so that he wouldn't trigger the metal alarm. He also placed a jacket on top of his carry-on suitcase to try and place another layer between the X-ray machine and his stash of pills. Things were moving along just fine. He retrieved his phone and watch and was about to grab his bag when a security officer moved toward him and took his bag from the moving belt for further examination.

Craig's blood ran cold, and he immediately began to sweat again. "CALM DOWN, CALM DOWN," he shouted inside his brain. The bag was taken to an area behind a screen to provide privacy to the guards as they inspected the contents. Craig was ushered over to the table and watched as they opened the bag. "DAMN, I'M BUSTED," he railed in his brain.

The security officer's gloved hands slowly opened the suitcase. At the top of the pile of clothing was a shocking pink sequined and feathered negligée. The officer lifted it slightly to reveal a bright yellow sequined negligée, also with feather flourishes beneath it. Each piece was pulled back to reveal yet another similarly sequined naughty-wear. All of them size large. The two officers conducting the search asked if Craig was transporting all these pieces for sale in the U.S., which would not be permitted since he had not listed anything as commercial goods.

Craig explained that all these pieces were, in fact, for his own personal use. The two officers looked skeptical and wanted to remove all of them for further inspection. Craig reiterated that these pieces were part of his own personal wardrobe. One officer moved his hands under all the clothing as if he were going to pull them all out of the suitcase. Craig immediately lifted his oversized sweatshirt to reveal that he was wearing a similar sequined and feathered bra underneath his top.

"I love the feel of these feathers against my skin. They make me feel soooooo sexy! Would you guys like to try one on so you can feel it for yourselves?"

The officer closest to the suitcase quickly shut and zippered the bag. The two officers were trying hard to hide their emotions as they pointed Craig to the security exit into the airport terminal. As he moved out of the security area, he could hear the two guards laughing loudly, mocking his comments about feeling "soooo sexy." This time, he was laughing with them. His plan had allowed him to get five thousand illicit pills past customs and security.

For a good portion of the previous day, Craig had removed all of the pills from the blister packs and meticulously taped them with the athletic tape he had received from the concierge to the inside of the clothing. The metal sequins, he correctly calculated, would distort the shape of the pills that were taped underneath. He was home free, expecting that his numerous trips to Taipei would allow him to quickly move through customs at O'Hare airport. Again, he was correct.

During the black car ride back to Clanford, Craig sipped a split of champagne that was provided by the driver. He played over and over in his mind the confrontation with the security officers at the Taipei airport and laughed to himself. What a genius move on his part. Looking out the window, he was reminded of what Emma said about finally being on a good path forward. He couldn't argue with her on that. The Mayfields were rising again. He smiled at the thought of showing Emma his new wardrobe. She would be so jealous!

Chapter Fourteen

Man-Up! Incorporated

Unbelievably, it had only been a week since the grand re-opening disaster at Twink's High Fashion Boutique. To Craig and Emma, it seemed like a lifetime ago. So much had transpired in only seven days.

Craig and Emma met Twink at her shop at 7 a.m. sharp. Emma's mom had agreed to take the boys for the day. Craig brought along the pills still attached to the athletic tape. Since he wasn't sure what type of packaging they were going to place the pills in, he figured it was safer to keep them secured and only make one transfer. He protected his stash as if it were gold bullion. On an equivalent weight basis, they were much more valuable than gold.

Craig emptied the pills onto a worktable in the backroom, and Emma and Twink joined him. Twink, as usual, had her cigarette and coffee in hand. Twink started in first.

"I've been thinking about how best to apportion these pills to make sure everyone who wants them will be allocated some number. We originally talked about giving Fluffy and her crew five pills each to start. I was wondering, Craig, if you think they will get the same benefits if we provide each of them four pills instead of five per week?"

"Twink, I'm not sure. When I took them, I was popping one per night. I finally stopped taking them when I came clean on my drinking problem."

"So, even when you quit, you were able to stay as fit as you had become on the pills?"

"To be honest, when I stopped taking the pills, I had already started eating better and exercising every day. I can't say for sure if I needed to keep taking the pills if I hadn't changed up my eating habits."

Emma remained silent as Twink and Craig continued their discussion.

"Craig, I think we should start with four and require the women taking them to give us a report back on their weight loss at the end of the first week. This will be a condition for receiving the next batch. If we see some considerable weight loss, then we will stick to the four-per-week schedule. If they don't realize any benefits from the pills, then we will up the dose."

"Twink, I think that is a great idea. That way we can make sure we have enough to spread around and last us at least through the Auxiliary luncheon in May."

The next question related to what kind of packaging they would place the pills in. Little baggies were out of the question. They didn't want to draw attention to the fact that these pills were produced in an Asian back alley sweat shop. Twink walked back into the sales room and returned with a small box in hand. Inside the box were the small linen envelopes that Twink used to present customers with her outrageous purchase receipts. The envelopes were off-white, about three inches wide and two inches tall, and had a gold embossed script letter "T" surrounded by a wreath on the front side. The envelopes would be both discreet and classy.

The three new business partners slowly removed the pills from the tape and placed the appropriate amount in each of the envelopes. Twink then placed them into a larger box and promised to keep them in the wall safe in her office.

"Twink, do you really think that we can charge $1,000 each for these pills? That seems like such a crazy amount."

"As I mentioned to Emma last week, these women are desperate for a weight loss solution, and the price is a pittance to them. I already alerted Fluffy that she and her girls are to bring cash when we meet later this morning to complete the transaction."

Craig couldn't refrain from smiling really hard. He looked over at Emma, who was smiling just as enthusiastically. Twink told them that she would collect the $20,000 from the women when they picked up the pills and replace her original $9,000 investment back into her safe. Craig's travel expenses had totaled around $6,000, which Twink would take to pay Suzanne. That left $5,000 profit after all startup expenses were covered. Twink told Emma she would drop off the cash later that afternoon. Craig and Emma couldn't believe what they were hearing. $5,000 in cash today, with even more next week when the group will hopefully be expanded. In its very first day of operations, Man-Up Inc. had become a profitable business!

***

At precisely 11 a.m., Fluffy and crew arrived at Twink's as instructed. Each had $4,000 in $100 bills in their designer bags. Once inside and after exchanging the requisite pleasantries, Twink got down to business.

"I have a small envelope with four pink pills for each of you. This will be your first week's supply. Take one today and then every other day until next Friday. I want you to weigh yourselves today before you take the pills and then again on Friday evening. In order to receive a second allotment next Saturday, you have to give me back precise weight readings. No fudging allowed. If these prove successful for each of you, we will expand the group to more of the Auxiliary membership."

Fluffy immediately protested, "Why the hell should we share this with anyone else? Why can't we just keep them to ourselves? The others can figure out how to lose weight on their own."

Twink was quick to scold, "Fluffy, Darling. Although being a selfish bitch is in your job description as the Women's Auxiliary President, that doesn't fly here. First, everyone deserves the right to get their figures back. This pandemic thing has been horrible for us all. Second, and more importantly, I have a shop full of expensive clothing that I need to sell to your membership. If they don't get skinny, I'm stuck with millions of dollars of inventory. So, my dear, it would be in your best interest to shut your selfish mouth and get your fat ass out of my shop. If I hear any repercussions about this, you will be the first to be cut off!"

Fluffy, as well as her friends, stood shocked at Twink's aggressive behavior. Did she know who she was speaking to? Twink did know who she was speaking to, and Twink was the ONLY woman in Clanford who could get away with dressing down Fluffy as she did. Twink knew she held the keys to the kingdom of couture that all the society ladies of Clanford clamored to be part of. Twink had anticipated Fluffy's response and had prepared the verbal spanking in advance. She needed to make sure Fluffy understood that Twink would be calling all the shots with regard to the weight loss pills, no questions asked.

***

The first trial week went exceptionally well. Each of the women reported back to Twink's at 11 a.m. again on the following Saturday. The weight loss averaged 6.8 pounds across the five women, with a high of 8.1 and a low of 5.7 pounds. Fluffy was on the low end but not the lowest. Twink asked if anyone had suffered any adverse side effects, and all reported none. That was very good news. Twink pulled out the next five envelopes and collected the $20,000 in cash. Although she had many of the membership women in her database, she told Fluffy in advance to bring an updated list of the full membership along with current email addresses. Again, she warned Fluffy there had better not be any omissions or general monkey business or ELSE!

When the women left, Twink called Emma and had her report to the boutique immediately. When she arrived, Twink handed her the cash in a large manilla envelope, and Emma became weak at the knees at the thought of that amount of money for her. She quickly regained her composure because Twink had work for her to do. Twink handed her the Auxiliary membership information, which totaled one hundred and fifteen members. This, of course, included the original five guinea pigs. The remaining one hundred and ten women would be divided alphabetically into two groups of fifty-five. Emma was to take the list and place every other name into either the A or B list. The A list will be contacted today to assess their interest in participating in the program. Group B would have to wait a week, given the logistics of getting so many women through the shop at once.

Emma began emailing the women in Group A. Word had spread the previous week when the original five began the program, and everyone was anticipating an invitation to participate. The email instructed the women to meet at Twink's at 4 p.m. with the required cash. The local branch of the Clanford National Bank had run out of $100 bills earlier in the week when the women started seeking cash in anticipation of getting into the program. The line outside Twink's started forming at 2 p.m., and once again, Twink was required to let the women in early to avoid complaints from the other local retailers. Fifty-two women in total arrived, and an additional two hundred and eight pills were dispatched. Emma nervously accepted the additional $208,000! She offered Twink the money, and Twink graciously declined. Twink was worth over $100 million, and this amount meant nothing to her in reality. She asked Twink to drive her home because she was still shaking from the thought of her financial windfall.

That night, Emma and Craig sat at the dining room table staring at the cash pile. On Monday, Craig would go down to Clanford National Bank and make a $200,000 payment on their $600,000 mortgage balance. He would also pay off the $18,000 that had accumulated on the home equity line. They were on their way to financial security again, and Emma could not have been happier. Craig expressed his concern about all the cash and the need to figure out a way to get it back into the banking system. He would consult with a friend of his on Monday as well.

***

Starbucks was its usually busy self when Craig arrived at 8:30 a.m. on Monday. After a cursory glance across the dining area, he spotted his friend Brian Gaines sitting at a small table in the back. Brian already had a cup in front of him, so Craig placed his order and joined him a few minutes later. Craig was careful to give Brian just enough information to figure out a way to handle the cash correctly. Craig told Brian that he and Emma were providing weight loss consulting to a group of women in Clanford. The women preferred to pay cash for these services to avoid their husbands seeing a credit card charge. They were quietly trying to lose the few extra pounds they had acquired during COVID-19 without revealing anything to their spouses.

Brian had started his career as an accountant with PWC in Chicago but had returned to Clanford about three years earlier to join a local CPA firm that focused on small business accounting and payroll services. Brian listened intently to Craig's description and immediately saw the opportunity to add Craig and Emma's new business to his stable of clients.

"Craig, we can set up a simple LLC structure for your business with you and Emma as the sole partners. We can also set up an online payment platform that would allow your clients to make cash payments directly into your corporate checking account."

"Ooh...we haven't gotten that far yet with setting up any accounts. How should I do this?"

"Craig, all you need to give me is your or Emma's social security number and date of birth to get the LLC opened. Then I will work with Ken Naples at Clanford National to get your accounts set up. Ken is the head of the small business group over there. I can have everything prepared for you to sign in my office and I will ask Ken to join so he can go over his other services that might be helpful. What's the name of this new venture?"

Craig froze. He didn't anticipate being asked this question. He quickly thought through some options and blurted out, "Obesity Management Group? Yes, Obesity Management Group, we will go by the acronym OMG!"

Brian gave a half smile. Craig couldn't believe how simple this all was, "How quickly can we get this done?"

"I will have everything ready by Wednesday afternoon. Why don't you and Emma plan to meet me at my office at 3 p.m? We can finalize everything then."

With the business matters settled Craig and Brian exchanged stories of their respective young families while they finished their coffees. Craig walked out with Brian, shook hands on the sidewalk, and parted in opposite directions.

When Craig arrived home, Emma was busy building an Excel spreadsheet to keep track of all their new customers and the schedule for pill distribution and payments. Craig went over the details of his meeting with Brian and explained that she would need to direct the ladies to use the online portal to make payments going forward. Emma chuckled when Craig divulged the name of the new business, OMG! LLC. Payments would show up as having been made to OMG!

After going through the numbers, Emma realized that the original five thousand pills would last only through the third week in April. Craig would need to make another trip back to Taipei no later than the last week in March, which was six weeks away. Craig cringed at the thought of going through all the bullshit again, but Emma reminded him what an additional ten thousand pill sales meant for their family's bottom line, even after taxes given the new scheme. Emma also had reached out to Twink to let her know that she would be over Thursday night to fill the now one hundred and ten pill packets for this week's distribution. She suggested that they split the group between Friday and Saturday and that the email requesting payment would also give a fifteen-minute window for pick-up to lessen the risk that other Clanford residents would catch on to this new enterprise.

As the first three weeks passed, the reported weight levels continued to decline across all the women. Twink was encouraged that this may be working and decided she would re-open the shop on April 1st and try, once again, to outfit the society ladies of Clanford for the season. During the last week of March, she would do a random weight sampling of the ladies as they showed up to receive their weekly fix. The women who had either achieved their desired weight loss or were clearly on track to do so would be invited back first to shop the inventory. Twink deliberately but quietly put the word out through the grapevine to encourage stronger diligence in their weight loss journeys. The first women allowed in would have first pick of the couture.

As the second week of March approached, several women, including Fluffy, approached Twink separately to request a slight upsize in their weekly dose. All had been making good progress but felt that an additional one or two pills per week would help them turbocharge their fat shedding. Fluffy, especially, was terrified that she would not be in the first group to be permitted in on April 1st. Twink spoke to Emma and Craig, and being the entrepreneurs that they were and fully realizing that the price of Man-Up pills was totally price inelastic, raised the weekly toll for these women to $5,000. Not one of them flinched!

***

The third week of March arrived, and Craig was packing his bag for his return trip to Taipei. As the co-CEO of the burgeoning new operation, Craig felt deserving of a first-class seat on this trip as well as a luxury suite at the Mandarin Oriental. Prior to his flight, he had reached out to Mr. Wu to request his assistance once again. Craig hid $20,000, this time in his carry-on suitcase and backpack, and lied on the arrival form that he was not bringing in cash in excess of $10,000. He also packed his special lingerie for the trip home.

After catching a quick shower and breakfast upon arrival at the Mandarin Oriental, he met Mr. Wu outside the front entrance, and they repeated their trek to the pill manufacturer. Upon their arrival, the owner looked up at Craig and had to stifle a laugh. Mr. Wu informed the owner that they would need ten thousand pills this time and would once again pay in U.S. currency. He also asked that they not put them in blister packs, a small box would work just fine. The owner agreed to the same terms but instructed Craig that he would need at least three days, maybe four, to complete the order. He would contact Mr. Wu when the order was finished and when they could collect the pills.

To show his appreciation for all his help, Craig paid Mr. Wu the equivalent of $3,000 U.S. this time and treated him to fine dinners each night while they waited for the order to be completed. Craig treated himself to daily massages in the spa. You need to look and feel like a successful CEO, he thought to himself. Finally, he received a call from Mr. Wu, and the transaction was completed.

It took Craig the better part of a day to tape all the pills into the lingerie pieces. As he dressed for the long flight home, he once again put on his insurance policy in case of a bag inspection. He was much more relaxed as he entered the airport security line this time. That changed quickly when he noticed that one of the inspection officers from his previous trip was working his line.

"Shit, just my fucking luck!" he whispered to himself.

Craig entered the line, placed his bags on the belt, and proceeded through. As he got past the metal detector, he saw the original inspector begin to move his way. Craig kept his head down and didn't make eye contact. The inspector came to the other side of the belt and stopped Craig's bag.

"Here we go again," he muttered.

The inspector was now directly across from Craig, waiting for him to make eye contact. Craig finally looked up. What happened next floored Craig. The inspector gave him a big smile, put his hand up to his chest, and started twisting his own nipple while winking continuously at Craig. Trying to decipher in his brain what the fuck was actually happening, he smiled and winked back at the man, putting his hand up to his own nipple. The inspector raised his eyebrows and pushed the bag down the line for Craig to retrieve. Craig complied and headed directly for the exit to the terminal.

Home free once more!

***

Friday, April 1st, had finally arrived. How appropriate Twink thought to be opening her store for these starved women on April Fool's Day. As expected, Fluffy had been given the privilege of being the first permitted in the store with the initial group of ten. Fluffy's weight loss had been impressive. Never in her entire adult life did she tip the scale at one hundred and fifteen pounds. Even with her short stature, she was looking awesome and wanted everyone to know. She spared little time gathering piles of clothing to try on. Emma, who was directed to help her, was getting a sore arm hoisting so many togs over the dressing room door. The final tally for her spring wardrobe exceeded $200,000. As was the custom, all the outfits were boxed and wrapped and would be delivered to Fluffy's home later in the day.

The remainder of the day was just as hectic as the beginning. Twink couldn't help but direct several shamings that day, mostly to retain her reputation. She was, however, mostly pleased with how the day went and the volume of clothing sold. The three saleswomen were exhausted by the time the doors were closed at 6 p.m. Twink cracked a bottle of Veuve, which she and two of the women polished off in no time. Emma, given her pregnancy, sipped on a small bottle of Perrier. Twink had kept a running total of the sales and retreated to her office to cut the commission checks for the women. Emma slipped behind her and whispered into her ear to divide the total by just two, not three, so the others would receive larger checks.

Twink turned around and touched Emma's arm and smiled warmly. She knew Emma was a class act.

With just a month to go until the opening lunch at Butternut, the women of Clanford Society were now be-dressed, be-shod, and be-jeweled in the finest couture available in the country, if not the world, all thanks to Twink's High Fashion Boutique. Anticipation for the upcoming event would grow daily until it reached a fever pitch by the first of May.

Chapter Fifteen

Fluffy could not have ordered a more beautiful day for the opening luncheon, although given her personal means she may have at least tried if Mother Nature had not cooperated. No detail was spared in preparing the club, and especially the Grand Ballroom, for Fluffy's coronation. As was the custom, a wooden platform precisely eighteen inches off of the ground was constructed in the center of the room in front of the Palladian windows. A lectern was placed on the platform from which Fluffy would deliver her State of the Auxiliary Board speech ahead of the seated luncheon. Rows of chairs faced the podium with a center aisle carved out for Fluffy's entrance. The entire meeting had been highly choreographed by Fluffy and her first and second vice chairs, Clare Johnson and Melinda Walsh. Once Fluffy gave her opening speech, Clare and Melinda would cover all the housekeeping issues of the board meeting. Fluffy would address her eager board members juxtaposed against the sweeping landscape of Butternut with its blooming dogwoods, crab apples, and cherry blossom trees. The blossoming beauties along the fairway would provide a full-body halo of spring beauty behind her color-coordinated outfit.

Fluffy arrived two hours early to meet with William, the club manager, Letticia, the club chef, and Jeff Leaffy a florist from Europe, to bark out her final marching orders. Fluffy had personally hired Jeff, who had become famous for his floral presentations in the lobby of the Four Seasons Hotel in Paris. Jeff and his crew had arrived several days earlier and were staying with Fluffy at her estate. Rumors of an extravagant floral display being created at Butternut that had been spreading through town ahead of the event were confirmed when a chartered cargo plane arrived at the Clanford Private Airport filled with shipping containers of spring flowers from Holland. The grand entry, foyer, and staircases were transformed into an English garden replete with boxwood topiaries. The theme carried through into the grand ballroom where the bar was adorned with flower arrangement ice sculptures masterfully created by a Norwegian ice sculptor, also engaged for the event on Fluffy's personal account. She also hired a photographer and videographer to record the full event for the club historian.

Although Fluffy had been more than courteous with Jeff and his team, she threatened mayhem and job loss to William and Letticia if everything did not go off precisely as planned. The ice sculptor spoke zero English, so he just went about his work oblivious to Fluffy's tirades. At zero minus forty-five minutes to game time, Fluffy excused herself to a private room where her hairdresser and make-up artist were awaiting her for final primping. The rest of the club staff drew a huge sigh of relief when Fluffy was finally ensconced behind closed doors.

At 11:30 a.m., the club gates were opened, and the line of cars began the trek up the long driveway to the club entry to deposit their precious human cargo at the door. Arrival had also been choreographed as well with the governing board members and emeritus presidents arriving first, followed by the regular members in order of club tenure. The ladies were directed through the entry hallway and up the left staircase where they were met by Fluffy, who was flanked by Clare and Melinda, standing precisely three steps behind. Air kisses, along with high praise for Fluffy's wardrobe choice and club decorations, were exchanged as the women were processed through the receiving line. Waiters with trays of Peach Bellinis (Fluffy's favorite spring aperitif) delivered the ladies their first drink along with instructions to enter the grand ballroom so the receiving line could continue without delay.

The ladies gathered in small groups for smalltalk, mostly in line with the social pecking order. Even in the highest stratus of society, there was still a well-defined pecking order, and every woman was well aware of where they fell within it. Almost all the conversation revolved around gratuitous compliments of each other's outfits, each silently confident that they had outclassed everyone in the room. Waiters continued to silently move about with additional drinks and trays of canapés. The canapés would be eaten later by the staff, given that no one would dare be seen foisting food into their mouths ahead of the luncheon program. Round luncheon tables had been set up at the back of the large ballroom where the ladies would "lunch" at the conclusion of the business presentation. Again, Fluffy had spared no expense, neither the club's nor her own, in designing the place settings, florals and seating for the luncheon.

Fluffy was in her glory! After completing her duty on the receiving line, she mingled with the entire Auxiliary membership being aware of the requirement to speak first to the more senior ladies of the club. Everyone was all smiles, enveloped in the glow of social achievement. If the world ended that day, they would all die happy and contented socialites.

At precisely 12:30 p.m., the chime ringers entered the room to alert the ladies that they should take their assigned seats in front of the podium for the beginning of the program. Clare and Melinda walked up the aisle created between the rows of chairs with Fluffy, leather bound and gold embossed folio in hand, lagging by exactly ten feet to confirm her royal status. She ascended the platform and opened her folio on the lectern, all the while smiling as she scanned the ladies before making sure to give a nose crinkle and wink to nobody in particular so she seemed truly connected to "her people."

And then it began....

Fluffy looked down at her prepared remarks, which had been typed out in bold eighteen-font lettering to ensure she would not have to struggle to read them without her reading glasses. She looked up and then looked down again.

Melinda and Clare watched from behind her in their assigned seats on the dais, smiling in full support of their new leader.

Fluffy's shoulders shook slightly, and she quickly stymied the involuntary impulse. She thought to herself it must be nerves and concentrated even harder on the prepared remarks before her. She was about to begin again when she stopped, looked down, then up and smiled to the crowd who was awaiting her every word. Clare and Melinda looked at each other with slight concern on Fluffy's slow start. A couple of the women in the audience shifted in their seats, and a quick, high-pitched fart was expelled from someone in the emeritus section. No one dared acknowledge this faux pas, although many of the young members were holding their sphincters tight to avoid any risk of doing the same as they tried not to chuckle.

Fluffy, again, tried to steady herself so she could begin her speech. She was unaware of the time-lapse that was beginning to cause some concern with the membership. She held tight to the sides of the lectern and looked down once again to begin reading. Nothing. Clare was on the cusp of getting up to help her but feared a strong retribution from Fluffy if she did so.

Slowly and in growing volume, Fluffy began to groan.

"hmmm, hhhmmMMM, HHHMMMHHHMMMMMOOOOO!"

Heavy inhales with deep exhales, audible to the entire room. Fluffy swayed back and forth as if she was in a trance. She wildly licked her lips and began again.

"OOOOOOOOOOOOHHHHHHHHHHH,	HMMMMMMM-MMM,OHHHHHHH WOWWWWWWWWW!"

Fluffy was now rocking back in forth, hands firmly attached to the lectern, which seemed, at least at that moment, to keep her from shifting from side to side.

She laughed out loud in a long, guttural, deep-throated cackle. She continued to seem trancelike but, at the same time, seemed to be greatly enjoying whatever was happening to her.

"OHOHOH,MMMMMMM,YEEEESSSSSS,YEEEESSSSSS, OOOOOOHHHHHHH MMMMMYYYYYY!"

Clare and Melinda were on their feet but avoided getting too close to her for fear of being hurt. The ladies in the front two rows had retreated to the back of the room as well. One of the older women was quickly identified as the farter when she let an even bigger one rip as she headed for the exit.

Fluffy continued as she was now biting her lower lip and tilting her head back to the point where it looked like it might detach.

"UHHHHHHH! UUUUHHHHHHHHH! UUUUUH-HHHH!!!!"

The ballroom was clearing at a rapid pace. One woman screamed that someone needed to get an exorcist right away. Chairs were toppled, and the beautifully set lunch tables were tipped over as the women pushed each other aside to make it out of the room. As the women exited, William was trying to make his way up the staircase against a sea of satin, velvet, and netting. He was trampled by the stampede of stilettos.

Back in the ballroom, Clare and Melinda stood in shock as Fluffy continued her wild movements and moaning. Then suddenly, she grew quiet. Her head fell back into its normal position, and she looked intently across the room but seemed indifferent to the wild scene unfolding before her. She stiffened at the knees and spread her legs as if to steady herself against some kind of anticipated body blow. Then, her hips began to shake. Her torso began to undulate like a belly dancer. Her hands began to move away from the sides of the podium, but surprisingly, she did not lose her balance. Her body waved back and forth from front to back and the movement seemed to climb up her torso into her chest with each iteration. All of a sudden, with precise choreography, her hands flew up toward the ceiling, her fingers sprawled in complete starfish, her head flew back, mouth agape, and she began to scream,

"WWWWWWWWWWWWWWWWWWWHHHHHHH-H H H H H H H H H H H H - HAAAAAAAAAAAAAAAAAAAAAAAAAAAAHHHHHHH-HHHHHHHHHH!!!!!!!"

It was one long, boisterous scream that seemed to emanate from her toes. It was loud and high-pitched and converted mid-scream to a full-throated laugh. And then, in honor of her Southern Baptist conversion, Fluffy screamed a command.....

"PRAISSSSSSE JAAAASSSUUUSSSSS!"

With that, her stiffened body, hands still splayed open-palmed, fell backward on the platform, just missing the two chairs recently vacated by her frightened lieutenants. Her body laid on the platform in the position of an open jumping jack with a puddle of liquid streaming onto the floor from underneath her Italian designer dress.

The few women remaining in the room stood in stunned silence, unable to move. Clare and Melinda, who had sought cover behind the ice sculptures during Fluffy's out-of-body experience, quickly returned to her side. At first, they both feared she was dead, but immediately realized their error when they saw Fluffy's chest rise and fall in deep breaths. They knelt on either side of her carefully to avoid the growing puddle of God knew what.

Clare shook Fluffy's shoulder lightly and softly spoke to her, "Fluffy, it's me, Clare. Are you okay? Do you know where you are? Do you know what just happened to you?"

Fluffy began to moan and moved her head from side to side. She slowly opened her eyes, and a huge smile broadened across her face. She tried to sit up but faltered at first. Clare and Melinda put their hands behind her shoulders and helped her into a sitting position. Fluffy was oblivious to the expanding liquid she was sitting in.

Melinda started in, "Fluffy, Darling, we think you had some sort of seizure when you were beginning your speech. Has anything like that ever happened to you before? Do you have a history of seizures?"

Fluffy groggily responded, "No, not a seizure."

Melinda continued her questioning, "So, you've never had a seizure? Do you know where you are?"

Fluffy was still smiling as she tried to re-engage her capacity to speak, "It was not a seizure. I came."

Now, it was Clare's turn again, "Fluffy, that's good. You recognize you came to the Butternut Club for the Auxiliary luncheon. You are sitting in the Grand Ballroom. It seems you are beginning to recognize your surroundings. That's good!"

"No, you dip-shit!" Fluffy snapped. "I came, I came!"

Both Clare and Melinda looked at each other and realized she was still confused. Melinda repeated Clare's words and said, "Yes, you came to the Butternut Club for the opening luncheon."

"Motherfucker, can't you understand me?" Fluffy was now in a much more irritated state. "I came! I had a huge orgasm. I came like I have never done before. It was like out of a science fiction movie. This kind of thing just never happens on our earth!" Fluffy smiled as she remembered the experience but quickly turned on her lieutenants, "Get me the fuck up! I need to walk this off!"

Just as she was screaming these orders, the emergency squad entered the room. The call to 911 detailed the scene unfolding at the club with a prominent member in distress. The best and brightest needed to be sent right away. The arrival team included two ambulances, two firetrucks, and four patrol cars. Needless to say, anyone else having a medical emergency throughout town would have to wait.

The paramedics immediately took note of the aftermath of chaos as they approached the platform. Chairs and tables turned over, high-heeled shoes littering the floor (the women were smart enough to realize that a quick evacuation required bare feet), as well as the volume of trampled flowers that made one of the first responders lose his footing as he crossed the floor. At first, Fluffy began to bitch that the EMS was there.

"I'm fucking fine! I don't need any help! Just find my purse and get me my goddam car keys and cell phone."

One of the paramedics was righting a chair for her to sit on as the other opened his emergency supply box to bring out the blood pressure cuff to begin taking Fluffy's vitals. When Fluffy realized both were well-toned, thirty-something hunks with muscles bulging through their tight white shirts, she relented, "Okay, men, maybe you should check me out."

Both her blood pressure and heart rate remained elevated, and the fire chief who had entered the room during the exam insisted that Fluffy be taken to St. Gerard's for a thorough examination.

Fluffy cooed, "Well, if you insist. Maybe you two should lift me onto the gurney. I'm still a little weak."

Fluffy was gently placed on the transport and wheeled out to the ambulance. Many of the board members were standing barefoot on the front lawn across from the main entrance, awaiting both word on their fearless leader and the opportunity to gather their purses and shoes from the ballroom. Fluffy closed her eyes as she exited the entrance on the gurney to heighten the drama of the afternoon. She chuckled to herself, thinking that many of these women would already be thinking about the realignment of power if she was taking her last breath. Fluffy whispered to the paramedic sitting across on the bench that she would expect full lights and sirens as well as a police escort to St. Gerard's. Her request was obliged without any protestation.

Back inside the club, William was being bandaged for the injuries he sustained during the stampede down the stairs. He would be carrying both the physical and mental scars of that day throughout the rest of his life. Letticia sat in her office, chuckling with her sous chef about the afternoon events.

"Now, what the fuck am I going to do with one hundred and fifteen plates of poached salmon and steamed broccolini? These skinny white chicks pick the damnedest things to eat!"

Clare and Melinda followed the ambulance to the hospital. En route, they spoke about everything that had unfolded over the last hour. They were both still suffering the effects of shock from witnessing all the mayhem.

Clare spoke first, "What do you think Fluffy was trying to tell us about her seizure, Melinda? Do you think she just thought she had an orgasm? Is that kind of orgasm a real thing?"

They both looked at each other and began to laugh out loud. They tried to suppress the laughter, but it only increased the intensity of their emotion. Melinda was driving and pulled over because tears had filled her eyes to the point of blurring her vision. Clare literally rolled with laughter in the passenger seat. They both tried to speak but the level of laughter prevented any words. Finally, Melinda caught her breath.

"What the serious fuck was that all about? She said she came!!" Laughter again.

"Oh, hahahahaha! She actually pissed herself. Did you see that? This might be the end of Fluffy. You can't piss yourself in public and keep the presidency of the auxiliary. Seizure or no seizure. That means that one of us will get to take her spot."

They both immediately started to scheme in their minds how they would effectively knock the other out of contention. Social climbing was a blood sport in Clanford.

***

C.J. was lining up his eagle putt on the thirteenth hole, par four, when Billy Walden, the golf course manager yelled his name as he hastily approached in his golf cart.

"Fuckin-A!" C.J. screamed as he dragged the putter across the green, sending the ball far right of the cup, "This better be something good, Billy! You just made me miss an eagle. FFFUUUCCCKKK!"

Billy ignored the tirade, "Mr Williams, you need to come with me right away. Your wife had a medical emergency during the luncheon and has been taken by ambulance to St. Gerard's. We have a police car waiting to get you there as quickly as possible."

C.J. was completely irritated that he was being pulled off the course mid-game. "What kind of medical emergency?" He asked as he threw his clubs in the back ofBilly's cart. "Did she break a nail?

Billy suppressed a laugh and replied, "No, it must have been quite serious. A waiter told me the Auxiliary board members were running and screaming out of the club."

C.J. remained unimpressed and still agitated. He knew Fluffy could send women running and screaming with the threat of social ostracism for some very minor social infraction. He told the Clanford police officer there was no need for a ride to St. Gerard's. He would drive there on his own. After the police officer left the club, C.J. showered, dressed, and had a sandwich and three beers at the bar. He didn't want to arrive at the hospital unprepared for whatever drama would ensue.

***

Melinda and Clare were seated in the waiting room when C.J. arrived. They gave him a quick synopsis of the afternoon's events but intentionally left out the part about the orgasm. They had no idea of what went on at the Williams home, specifically in the bedroom, and had no intention of invoking any details through a discussion about Fluffy's "fluffy parts." C.J. told them that they should leave and he would call them when he knew more about Fluffy's condition. On the ride back to the club to retrieve Clare's car, they both burst out again in uncontrollable laughter. In unison, they said, "She said she came!!!! Hahahahahahaha!!"

***

Fluffy's emergency room cube was empty when C.J. eventually made his way back. The nurse said Fluffy had been sent down for some X-rays and a CAT scan of her head to make sure there weren't any lingering issues from the "seizure."

C.J. plopped himself down in the single chair allocated to the room and was fast asleep when the three beers from lunch took their desired effect on his brain. When Fluffy was wheeled back into the room, C.J. did not budge.

After the attendant left the room, Fluffy pounced, "C.J., you piece of shit, how the fuck can you be asleep at a time like this? The whole room smells like a brewery!"

C.J. lifted his hat above his eyes and said to Fluffy, "I'm so fucking happy to see you too, darling."

Just as she was about to let him have it even more, Dr. Lovejoy, head of Emergency Room Medicine, entered the room. The paramedics made sure to alert the staff just who they had brought in for treatment. Like Fluffy, Dr. Lovejoy was a trust fund baby but not nearly to the same level of wealth that she had been "trusted." As such, he was well aware of the social foundation in Clanford and specifically at Butternut, where he was also a member.

"My dear, Fluffy, it seems you had a very unexpected episode this afternoon. How are you feeling now?"

Well, doctor, my head hurts a bit from smacking it when I fell, but other than that, I feel pretty good."

Lovejoy continued, "That's great, Fluffy. Your X-rays have comeback negative for any fractures, and I'm still waiting for the results from the cranial CAT scan. It seems from the accounts of people who were with you describing your actions you most likely suffered a grand mal seizure. I will want to have you admitted for some more tests so we can figure out what may have triggered this. By the way, Fluffy, did you have anything to eat out of the usual before this all went down?"

"Eat? Dr.Lovejoy, don't you understand that Butternut women NEVER eat!"

Once again, he became quiet as he tried to figure out the seriousness of this and her previous comments. Maybe she was still suffering the effects of the seizure.

In reality, Fluffy's CAT scan had come back, and the results showed the entire frontal lobe of her brain had lit up like a Hiroshima heat map after the A-bomb was dropped. That part of her brain appeared so energized that he was having the machine inspected for mechanical malfunction. He didn't want to alarm her just in case it turned out to be a true reading for fear the news might cause her brain to explode. Fluffy would not abide by any overnight stay at the hospital. She wanted to set the record straight.

"Dr. Lovejoy, I did not have a seizure. I had a full-body orgasm!"

Immediately, C.J. sobered up when he heard the word orgasm being used in mixed company. Lovejoy quickly stifled a chuckle and did his best to intone a serious doctor being concerned voice.

"Fluffy, what do you mean by that?"

Frustrated, Fluffy replied, "What I mean is that I had an orgasm, I came, a boot knocker. How else can I say it? My world was rocked. Do you get it now?? I didn't have a fucking seizure. I had an orgasm so hard that it made me scream and drop over. I have never felt anything like this before in my whole life."

The good doctor gave a side-eye glance to C.J., whose mouth hung wide open. Lovejoy had learned of the screaming part from the report, which technically did not fit with a classic seizure. He wanted to ask more questions but Fluffy would have none of it.

"I have no fucking idea what gave me that wonderful orgasm, but I can tell you for sure it had nothing to do with any seizure. If you don't mind, I would like to get out of here. Hand me my clothes, C.J., and get your ass home," Fluffy continued.

As usual, C.J. did as he was told and quickly handed Fluffy her urine-soaked dress and shoes. Dr. Lovejoy was not as quick to dismiss all that had happened. He was going to spend some time trying to better understand the circumstances around the day's events.

Chapter Sixteen

The news of the day's events spread through Clanford with lightning speed. The cell phone transmission towers were stretched to their very limits and bordered on the risk of a complete collapse. Ladies in one conversation were put on hold and forgotten as the next call came in. Each new story took on added details most of them embellished beyond recognition. Half of Clanford was convinced that Fluffy Williams was dead, rest her soul. Another storyline making the rounds insisted that thirty-some women were dead or injured from the stampede that ensued during Fluffy's seizure. Although the story outcomes were all different, they all started with eyewitness accounts of the physical gymnastics of the queen bee of Clanford.

And the queen bee was lying low. She had the assistant to her assistant hold all calls and definitely not accept any visitors. Fluffy was smart enough to know that she, and only she, needed to control the conversation around what exactly had happened. She took refuge in her master bedroom, which was a separate room from C.J.'s master bedroom. With a bottle of her favorite Sauvignon Blanc, she began to plot her response.

The first people to be contacted were the photographer and videographer. Her henchman would be dispatched the following morning to get full possession of all photo images and video. Just to ensure full compliance, a message of never doing business again in Clanford would be delivered to the two small businesses if they failed to comply fully. Both, Fluffy anticipated, would immediately realize the risk to their livelihoods and fall in line.

Next, Fluffy's senior assistant would meet with William and Letticia at Butternut to discuss their "recollections" of the prior day. Both would be instructed to meet with their entire staff, those present at the luncheon, and those who were not even working but more than likely had already been given blow-by-blow accounts to demand signed Non-Disclosure Statements or risk immediate firing without any possible references. William would be compliant, but Letticia might be a wild card, Fluffy thought.

Another Fluffy representative would meet with the Fire Chief and commit a large donation to the Fire Safety Board's Annual Fire Ball and offer the Butternut Club as this year's venue. This would be a real coup for the Chief, given ninety five percent of the usual attendees would never ever have the opportunity again to see the inside of the club. Only Fluffy carried the weight inside the club to be able to make such an offer. The Chief, in return, would assure Fluffy that none of his crew would divulge any details of the day.

Fluffy felt confident that the HIPAA laws would protect her against wagging tongues at St. Gerard's. She did, however, also plan to have a call with the hospital administrator first thing in the morning to remind her of her own and her mother's senior positions on the hospital board and the level of financial support they gave annually to the St. Gerard Hospital Foundation.

The last line of defense was the Auxiliary Board membership themselves. Here is where Fluffy may have been a little too naive. She assumed, quite incorrectly, that the ladies of Clanford society would demonstrate the utmost degree of discretion if they were asked any details about Fluffy's medical emergency. The women were from the finest families and would never participate in any type of gossip or innuendo that would defame the duly elected president of their social sorority. They were clearly a class above all that type of plebeian behavior.

Wrong!

Fluffy knew all too well the road to the highest ranks of social standing. It was a pathway paved in the crushed bones of social rivals. Getting to the top was ugly, but the fall from the top was even uglier. Fluffy had assumed that she had been well supported in her rise to the pinnacle of the Clanford in-crowd. In reality, most saw the clear advantage she had inherited as the daughter of Marguerite. Many correctly knew that trying to challenge her on her way up could prove socially fatal for them. They gladly feigned total allegiance to the up-and-coming doyenne because it served their own social position and strategies to align with the leader. Deep down, her fellow members knew she was a raging bitch and were aware of her whorish reputation from college. Any sign of weakness in her total control of the social stratum would be exploited by those who felt they were better suited to the role and would bring decorum back to the

Auxiliary membership. The two best positioned to initiate the coup were her two right-hand ladies-in-waiting, Melinda and Clare.

Melinda and Clare, who had observed everything firsthand, had vested interests in seeing Fluffy go down. They met again over drinks that night at a local dive bar where no one who knew anyone would recognize them. Melinda brought her iPad so they could memorialize in detail everything that had occurred. They started with how bitchy she had been to the staff that morning and how she was railing against everyone, including themselves, who weren't continuing to praise her for the club's presentation ahead of the luncheon. They moved on to the receiving line, where she frequently made a face back at them after greeting one of the members she didn't care for. The finger-to-mouth puking sign was her favorite.

Her choreographed entrance to the podium was laughable at best. Fluffy truly believed the luncheon to be a coronation into her position as "queen" of Clanford society. Melinda was busy typing while Clare narrated their collective memory of the events. They documented the body movements, the moaning and laughing, the undulating belly, and the arm stretching high into the air with her fingers splayed. They both burst out in laughter again when they recounted the final moments of her performance.

"She fucking screamed like she was being ax murdered in a voice nor octave I've never heard before."

Recounted Clare, "The icing on the cake, hahahahahaha, was the Praise Jesus! I thought I was at a fucking revival!"

Melinda screeched as she once again was in a full belly laugh, "I'm going to call that move a PJ. Hahahaha a PJ!"

"Be careful, Melinda. Fluffy might think you are saying BJ, which is something she is quite familiar with!!"

The two of them were laughing so hard that the other patrons in the bar began to stare. They tried to calm themselves, but one of them would ultimately crack up and send the other into hysterics.

"This is just too good to be true!" Clare barked.

"This, along with her soiling her fancy Dolce dress, will give us all that we need to insist she step down from her position in the membership."

Two more glasses of wine were ordered, and the women continued to plot. The plan would be to call the more senior women of the Auxiliary and recant the details of everything that happened. Many of them were still in slight shock from the chaos that ensued as if a fire had been started in the front of the ballroom and everyone was running for their lives. They would embellish where needed to enhance the dialogue so that this kind of "scene" could never happen again. It might take years to claw back the high esteem the membership had been held in throughout Clanford. One could not risk the leadership of a woman who clearly could not maintain her dignity in the face of an emergency. Then they would drop the bomb of Fluffy's insistence that she had had an extreme orgasm, not a seizure. The O-word should never have been spoken by a woman of her position. Polite company should not even know the word exists. Clare and Melinda knew well that the wagging tongues of this subset of women would guarantee full delivery of their script to the rest of the Auxiliary membership.

They held the first meeting with ten of the more senior members at Melinda's home the following afternoon. They had called them and said they needed to discuss a matter of great importance regarding the reputation of the Women's Auxiliary Board. As Melinda's housemaid poured tea and offered cookies (no one touched them, of course), they laid out the whole ugly tale for the women to digest with their Chamomile. Two elderly members nearly fainted at the utterance of the O-word, which Clare spelled out to ensure these ladies knew she would never speak such a vulgar term. One was concerned that Marguerite had not been invited to hear this with her own ears. Clare assured her that either she or Melinda would meet with Marguerite at "the appropriate time." Both quietly knew that Marguerite would be used to lay the fatal blow, but that would happen in due time as events unfolded.

Within twenty-four hours, the entire membership and half of the Clanford "regular folks" had been made aware of the events of the opening luncheon in full detail. The insiders were aghast at the actions of their President-elect while the townies were splitting their sides in laughter about the rich bitch who came in public. The discretion that Fluffy had counted on to bury the story was nowhere in sight. Her story laid bare just like her wet undies on the platform of the grand ballroom.

Chapter Seventeen

CLEAN UP IN AISLES THREE, FOUR...

Shelly Watson arrived at the Clanford Piggly Wiggly just before 7 a.m. on Monday, just like she had for the previous thirty-nine years. Shelly had risen from high school bagger to opening manager over her long, uninterrupted tenure at the Pig. She ruled the morning shift with an iron fist. All the brand delivery trade and the food distributors who made morning deliveries and stocked their dedicated aisle shelves feared retribution for any false move. The store personnel avoided her wrath like the plague. When Shelly spoke or mostly screamed, everyone listened.

She ruled her 7 a.m. to 3 p.m. kingdom from a glass-walled office on the second floor of the store that allowed her a view of the grocery aisles that ran perpendicular to the front wall of the building. The areas that were not within her direct sight line were covered by closed-circuit cameras. She had a view of every square inch of the store and the stock area from her perch, and everyone who worked for or in the store knew it. Customers were regularly terrorized by the PA system with her booming voice chastising them for snatching a grape for a quick taste, reaching to the back of the refrigerated case for the most recent shipment of milk with the longest expiration date ("Please take the milk at the front of the display, we will not be liable for any arm injuries from trying to reach behind") or god forbid, a broken jar of Ragu ("clean-up in Aisle five!").

Shelly was an interesting character. She was a large woman with short, cropped hair who preferred stretch-waisted pants and baby doll tops mostly to hide her wide girth. She had convinced district management years before to provide her with XXL white tops embroidered with the Piggly Wiggly logo on one breast and her name on the other with the title of Shift Manager below it. Although, as a union employee, she had made decent money over the years, she lived an hour's drive away near Waukegan in a double-wide trailer that she had inherited from her parents. She was an only child, so when her parents perished in a tornado that blew apart their Florida double-wide just outside of Orlando fifteen years prior, she was the sole heiress to their "estate." She told friends that she was comforted by the fact that when the only remains found of her parents or her parents' belongings was her mother's dismembered arm on Main Street in Disney World the morning after the storm, it was still clutching a Pabst Blue Ribbon long-neck. Her mother was a true redneck up to the very end.

Shelly knew well the worlds apart life she lived from the women of Clanford. While she drove a ten-year-old Honda Civic, they drove around town in BMW, Porsche, Mercedes, Audi, and Bentley SUVs. They arrived at the store well dressed and coiffed, bringing young toddlers and infants well-dressed, although usually not well trained. There was nothing Shelly hated more than small children running through her aisles, wreaking havoc, and pulling items off the lower shelves. She was never shy to admonish a new mother over the PA for her child's indiscretion. Occasionally, bringing a mother to tears was the highlight of her day.

Shelly was pragmatic and fully understood that these women's dollars were the lifeblood of the store. The Clanford Piggly Wiggly was one of the most profitable in the whole system, with the average register receipt being the highest in the company. Shelly nicknamed these women the "fancies." They wore fancy clothes, they pushed fancy strollers, they bought fancy foods and most notably, they binged on fancy wines. Shelly made the unilateral decision to up-charge her entire wine selection 25% above prices dictated by corporate policy. When she was called out for it by a district manager, she pointed out that her wine volume exceeded that of every other in-store wine operation comparable. The wine thing Shelly never really understood. She only drank PBRs, just like her mother.

Monday mornings were historically the busiest day of shopping at the Pig. The wealthy families of Clanford usually dined out at the many restaurants available in town over the weekend, so Mondays were grocery replenishment days. The busiest hour was usually between 8:30 and 9:30 a.m. when the moms came in after dropping their fancy brats at their fancy schools. During this hour, Shelly was on her feet, constantly working her large frame back and forth across the office window, watching closely for any infractions down below.

This particular morning at 9 a.m., the store was especially crowded, with the young wives making their way through their shopping lists. Shelly had been busy following a mom of young twins as they perused the ice cream novelty section. She was ready to pounce if the little shits even thought of pulling anything out of the case. It started with a light chorus of "ohhhs" and "ohh myyys" emanating from aisle three. Shelly gave up on the twins and moved back across her office to observe what was happening in the condiment aisle. A young woman with blond hair and dressed in a tennis shift was standing in the middle of the aisle encircled by four other moms. Shelly heard a loud moan and then a long, cackling laugh. She strained her eyes to see what was happening but could not make out all the details. She grabbed her trusty binoculars and focused directly on the pencil-thin blond (God, how she hated women like her).

She was standing in the aisle with her hands at her side. She was definitely laughing or possibly crying. Either way, she was very emotional. Shelly was transfixed. The woman's vocals increased in volume, and she began to move her body forward and then backward very rhythmically from her hips up through her chest. Shelly was frozen. She knew she should be calling 911, but she couldn't pull her eyes away from the scene. Just then, the woman's hands went straight up in the air, fingers starfishing. The woman threw her head back, laughed again, and let out a long and boisterous scream (which made Shelly dribble in her lycra pants), finishing with a full, throated Praise Jesus! (Yes, the PJ!) then dropped her body to the floor.

Shelly couldn't move. She had been trained in CPR but was so shocked by what had just unfolded in front of her that she was paralyzed. Finally, she regained her senses and screamed into the microphone in a voice that shook the walls, "CLEAN UP IN AISLE THREE!!"

She raced (a relative term because her BMI made racing, let alone fast walking, pretty much impossible) down the stairs and out into the store, screaming orders as she approached the scene.

"Call 911! Clear the aisle! Give the woman some air!"

When she finally made her way to the woman, she had been helped into a sitting position on the floor by some other moms. She was sitting in a puddle of urine but didn't seem to notice. She had a huge smile across her face, which belied any sense of panic or pain.

Shelly started in, "My dear, are you okay? How are you feeling? It looks like you had a seizure, from what I saw from my office upstairs. An ambulance is on the way."

The woman seemed a little out of it but was still smiling broadly. A smile that a friendly drunk might have on their plastered face. She finally spoke a few words, "I came!"

Each of the women attending to her, as well as Shelly, looked quizzically at her and each other.

Shelly asked, "What did you say? You came? Yes, you did come. You came to the Piggly Wiggly to grocery shop this morning. You seemed to have a seizure, but it had nothing to do with the store. We have no liability here!"

The woman's smile grew wider across her taught face, "I came! I came! I had a mother-fucking, earth-moving orgasm! I caaaaammmmmmeeeee!"

Every woman around her was shocked by her statement. Several were also young moms and tried hard to hide their smiles, wondering silently what she was feeling. Shelly was lightheaded from all the unexpected physical movement so early in the morning. She asked one of the stockers to bring her a chair from the front desk area.

EMS arrived and began attending to the woman. Although she tried to refuse treatment, Shelly insisted that for liability purposes, she had to leave the store via the gurney. She could decide to jump off once she was off Piggly Wiggly's property if she liked.

Shelly was still in the chair, recuperating from all the excitement, when a similar scene started to unfold in the "parade of foreign foods" aisle, Aisle Six. Shelly scrambled to her feet and was heading three aisles down, screaming the whole way for people to get the fuck out of her way. She was clearly becoming unhinged. She made the turn onto aisle six just as the hideous scream came rushing down the aisle toward her, and the exuberant "Praise Jesus!" was being let loose by the unsuspecting "fancy." This time, it was also a rail-thin brunette decked out in designer athleisure wear. Same story, the same outcome. The urine streaming under the shelf featuring the Taco Tuesday specials by Old El Paso.

"CLEAN UP IN ASILE SIX!!!" This time, Shelly screamed the message unassisted by the PA system. She held tight to the end cap, hoping to let the wave of lightheadedness pass. She really wasn't used to this kind of excitement. But this was her store from 7 a.m. to 3 p.m., and she was going to defend its contents and its customers.

Within minutes, another wave of "ohhhh nooooos" was heard coming from the produce section. Shelly saw the crowd shift momentum in that same direction to check out the action by the watermelons. Sweating now and unsteady on her feet, Shelly screamed for one of the baggers to bring her the electric riding grocery cart reserved for the handicapped customers. When it arrived, Shelly plopped her sweaty ass in the seat and started heading for produce, screaming at customers to get out of her way and oblivious to just how close she was coming to running some of them over. Before she could make it to the watermelons, the scream and then the PJ! All Shelly could think of was the old Queen song, "Another One Bites the Dust."

Shelly did a quick three-point turn and headed to the front of the store to close the entrance to any new customers. Something was happening unique to her location, and she needed to figure out what was causing it. Closing the entrance made no difference. In the time it took for her to reach the front of the store, six more women were succumbing to the mind-bending orgasms. As a result, there would be the need for "clean-ups" in aisles one, four, seven, eight, frozen pizzas, and the butcher shop. In total, nine women were whisked off to St. Gerard's, all with soaked drawers and huge smiles on their faces.

Because of the volume of ambulances called in such a short timeframe, the chief of police arrived at the Pig with three other squad cars to get a sense of what was going on. When he found Shelly slumped over the handles of her electric cart, she was crying and seemed close to hysterics.

"Shelly, what the hell is going on here?" The chief demanded.

"I have no fucking idea, chief! These skinny ass women started dropping like flies, screaming, hollering, and pissin' themselves, all the while saying that they were having these fantastic orgasms. Right here in the middle of the store. I think there were eight or nine in total."

The chief interjected, "Nine, Shelly."

"Jesus H. Christ, what the hell is happening in this town? If corporate finds out about this, I might lose my job and my pension. Why did they choose my store to bring all this nonsense into? I think it was kind of a prank, like one of those Funniest Videos spoofs. I didn't see any cameras, but this was just too fucking coincidental to be real, chief."

"Shelly, I have no idea what is happening, but my men are going to interview some of the women who witnessed all of this, and maybe we will find out what this was really all about. In the meantime, you better get up to your office and rest yourself. You look like you were hit by a truck. Everything will be back to normal here in no time. I will make sure your people get things back to just how you like everything, ship shape."

Shelly thanked the chief and motored over the the elevator that allowed access to the second floor. She walked into her office and plopped down on her chair. She put her head on her desk and started to cry. Once she regained her strength, she would call corporate and tell them she was leaving sick. This would be the first day in her thirty-nine-year career that she would leave before her shift ended. And all because of those damn fancies!

***

Dr. Lovejoy was more than shocked to see the continuous flow of women patients into the ER that morning, all exhibiting the same symptoms as Fluffy three days prior. He interviewed all nine of the women taking copious notes on recent diet, exercise, medications, and family histories. At this point, none of the women had divulged to the good doctor that they were taking a little pink pill of unknown origin that was making them lose an incredible amount of weight in a short period of time. They were told by the trusted Twink to keep this all secret and they were respecting her requested tight lips.

***

Emma was putting the boys in the bathtub when she received a call from her friend Bobbie, who worked at the Piggly Wiggly as a cashier. Bobbie and Emma grew up together, and both came from families where the parents were both teachers. The week before, Emma had ended up in Bobbie's cashier line and they promised to catch up over coffee soon. Bobbie was following up to see if Emma could meet the next morning, Bobbie's day off. Emma was free, so they agreed on a time and place to meet.

When Emma arrived a few minutes late, Bobbie was already sitting at one of the coffee shop tables with a small coffee with oat milk for Emma.

She knew what Emma's routine was given her pregnancy. They embraced when Emma arrived at the table. Bobbie spoke first.

"Emma, you look wonderful. How are you feeling? How far along are you?"

Emma replied, "I'm going on twenty-five weeks. Feeling tired most of the time because I'm chasing after the two boys. Craig has been a big help so I'm grateful for that.I just feel so big this time!"

"You really do look good, Em. I'm serious."

Emma continued, "How are things with you, Bobbie? Are you still dating that guy who owns the construction company? What's his name, Tim?"

"No, Ted. And yes, we are still dating. I really like him, but we are having a hard time getting our schedules to sync. He's committed to take me away for a week this summer up to northern Wisconsin where his family has a cottage on a lake. I hope that will give us a chance to get a little better connected."

"How's work at the Piggly Wiggly?" Emma asked.

"Well, usually it's as boring as hell, but yesterday we had a real shit show take place with all of these women screaming, gyrating, pissing themselves, and then falling over. Nine women in about forty-five minutes. All of them are from the Butternut Club. Skinny little things that seemed to all get sick at once. Maybe they had a bad meal or something at the club over the weekend. The chief of police is investigating."

Emma was surprised she hadn't heard anything about it but figured it was because she was usually fast asleep long before the evening news came on at 10 p.m. They spoke for about an hour and then left because Bobbie had a ton of errands to run on her day off.

On the ride home, Emma thought more about Bobbie's story regarding the women afflicted at the store. Her description of the women as "skinny little things from the ButternutClub" caught Emma's attention. Could there be some connection with the diet pills? She wondered. No, of course not. It was just a coincidence. She forced the thoughts from her mind as she pulled into the driveway and parked the minivan.

***

Twink was having tea with Marguerite, planning their upcoming trip to Paris for a private shopping jaunt for her summer wardrobe. Twink feigned ignorance when Marguerite gave a much more genteel description of the "small situation" that had happened to Fluffy during the opening luncheon. Twink sat quietly as she absorbed a very much water-downed version of the actual events. Marguerite blamed her fainting spell on Fluffy's menstrual cycle and said that earlier in her own life, she had also been afflicted with a similar curse. Twink was working hard to suppress a smile.

Marguerite did, however, inform Twink of the happenings at the Piggly Wiggly the prior day, of which Twink was completely unaware. It seems one of her assistant's assistants was shopping at "that dreadful place" right about the time that all of the action was going down. She was an eyewitness to the whole episode and shared it with her boss, who shared it with Marguerite. Twink was now aware that nine women from Butternut had been rushed to the hospital for all these atrocious symptoms and behavior. Marguerite clearly had not been given the juicy information about the orgasms, so Twink only heard about the fainting spells and incontinence. Twink made a mental note to call over William at Butternut after tea to see if he might know which members had been afflicted at the local grocery store. She was curious but not yet concerned.

***

Unbeknownst to the many women afflicted in public, Twink, Emma, Craig as well as Dr. Lovejoy and the management team at Butternut, the same scene was playing out in many homes beginning that same weekend. Frightened husbands, children, cats, and dogs were all running for cover at the sights and sounds of these "attacks" in kitchens, family rooms, bedrooms, bathrooms, and outside yards and patios. Although a few had contacted their own internists to inquire about their afflictions, most viewed them as one-off occurrences, most likely caused by the increased stress around the Auxiliary opening luncheon. They were firm believers in the adage: "discretion is the better part of valor."

Chapter Eighteen

HAND HELDS AT THE THRIFT STORE

Arlene Grey was a Monday morning volunteer at the St. Gerard's Hospital Thrift Store. She had been a long-time fixture at the store for just shy of twenty-five years. In fact, she was looking forward to receiving her Quarter Century Club pin in July. Monday mornings were reserved for intake. Monday was the only day the benevolent citizens of Clanford could drop off their cast-offs for charitable recycling. Women came from all over the extended area to shop for the high-end clothing, bags, and shoes that had fallen out of fashion favor.

The past four Mondays had been unusually heavy days for drop- offs as the newly slimmed-down social scene was discarding their "fat wear." This particular Monday was two weeks past the Butternut "event." Just like the most recent Mondays, Arlene stressed about the mere volume of clothing that needed to be sorted, sized, and priced before it could be sent to the retail store. All her sorting tables were piled high with the newly arrived clothing, leaving her very little space to work.

Some other arrivals were also causing Arlene some dyspepsia. Tucked neatly into the bundles of clothing that arrived were some strange kinds of cylindrical gadgets, some with and some without long cords and plugs. It appeared that they were being intentionally hidden in the stacks of donations. They ranged in size from small to larger, and the colors varied from bright and shiny to soft pastels. One in particular was very large, black, and had a large bulb-like top. (Apparently, the sensational side effects of the man-up pills were eliminating the need for mechanical assistance.)

It was also well known amongst the other Thrift Store volunteers that Arlene suffered a lifelong affliction with OCD. All the clothing was folded or hung in a particular manner. All clothing was arranged first by size and then by its place on the color wheel spectrum.

These new "gadgets" were adding a wrinkle to Arlene's usual daily routine. None of them seemed to be exactly the same, which made it difficult to prepare the appropriate space in the retail store. Arlene would ask Bonnie, the well-meaning and well-tattooed, thirty-something fellow volunteer who ran the front of the store, what exactly these items were. She grabbed a handful of them and walked to the sales counter.

"Bonnie, dear, what do you make of these? I've never seen anything like them before," Arlene inquired.

Bonnie, eating an apple and perusing a Vogue magazine that had found its way into one of the larger bunches of clothes, looked up quickly and then retreated to her magazine, "Those are hand-helds."

Arlene made a puckered-up face. Hand-helds? The only hand-helds she had ever heard of or had seen before were the hand-helds at the Pita Palace next to the Starbucks in town. She queried Bonnie further.

"Why are they called hand-helds?" asked Arlene.

Bonnie, still with her nose in the Vogue, replied, "People hold them for self-pleasure."

Arlene was now even more confused. She liked the hand-held pita sandwiches at the Pita Palace, especially the Pita Supreme with its crunchy vegetables and generous tahini sauce, but she wouldn't necessarily describe eating one as pleasurable. Delicious for sure, but not "pleasurable."

She walked back into the workroom area, set them on top of a pile of unsorted clothing, and searched the store room for a container to put them in. She stumbled across a clear plastic storage box. Given the differing lengths and the fact that some had electric cords attached, she at first found it difficult to arrange them in the box efficiently. She wrapped the cords tightly around the shafts of the electric ones and placed them in the bottom of the container. Next, she placed what appeared to be battery-operated versions on top of them in the box arranged by color. For the most part, she was pleased with the presentation and was about to carry the box into the retail store for placement. She quickly noticed the large black gadget was still sitting on top of the clothing but seemed too big to fit into her neatly organized box. No matter how she tried to make it work, the big black one just wouldn't fit into her smallish box. She grew frustrated and decided to see why the heck it had a long plug on it. She found an outlet next to the light switch and plugged it in. A red button on the side appeared to be an on/off switch. When she turned it on, the wildly pulsating appliance jumped out of her hand, landed on the floor, and was spinning and gyrating in circles. As the vibrations intensified, the lights in the store began to flicker. Arlene was mortified and tried to pick it up to no avail. The lights were now buzzing as they fluttered from bright to almost total darkness. Bonnie yelled from the front counter.

"Arlene! What the hell is going on back there? Seems we keep losing power. Are you okay?"

Arlene dove for the cord and yanked it from the wall.

Immediately, the lights returned to their normal wattage.

"Everything is good back here, must have been some sort of power surge in town or something."

Arlene tossed the black beauty into the trash and regained her composure. She neatly wrote a tag on the front of the box, which read: "Hand-Helds Mix or Match $1.00 each," and placed it on the shelf above the hairdryers and curling irons.

As she spent the remainder of the afternoon sorting clothing, she made a mental note to stop at the Pita Palace on the way home.

Chapter Nineteen

MOTHER'S DAY PROGRAM AT THE ACADEMY

The annual Mother's Day Program was always presented on the Friday before Mother's Day at the Clanford Academy Day School. The Halloween Costume Pageant, The Thanksgiving Play, and The Christmas Sing-Along all paled in comparison to the time, money, and effort expended on the Mother's Day Extravaganza. That was because the C.A.D.S. moms were the "best moms evvaaaaaa!"

This year was no exception. Preparations had begun immediately after the winter break in February. Melinda, who had three children throughout the K-12 program, was named chairwoman of this spring's event. After its two-year absence because of the COVID lockdown, this year's program would be a spectacular tribute to the rebirth of the community after the dark days of the pandemic. Not unlike Fluffy's well-choreographed coronation into the Auxiliary presidency,

Melinda's directorship of the Mother's Day line-up would solidify her position in the highest ranks of Clanford society. She was determined to make her production the most arresting of all the previous programs.

To that end, Melinda retained Broadway-acclaimed and Tony Award-winning choreographer Madame Bijou to develop and direct all the dance ensembles. Melinda was secretly scheming with Madame to create a role for her in the grande finale, assuring her new hire that she had retained all her skills from her dance line days in college. In addition, she called in a favor from an old family friend of her mother, James Christopher Washington, renowned Broadway musical composer and director. Melinda's mother had spent her early twenties as an understudy for several musicals on Broadway and was rumored to have been one of hundreds of paramours of "JC." No one knew for sure what "favors" were being called in but one could only imagine. Melinda's mother demanded that she be present during all the meetings with JC, mostly to make sure Melinda didn't take any attention away from her.

During the first meeting with Madame Bijou and JC, Melinda outlined song titles for which she would expect the talented duo to create both music and choreography (both rolled their eyes in unison). The initial four titles, the brain children of Melinda and Melinda alone, were:

"Our Skinny Mommies Love Us Tons"

"Riding With Mommy in Her Range Rover"

"Kale, Quinoa, and Kashi"

"Las Niñeras Hacen Girar El Mundo" (English translation: Nannies Make the World Go Round)

The last, sung entirely in Spanish by the eighth graders, would be a tribute to the many nannies in the audience that day who worked tirelessly to keep the next generation of social stars cleaned, coiffed, clothed, and most importantly, kept out of sight. The Nanny trade in Clanford was a lucrative one, with most receiving not only hefty paychecks but also their own cars and defined-benefit pension plans. The most common "company cars" driven by the south of the border governesses were the Kia Soul. The nanny's cubed-shaped autos were seen throughout town transporting their charges to and from school, sporting events, and general mind-expanding activities. They likewise were seen at the beginning and end of the day caravanning to the more reasonably priced areas outside of Clanford.

Melinda had convinced the school administrators that the children be permitted to practice one hour at each end of the day to make sure they were well versed in all their duties. She carried a detached wooden broom handle and pounded it incessantly while pacing back and forth in front of the stage, trying to keep the music and dance steps in time. The children, as well as the teaching staff, were sworn to complete secrecy to ensure the program had the ultimate surprise effect on their beloved mothers.

Classes were canceled on the Thursday prior to the show for two rounds of full-dress rehearsal. Melinda was worked into a frenzy, screaming orders and directions at everyone, including Madame Bijou and JC, who would happily depart Clanford as soon as the show was over and never return. The rehearsals went off flawlessly, and everything seemed in place for the grandest of grand Mother's Day Extravaganza of all time!

***

Because Clare Johnson's children were older and had already graduated C.A.D.S., she had not been privy to the show's development or content.

Given Fluffy's still dented reputation and questionable return to the top of the Women's Auxiliary Board, Clare knew that a possible Melinda triumph in her school program might vault her into first place in the race for Fluffy's role as Board President. Clare would quickly need to devise a plan to try and thwart that from occurring by sabotaging the Extravaganza.

Clare's first job out of college was pharmaceutical sales back when that was the primary distribution of information about the attributes and efficacy of specific medicines. Her major field of study in college was biology, and she took a keen interest in understanding the nuances of the pills she was hocking to the doctors in her territory. Her company's focus was on painkillers, just as that field was exploding with new and different options for chronic pain. She read extensively about her products, given their newness, and understood very well how metabolism played a role in the side effects of the drugs. Even though the initial use of her product had extremely strong impacts, they seemed to build up in one's system over time, leading to some unexpected and detrimental side effects. Clare was very conscientious about her work and made sure to give full disclosure to the doctors she met with daily about the need to taper the drug if and when the side effects began to occur.

After Fluffy's episode and the subsequent episodes of some other club members, Clare began to think about the little pink pills that everyone, including she, had been talking about for weight loss. Initially, she was a little leery of taking the unmarked pills, given her background and knowledge of the industry, but she put those thoughts out of her head as she began to drop weight at an unbelievable rate. Over the last couple of weeks as the "episodes" were increasing in number, she began to think again about metabolism and side effects. She recounted in her mind that all the women had started the drugs within roughly two weeks' time at the beginning of February. Somehow, regardless of size or age, everyone was given the same allocation of pills on a weekly basis. To her knowledge, no one's dose had ever been adjusted. It was a pay-to-play scheme to lose weight, and everyone was willing to pay.

As she further analyzed the situation, she realized that it was around the eight-week mark of taking the Little Pink Beauties that the extreme side effects began to occur. It all had to do with metabolism! Whatever these pills were made of was most likely being metabolized in their bodies at a decreasing rate. They had a buildup of this pink shit in their systems, and it was manifesting itself in the seizures and more. She immediately thought she should start alerting the women to the dangers of these pills, most likely by reaching out to Twink. But then she thought again. Maybe this was the path to making sure Melinda didn't succeed with her Mother's Day Extravaganza. And so, a plot was hatched.

Melinda knew well that her "bestie," Clare, was a huge fan of all-natural energy drinks and water. Clare would often introduce her to the latest craze in power and energy supplements, snacks, and drinks. On the day of the dress rehearsal, Clare arrived at the C.A.D.S. auditorium with a bouquet of flowers and a large Nalgene bottle of the "latest energy" supplement for Melinda. Air kisses were exchanged, and Clare feigned enthusiasm for the upcoming show. She said she wouldn't stay to watch because she wanted to be in the front row on Friday for the full production. She did tell Melinda, however, that she should make sure to drink the entire bottle of the latest "power drink" that her trainer had introduced to her the previous week. She herself had used it and couldn't believe how much energy and clarity it had given her. The secret was to drink the entire thirty-two ounces within a fifteen-minute time frame. Clare suggested Melinda drink the liquid right before the first curtain went up so she would be fully energized to direct her wonderful show. Melinda was soooo appreciative of Clare's kindness. She couldn't wait for her to see the play on Friday. As Clare left the auditorium, she couldn't help but feel a little guilty about her plan but quickly extinguished those thoughts from her brain. Too much was at stake with the possibility of being Auxiliary president. All's fair in love and status...

***

The day of the Extravaganza had finally arrived. Melinda took a page out of Fluffy's playbook and hired her hairdresser and make-up girl to be at the auditorium for final touch-ups. All her helpers were assembling the children by grade and performance number in the hallways outside of the main stage area. There was a huge buzz of excitement moving through the student body, but none was more excited than Melinda. Melinda's phone calendar notice alerted her, as programmed, to drink her full Nalgene of the special energy drink that Clare had so generously provided her.

In the auditorium, the mothers were falling into lines to enter the auditorium, where they would be seated by class grade. The senior's moms would be in the front two rows, and the rest would follow accordingly. About one-third of the auditorium was filled when an eruption started in the seventh-grade section. A skinny brunette dressed in a pink tank dress, color-matched Louboutin four-inch heels began to gyrate as she entered her row. By now, most of the women in the "diet plan" were used to the drill that would soon follow. Several immediately ran over to stand by her side while she swung front to back, undulated up and down, and splayed her hands to the ceiling. The loud and long, high-pitched scream followed as expected, upsetting many of the women who were unaware of these incidents. At exactly the point when she did the anticipated "PJ," they moved behind her, grabbed her as she fell, and log carried her out the door. Before they made it to the exit, a fourth-grade mother from the Butternut group began her "episode" as another group of dieters headed toward her to manage her out as seamlessly as possible. A third-grade mom was next, followed by a kindergarten mother of twins. All in all, six women provided the opening act for the real show which was just moments away from starting. Many of the women in the audience sat in silent shock, trying to take in all of the commotions that seemed to some of the more "statused" crowd an ordinary and normal occurrence. Many of the women in the audience were fanning themselves with the programs, half afraid of what was going to happen next.

When the intro music began (played in the orchestra pit by the Clanford Orchestra Band, of course), nerves in the room began to settle down, and the audience of mostly women resettled their well- dressed asses into the plush velveteen seats. The curtain was raised and the first act of the meticulously choreographed twelve acts was underway. Like a well-oiled machine, the groups of children were ushered onto the stage as the dance moves and musical lyrics embedded in their brains were robotically regurgitated to loud applause and cheering. The well-placed jokes in the program were well-received, and every mother in the audience could not have been more proud of their children. What a wonderful program! What a wonderful school! What a wonderful life!!!!

Because of her close friendship with Melinda, Clare had been given a reserved seat in the front row, center, along with the school administrator, academy benefactors, other V.I.P.s, as well as Melinda's husband and mother. Clare squirmed in her seat as she silently anticipated a repeat of Fluffy's highly public on-stage "performance." The timing was everything. The first eleven acts took roughly sixty-five minutes to complete with the grand finale scheduled to take another six minutes. The senior class women would be performing a Rockette-style dance line to a bespoke music number composed by J.C. The surprise part of the finale would be Melinda, dressed like the rest of the dancers, working her way from the side stage to the center for the final high kick number. She would join the seniors in the center of the line, arms clasped and fish-netted legs extended. Although only a few people were in the know, Clare had managed to extract the information from a classmate of one of her nieces.

As the curtain for the final act rose, Clare could hardly contain herself. She stretched her neck to try and find Melinda on the right side of the stage, waiting in the wings. Finally, she zeroed in on her, watching her face closely for any sign of distress. If the body movements were initiated before she was onstage, the full impact would be lost. Clare's heart pounded as she strained to see any sign of an impending quake. Melinda was beaming as she awaited her queue, a huge smile plastered across her face. The senior dance troupe was moving about the stage in perfect formation, shifting up and back so that each girl would have a chance to be up front for the professional photographer hired to take their pictures, but most importantly, Melinda's.

The time came for Melinda to shuffle in behind the dance line, bending low to get the maximum impact when she worked her way into the exact center of the line as they bent their bodies at the waist and then stood tall. The move went off flawlessly! As the group moved to the upward stance, the audience realized that Melinda was now at the center of the linc. The audience erupted in cheers and applause. Melinda was flush with excitement and pride. She worked hard to stay focused on the dance moves to avoid looking out of step. Bent at the waist and arched back as the right leg extended into a high kick. Melinda was in her glory, and she was eighteen again, the center of attention where she always strove to be. Then...it began!

Clare noticed the twitch in Melinda's left eye as she was literally only feet away from the front row of the auditorium. First her eye and then her nose. Melinda shook her head slightly, trying to force the twitches away. She focused on her smile and her dance steps. Within a few seconds, her left shoulder slumped just enough to cause the dance partner to her left to look over nervously. Melinda persevered. She clearly knew what was about to unfold but was trying her best to keep her shit (literally) together. Clare felt a tingle move down her spine as she watched her plan come to perfect fruition.

As the twitching metastasized throughout her body, she inadvertently grabbed hard onto the upper arms of her two closest dance line partners, evoking screams from the girls and frantic attempts to breakaway from her grasp. This, in turn, made these girls push away from their next-door partners, and the domino effect began.

Within seconds, the entire line was falling backward off their feet. The audience stood in disbelief as the girls, one by one, landed hard on the stage floor. Now, Melinda stood alone at the center of the stage.

Clare was hyperventilating as she watched the scene on stage unfold, silently congratulating herself for pulling off the perfect plan. Melinda's initial twitching subsided as she tried hard to regain control. She tightened her quads and calves in order to maintain her vertical stance. The power of the pills (especially a fivefold dose) was just too much for her. Melinda's body now began to quake, undulate, and sway. She was in full rapture, center stage under the glare of the overhead lighting. The "overdose," administered via the spiked power drink, was having an exponential impact on her symptoms. Her body movements mimicked a used car lot's inflatable tube man. She peed a stream of urine so violently it ricocheted off the stage floor and out into the front row seats. There was yet another call for an exorcist from the audience as her movements and screams reached a fevered pitch. It was during the crescendo of her "PJ" that she projectile-puked her stomach contents into the audience before dropping to the ground. Her mother and husband were immediately by her side, trying to console her, although she was laughing hysterically in a very disconnected manner. The children of all ages who had joined their moms in the audience ahead of the after-party in the gymnasium were too traumatized to leave their sides. Clare was still trying to wring Melinda's urine out of the front of her dress, given that she took a direct hit from the pee bomb. As she was exiting stage left, she thought to herself that maybe putting all five pills in Melinda's drink had been overkill. Immediately, she course-corrected her thoughts, reminding herself of the old adage, "Go big or go home!" There was no question now that Melinda would be going home. As she was being guided out the back exit of the auditorium (and just like Fluffy on opening luncheon day), Melinda told anyone and everyone who would listen that she came, yes, she came!

***

Word of Melinda's "possession" spread like wildfire through the town. Now, the regular citizens of Clanford had become aware of the events of not only the Mother's Day program but also the other similar "situations" that had been occurring over the previous three weeks. What were all these crazy socialites doing?

Twink was made aware later in the afternoon and immediately drove over to Emma and Craig's home, a sure sign of her concern given she usually summoned them to her shop for any business-related discussions. Emma was on the phone getting a blow-by-blow from one of her friends who had witnessed the whole event when Twink rang the bell. Craig, at this point, had been clueless about all these events. He was solely focused on the supply chain aspects and cash management of OMG! They had already passed the million-dollar revenue mark and were quickly heading to two million.

Oblivious to the no-smoking rule in the Mayfield home, Twink immediately lit up her Virginia Slim and took a seat at the kitchen table. Emma offered coffee but given it was not her beloved Néscafe, Twink declined and then started in, "After hearing about these "incidents," I think we can all agree that they are directly linked to our little backroom enterprise."

Emma nodded, and Craig looked bewildered.

He asked, "What incidents are we talking about?"

Twink immediately became frustrated with Craig and responded curtly, "Craig, there are women having seizures all over town, and I will bet you that each and every one of them is taking the man-up pills."

"Twink, why do you think these seizures are related to our pills?"

"Because all of the women who have had them, at least most of the ones I've heard about, are from the Women's Auxiliary at Butternut. The same women who are our clients."

Emma remained quiet but, in her mind, knew that the pills were having weird side effects on some of the women. Craig was silent also, but for a different reason. Suddenly, he had an intense flashback to the day that Mr. Chen came to the hotel and, after seeing him so hungover, introduced him to the pills. He also specifically remembered now that Mr. Chen said that women couldn't have them, "they make them go crazy!" Craig did not think now was the right time to divulge that little fact. Instead, he refocused and suggested a possible alternative possibility for the seizures.

"Let's hold on a minute, Twink. Maybe it's not the pills that are causing the problems but the effects of the rapid weight loss. Maybe these women aren't eating the right foods to keep their electrolytes and shit like that in order. Maybe they are being too aggressive and not getting the right number of calories and vitamins."

Emma liked that explanation. She herself had to take prenatal vitamins with her pregnancies to make sure her body was getting what it needed because the baby was living off her. Not all the women were having seizures, and the first was Fluffy, who had lost the most weight anyhow. It wasn't their fault. It was the stupid women who didn't know what balance meant.

Twink took a final long drag on her cigarette and blew the smoke above her head. Emma tried to dodge it the best she could. Twink was now in deep thought. Maybe Craig was right. Maybe the three of them needed to remind their customers that they had to make sure they were getting the right amount of nutrients every day. Maybe they should suggest a multivitamin or something like that for them to take.

"Craig, darling, you may be right. Let's tell the women that in order to get any allocation, even a single pill going forward, they have to start taking a multivitamin every day. If we find out that they are not doing as we suggest, they will be cut off permanently."

"No second chances. Emma, I will leave it to you to draft the appropriate note to send to everyone. Let's hope this does the trick. I wouldn't want to even think about the liability we all could face if our little remedy was actually making our ladies sick."

With that, Twink stood up and headed for the door. Emma was trying to catch up to thank her for coming over. Twink had already lit up another cigarette and was opening the car door when Emma reached her front door.

"Thank you, Twink. I will get the note out today! I will see you tomorrow at your shop."

Twink's hand flew up from her car window as she pulled out and disappeared down the road. Emma went back into the house and sat back at the table where Craig remained seated.

"Craig, what kind of liability was Twink talking about? Could we really get hit with some type of lawsuit?" asked Emma.

Craig thought about this for a little while before responding. He himself was thinking the exact thing but didn't want to worry Emma.

"Em, I don't think we would be held liable. We never packaged these pills and made some sort of medical or scientific claim about them. We told these women that these pills could help them lose weight. That is all, nothing more. They are the ones who are clamoring to get them. They don't even give a shit that we charge them $1,000 per pill! A fucking $1,000 per pill!!!! They can try and come after us, but I think they will be the ones who look like fools. The high price might just be our guarantee against getting any grief on this. What wife is going to tell her husband she has been dropping thousands of dollars per week to lose weight when she could just as easily keep her fucking mouth shut. Nope, the more I think about it, the more I'm pretty sure these women won't be coming after us."

Emma liked what she was hearing. The past two months had erased not only a huge amount of debt for them but also the constant pressure of uncertainty. They were now mortgage-free with more than half a million dollars in the bank. Their world had become easy, and she didn't want to risk that at all. In fact, she would be willing to stop selling the pills now and shut down the entire enterprise if it meant that they could keep the status quo. She told this to Craig. He stood up and kissed her on the head.

"Don't worry, Emma, just a few more months of this, and we will really be set. Come to think of it, some of these Butternut women we are helping may be willing to sponsor us into the club. We could join right after the baby is born and have the rest of the summer to enjoy all the club amenities."

Emma wasn't so sure about joining Butternut. It wasn't exactly her scene. That would be a discussion for a later time. For now, she would get the note out to the women with the next set of invoices due at the end of the week.

***

Dr. Lovejoy sat in his office just outside of the emergency room entrance at St. Gerard. He was looking at the notes he had taken on some sixteen women who had entered his ER with the same seizure symptoms over the past ten days. He was completely puzzled about this for two reasons. First, the women seemed very, very evasive when questioned about their symptoms and memories of the incidents. Every one of them blamed their temporary medical issues on not eating enough before they were stricken. Once they had a little something to eat, they would be fine, just fine. No need to worry, they all remarked, just a slight issue with their blood sugar. The second puzzling fact was that none of their blood work revealed any signs of being hyperglycemic. All their bloodwork and vital signs had come back normal. As his call light grew red on the panel beside the door and he began to return to the emergency room, he promised himself he would dig deeper to find out what was really happening to the women of Clanford.

Chapter Twenty

RUN, LADIES, RUN!

In keeping with the original mission to support unwed mothers, the SBH convent held a fundraising 5K run on campus every Mother's Day morning starting sharply at 7 a.m. One of the newer novices, who came from the branding team of a major advertising firm before taking her vows, renamed the event "The Running Nuns Fun Run." Although much of the operating expenses for the convent were covered annually by its historic endowment trust, the money raised each year at this event provided college scholarships for the new mothers, advancing their educations. Each year, the citizens of Clanford came out strong in support of the run.

The run/walk path began atop Humility Hill, proceeded to circle Lake Chastity, traversed through Poverty Pines, and ended in the common area in front of the Administration building. (A quick history of Lake Chastity. In the original days of the convent, there was no indoor plumbing, so the good sisters would bathe in the lake, weather permitting. To reinforce the all-important vow of chastity, the early mother superiors told the novitiates that bathing in the lake would eliminate all present and future sexual desire to help make the vow easier to adhere to. As time passed, the students and boarders became aware of the lake's supposed "healing waters" and stayed clear of any possible lake encounters. Even though the lake was spring-fed and had crystal clear water, no student ever ventured into the lake over the history of the convent. Somewhere along the line, the lake was nicknamed "Lake Flaccid" to keep the local boys out as well.

As custom would have it, the event began with the senior class boys dressed in the long black habits of the sisters and wearing short heeled, tie-up, black "nun shoes," leading the pack of runners at the sound of the starting horn. This year, being the first run since the pandemic shutdown was lifted, had drawn an unusually large crowd, all looking to enjoy the lovely May Day and the camaraderie of their fellow runners. Also present was a large contingent of some of the younger moms who were also members of the Butternut Women's Auxiliary.

Twink, who never ran or even quickly walked a day in her life, was also present at the starting line with a large check in one hand and her ever-present Virginia Slim in the other. Twink spoke briefly with Mother Superior, mostly about the weather and the feeling of excitement in the crowd experiencing a new found freedom. Twink's real motivation for coming to the run was to observe any possible "medical events" that might occur that day. She had a theory that exercise might be a deterrent from these now regular episodes that were happening to her clients and, if correct, would add an exercise requirement as the next directive along with the vitamins to the pink pill poppers. Twink also asked Emma and Craig to join her at the race. Emma would observe the race with Twink and Craig was going to run with the two boys in their baby jogger to have proximity to any possible events.

Humility Hill was the highest point on the SBH campus, that allowed a panoramic view of the entire property. One of the early Ford heirs had provided the funds for a stone grotto where hundreds of weddings had been officiated over the years. It was a beautiful part of the campus from which Twink and Emma would have an unobstructed view of the entirety of the fun run events.

"Emma, Darling," Twink started in. "I've been thinking more and more about these unfortunate episodes experienced by our clients, and I am growing increasingly concerned about the long-term safety implications of our little project."

"Twink, I have been worried too, but Craig assures me that he doesn't think that any of these women will admit to taking the pills or, more importantly, where they got them or how much they paid." Twink thought a moment and continued, "Craig makes a good point about it coming back on us, but I am concerned that there will be a bigger health issue here. For god's sake, Craig bought these from a back-alley drug pusher in some god-forsaken country."

Emma chuckled, "Twink, he bought them in Taiwan, which is not exactly a third-world country."

Twink remained unimpressed, "Let's just say we need to have an exit plan in place for this business if things get more complicated."

Emma realized that Twink's use of the term "more complicated" referred to more episodes of this unexplained side effect.

Twink smiled back at Emma and spoke, "Emma, I'm not looking to worry you, especially in your current state. Let's just drop the subject for now and enjoy watching this silly form of entertainment."

Emma chuckled again at Twink's description of one of the most popular forms of physical fitness. She smiled and, under her breath, repeated, "Silly form of entertainment, ha!"

***

The runners were lined up with the be-habited senior boys at the front, hooting and hollering in anticipation of a quick sprint at the sound of the horn. The pack of runners seemed at a historic high this year. The SBH nuns were stationed throughout the 5K course to attend to any possible injuries or difficulties. Craig was positioned about halfway back in the throng of runners beside other moms and dads pushing baby joggers.

The horn sounded, and the runners were off. Immediately, several of the senior boys tripped in the nun footwear and began rolling down the hill in great laughter with some of them immediately realizing the growing pain from a twisted ankle. Once the injured boys moved to the sidelines, the serious runners moved past in an effort to break personal best running times.

Twink and Emma followed the pack as it spread out across the course, much like watching a horse race. Both women were straining to watch for the women from their client list whom they knew were taking part in the race. It was not that difficult because most of them had chosen highly colorful, designer running gear and stood out from the usual Lulu Lemon crowd. Emma pointed out Cindy O'Gara as one of the more serious runners as she made her way toward the front of the group. She was wearing bright chartreuse-colored shorts and a tank with a multi-colored chartreuse dominant hair bow that was used to create a ponytail out of her long blond hair. Both Twink and Emma could see she was a serious runner who had perfect form and drive as she made her way past the more weekend-type runners.

As Twink concentrated on Cindy, Emma was able to spot two more of the Butternut crowd. Katie Casey and Diana Long. Like Cindy, they were both dressed in loud colored designer togs that allowed Emma to keep track of them as they moved along the course. Although not nearly as competitive as their fellow club member, they were both fully engaged in the race. In total, the initial inspection of the crowd revealed a total of six Butternutters that Emma and Twink knew were current clients of the pills.

Cindy O'Gara was a serious runner. She had run cross country in grade school, high school and at Smith College. Her daily routine in Clanford was a five to seven-mile run that she completed before her children even woke up. During this race, she had moved up to the serious group of runners, which numbered around thirty when she made a short foot fault. This immediately made her focus on her stride as she realigned her body without missing a beat. Within the next twenty yards, it happened a second and then a quick third time. Cindy was baffled, this had never happened to her before, and she was not about to give up the progress she had made during the race to back off and slow her pace. She pressed on even harder. Her legs began to wobble as she forced herself along and felt a hot rush of blood across her body. Her usually tightly controlled arms began to flail to the point that other runners were beginning to move away from her and provide her more room. Her disciplined running gait had turned into a clippitty-cloppitty, high-kneed motion that began to look cartoonish. As she felt the control of her extremities melt away, her body began the signature forward-to-backward undulations of her torso while still in motion. This seemed to be a first of its kind, given that the other stricken ladies had been standing still during the ordeal. Poor Cindy began to laugh loudly as she pushed herself even harder to move forward.

As she was watching the events unfold, Twink, speechless, grabbed Emma's arm and pointed toward the crowd that was opening up away from Cindy. Although Twink had heard bits and pieces of the events that had occurred, given her status in the community, the details were often softened when she received them. Twink's own body began to tighten as she was laser-focused on Cindy's episode. Emma felt Twink's grip tighten on her arm and tried to free herself from her grasp, all the while keeping focused on Cindy.

The runners in her immediate vicinity had moved meaningfully away from Cindy but were still fully engaged in the race. As the course moved through the campus a left-hand turn was looming as it approached Lake Chastity. Cindy's gallant efforts to regain her composure resulted in her body taking on an acute angle of almost fifty degrees as her upper torso was moving at a speed slightly faster than her legs. Her head was now bent back, and she was laughing as her full existence was racing to nowhere in particular. All at once her hands were thrown up above her head with her fingers splayed out. A PJ was now imminent as her scream began to build from her toes. Twink was transfixed. As luck would have it, the left-hand turn was upon Cindy as she crescendoed into full rapture. Just as her high-pitched scream reached its pinnacle, the running pack veered left, and Cindy ran full force into the lake. The momentum built up from a combination of her running skills, and the adrenalin-fueled orgasm pushed her a good twenty yards into the lake before she fell forward atop the water. Several runners, as well as two of the SBH sisters stationed nearby, quickly followed her into the lake to rescue her from certain drowning. As she was dragged onshore, Cindy gave a silly grin to Sister Mary Agnes, who was propping up her left arm and shoulder, and quietly said,

"I CCCCAAAAMMMMEEE!"

Both shocked and confused, Mary Agnes dropped her on her left side and high-tailed it back to the convent. From her elevated lookout position, Twink received the full force of the scream as it echoed across the lake and bounced off the nearby hills. With her mouth now the size of a largemouth bass, Twink dropped her cigarette and began to collapse as her knees gave out from beneath her. Quick action from Emma and Mother Superior kept her from face-planting to the ground. A folding chair and bottled water were administered to Twink immediately as she tried to regain her composure. Never, ever in her adventurous long life had Twink witnessed anything like what had just occurred, never! Emma, too, was shocked by what had just unraveled and felt a sharp pang move across her prepartum abdomen. She also quickly took a seat.

Runners farther back in the pack had no idea what had just occurred and were making their way more leisurely to the finish line. Craig was keeping a leisurely pace as well when he came upon another of the Butternut crowd going into similar orgasmic gymnastics. It was Diana Long (Craig wouldn't know her from Adam), who, like Cindy, was trying to overcompensate for the loss of control by increasing her pace and strength of stride. Her efforts, too, were futile, and the harder she tried, the more wildly her contortions and flailing increased. The crowd in her immediate vicinity had backed off as her symptoms expanded. Diana was now close to a full PJ and a full-throated scream. Simultaneously with this occurring, she assumed the acute angle lean and ran full speed into a nearby two-hundred-year-old white oak tree. The sequence of fast-moving events was PJ, scream, and head-on collision. Luckily for Diana, the large roots around the tree slowed her pace so that the contact between her head and the soft bark only left a large abrasion on her forehead. She popped back on the ground in a body-stiffened fall. Again, concerned fellow runners raced to her aid and were greeted with the now all too familiar response of

"I CCCAAAMMMEEE!"

Puzzled onlookers, after seeing her regain her faculties, resumed their running while the nuns who came to help radioed to the hilltop command center to send an ambulance. Diana was sitting up now, supporting herself with her arms back against the ground. Craig left the boys in the running buggy with a neighbor friend and approached the injured runner. Diana was still a bit giddy when Craig introduced himself and asked her what she thought had happened.

"I have no fucking idea what happened other than I just had the most mind-bending orgasm of my entire life!"

Both nuns, waiting for the EMS Service to arrive, quickly retreated from the scene.

Craig couldn't help himself, "Ma'am, did you just say an orgasm made you run yourself into that large tree?"

Diana was quickly losing her patience.

"Hey, numbnuts, are you fucking deaf or what? I said I had a fantastic orgasm, and I must have lost consciousness for a few seconds or something."

Again, Craig continued, "What do you think caused you to have such a large orgasm while you were running the race? Did you have something in your pocket that may have dislodged?"

Diana was now trying to get herself off the ground, "You motherfucker! What the hell do you think? I'm carrying a dildo in my front pocket or something?"

Craig now knew it was time to back off. He smiled at Diana and quickly moved through the crowd that had formed because of all the yelling and swearing to find his boys. He finished the race and went looking for Emma.

In addition to Cindy and Diana, there were also two other similar "medical emergencies" that had been reported during the race by two (you guessed it) Butternut Auxiliary Board members. Two of the four, including Cindy, had declined transport to the hospital and had left the race vertically.

While Mother Superior was at the finish line handing out ribbons and awards, Twink remained at the top of the hill, chain-smoking in an attempt to recalibrate from her eyewitness surveillance of the day's shit show. Emma, herself still on edge, wanted to reassure Twink but stayed clear of the smoke tornado engulfing her. Craig brought the boys to Emma, and they briefly exchanged their respective eye-witness experiences. Although both were still trying to process all the events, the immediate task at hand was to tend to Twink and make sure she was okay.

Craig approached Twink as she was about to light up another cigarette, "Twink, let me help you down the hill and into the parking lot. Why don't we leave your car here and you can ride with us back to the house for some lunch."

"Thank you, Craig, but that will be unnecessary. I am perfectly capable of making my way home but after what I saw today, the three of us must meet immediately to discuss how we can unwind all of this."

Craig was not about to challenge Twink so soon after what she had seen. Unwind was not something Craig had any intention of supporting. This cash cow still had plenty of legs and Craig intended to take full advantage. As he watched Twink graciously descend the hill, he knew that he would have to finesse any discussion of the day's events with Emma to ensure she was in support of his belief that they should continue to run the business. It would be a difficult task given Emma's kind heart and aversion to risk, but Craig knew the right cards to play when it came to his wife. Together, they corralled the boys, packed up the car, and headed home to enjoy the rest of an already too-eventful Mother's Day.

***

Dr. Lovejoy was on hand in the ER when two of four women from the race were wheeled in. By this time, he knew that neither would reveal any details to help him understand the pattern of these episodes. His own research, however, was beginning to uncover a linkage between the afflicted women. He knew now who he needed to speak to in order to unravel the mysterious Clanford "curse."

Chapter Twenty-One

DEATH CUMS IN THREES!

Oftentimes, curiosity kills the cat.

Number One.

Ann Franklin was a sixty-five-year-old, thrice divorced, dowdy, duck-footed, kyphotic, entitled, and mean-spirited member of Clanford's high society. She attained her prominent position in the most traditional of ways, nepotism. Ann was the sole child of Bertrand and Ernestine (the original Bert and Ernie) Franklin. Bertrand was a direct descendent of one of the original property rights investors and had mostly lived off his investments after college. In the early seventies, Bert was made aware of a quite unsavory affair that Ernie was engaged in with (pearl clutch) another woman! Although he brought his inheritance to the marriage, a more progressive judge from Chicago gave Ernie and her new partner half of Bert's net worth. Ernie and Barbra immediately escaped the suffocating backwater attitudes of Clanford and moved to San Francisco abandoning poor Ann for good.

Bert, although far from destitute, was determined to re-amass his lost fortune through active rather than passive wealth management. During this same period, the U.S. government was forcing the de-centralization of utility ownership in an effort to bring free market forces to this all-important sector of the economy. Electric, natural gas, water, and telephone monopolies were being disbanded in favor of private ownership. Bert, in his own right, was a smart guy and understood the opportunity of investing in this new form of utility ownership. He quickly made an outsized bid to take private all the public utilities in Clanford. His plan was to quietly recreate a monopolization of the combined utilities once the governmental oversight had ended. Oblivious to the potential impact of wrong-minded acronyms, he named his newly formed venture the Clanford Utility Network Trust, there after immortalized as C.U.N.T.

The advent of cellular phones and cable television, along with a steady upward trend in new housing formation in Clanford, turned the utility trust into a cash-generating dynamo. Bert transitioned from a doting father to a middle-aged playboy, spending his enormous wealth on all forms of conspicuous consumption. His most fervent passion was cigarette boat racing on Lake Michigan. With his signature young and buxom girlfriend at his side, he plied the waters of the Great Lake with the newest and fastest versions of his favorite boats. He became a top racer in the international cigarette boat circuit.

After her maternal abandonment and paternal indifference, Ann was raised by a governess from Switzerland named Inga. Although she tried to engage Ann in playgroups and team sports, Ann was an avowed loaner more concerned with her potential net worth than the boring drudgery of daily life as an heiress in waiting. After high school graduation, she attended Oberlin College, where she fortified her liberal chops and became even more distant and mean-spirited. After an unremarkable four years, she returned to Clanford to work for her father's utility trust.

As an entry-level analyst, she alienated almost everyone in her group with her greater-than-thou attitude and rudeness. As her father promoted her as a management trainee, she took on more responsibilities as well as direct reports. She was a ruthless manager who ruled with an iron fist in spite of the fact that almost all of her underlings were much smarter than she. Ann was indifferent to anyone's needs, exclusive of her own. She was reviled by everyone who worked for or with her. The trust was so profitable that her poor management skills never appeared to hurt the bottom line. As a result, she was continually promoted to increasingly responsible roles.

Upon graduation, Ann also became a junior member at Butternut. Her family was original founding members of the club, where the Franklin Library was only second in size and opulence to the Ford Library. She was not a very good golfer, although she claimed a handicap of 10. Her golf partners, as well as the golfers on the tee box awaiting their turn, quietly laughed at her exaggerated duck-footed stance and swing. It was not uncommon to hear a muffled quacking from a fellow golfer as she teed off. She was also a regular at the nineteenth hole bar, where she pounded glass after glass of Chardonnay. So aggressive was her drinking style that she was nicknamed the "booze hound" by the bartending staff. As could be expected, drunk Ann was exponentially meaner than sober Ann on any given day.

The week before her twenty-fifth birthday, Ann was summoned to the executive suite for an urgent meeting. When she arrived, she was met by her father's sober-faced best friend and attorney. There had been a boating accident during a race. Her father and twenty-two-year-old paramour were ejected from the boat during an aggressive turn maneuver and died instantly on impact. When they fished out the bodies, old Bert was found pantless with what appeared to be red lipstick on his penis. The twenty-two-year-old appeared to have a dislocated jaw. None of this was ever documented in the official coroner's report, but the funeral home employees had a good laugh on the matter.

Ann turned twenty-five on the day of her father's funeral. She was stoic, as expected, because she had never shown any emotion in her entire life. She went through the motions of the day, all the while calculating in her head the vast wealth she was about to inherit. There was a call from the attorney of the dead girl's family, looking for some type of compensation for her untimely death at the hands of a rogue boat pilot. Ann, in her usual venomous style, informed the attorney that if they wished to proceed with this shakedown, she would request that the girl's body be exhumed and her stomach contents analyzed to prove she was an active participant in the boat accident. No further communication was forthcoming from the family.

***

Over the subsequent forty years, Ann cemented her position in the Clanford social stratum because of her vast wealth and position as CEO of the utility trust. Fellow socialites resented her power as well as her demeanor. They were cordial because they had to be, but behind her back, she was the laughingstock of the Butternut social scene. Her three short marriages that all ended in divorce were rumored to have been with three gay men. Because all three signed non-disclosure statements along with pre-nuptial agreements, it was never confirmed that none of the three unions was ever consummated sexually, although many considered it a hard fact. Many members of the club strongly believed that old Ann married all three of these men because she liked to have a handsome and well-dressed escort on her arm for all the annual social events at the club. There were further rumors that each of the men was paid a "go away fee" to get lost after the dissolution, never to be seen or heard of again in Clanford.

At work, Ann was greatly feared but never respected by her employees. She seemed disproportionately hard-nosed toward the men who worked for her. They, in return, loathed the treatment they received. Her nickname amongst the male crowd was "Ben" (as in Ben Franklin) for her mannish body type and lack of any femininity whatsoever. She could be heard belching and farting in her office when the door was left open. Her other sobriquet was "Queen CUNT" given her leadership role in the utility trust. People who worked directly for her understood the drill well. Always praise her work, ideas, and ruminations, or compliment her style or "smart" outfit for the day. Remain quiet and undeterred when her wrath falls upon you.

Her "style" was a running joke amongst the female employees of the firm. Ann was the highest-paying client of Twink for over twenty years. She demanded exclusive showings of the upcoming season's fashions on her schedule, not Twink's. She also demanded that Twink close her shop one day each quarter so she could view and try on the latest fashions ahead of the rest of her clientele. Twink was much brighter than Ann gave her credit. Twink would search the fashion houses for the most outrageous of outfits to dress Ann. In Twink's world, many clients were categorized as either "pear" or "apple" shaped, given the physical make-up of their legs and torso. Ann was a "papple." Her stomach was rounded, and she had wide legs, hips and butt. The added challenge was the way her feet splayed outward as opposed to being aligned with each other. She was truly duck-footed. This physical attribute pushed her torso forward when she walked. Twink's "revenge" for the decades of bad behavior was to bring in outfits that accentuated her physical flaws rather than obscure them. Add high-heel pumps to the equation and her gait became comical. Once they were tried on, high praise from Twink and her assistants cemented the deal for Ann, who was too clueless to realize she was the butt of a running fashion joke for years. Twink also greatly inflated the prices because she knew she could. This was probably the only questionable business practice Twink ever engaged in.

Once she was done with men, Ann set forth to build an opulent mansion for herself and her pet cockatiel. The planning and construction took over three years and she purchased two homes in the center town area and demolished them both to make room for her manse. There was no limit to the gaudiness and lack of taste put into the home. Architecturally, it was a disaster. Three well-known architects came and went during the process, refusing to put their names on the home Ann would continue to modify on the fly. The end product was an eyesore to everyone but Ann and the bird. The interior decorating was just as bad, if not worse than the exterior facade. There were over 10,000 square feet of mismatched wood, stone, metalwork, fabrics, and rugs. It could have been the cover story for the inaugural issue of "Architectural Indigestion." Once again, Ann was oblivious to the talk behind her back on what a horrible piece of shit she had built. Her nightly routine consisted of sitting with her bird in the oversized living room, downing at least one, if not two, bottles of chardonnay, and telling the bird the highlights of the day. Ann, who kept all of her wealth in low-risk municipal bonds, also told the parrot, the closing trade balance of her portfolio.

Ann had chosen the talking bird as an alternative to the pet she had dreamed of since childhood, a white Persian cat. Upon purchasing an exclusively bred white Persian in her early thirties, she quickly realized she had a deathly allergy to the feline. As much as she tried to make the pet situation better (shots for her, antihistamines, special air filtration), she finally surrendered to her physical deficiencies and got rid of the cat. She chose the white cockatiel for several reasons. First, it was pure white, which is what was so attractive to her about the Persian cat. Second, it could learn to speak and actually have conversations (at least Ann thought that) with her as a substitute companion. Third, like a cat, it was low maintenance.

Ann purchased the albino cockatiel from a parrot breeder in Bolivia and had it shipped via a private jet to her home. It was love at first sight on Ann's part, and she named the bird "Pussy" to commemorate her unrequited love for the Persian cat. Ann and Pussy became great friends, and Pussy's vocabulary grew exponentially because of the constant nightly drunken jabber of Ann.

***

On the Wednesday following the Mother's Day run, Twink was scheduled to close her boutique to meet with Ann for her summer dressing. Twink had asked Emma to join her for the fittings so she could become acquainted with the Twink/Ann quarterly drill. When Ann arrived, Twink and Emma were having a conversation in the workroom and did not hear her come in. Ann was a consummate eavesdropper and quietly moved closer to the workroom to listen in on the women.

"Twink, I don't think we can ignore how effective our pink pills have been in helping the women at Butternut lose so much weight. Even with side effects, they seem overjoyed at the rapid loss and their ability to sustain it."

Twink responded, "Emma, darling, I don't disagree, but I think we need to move more cautiously going forward. We don't want any physical issues with these women."

Ann, let out what she thought was a silent fart that wasn't so silent. Both Twink and Emma were startled that Ann was in the next room, and they hadn't heard her come in. They ended their conversation and began to move out of the workroom. Ann quickly moved to a chair in the showroom acting like nothing happened.

Twink approached Ann with Emma right behind her.

"Ann, darling, how are you? I didn't hear you come in." She gave Ann air bisé kisses and grasped her hands, "It is so nice to see you, and I'm particularly excited about many of the outfits I have picked for the summer season. Ann, this is my new assistant, Emma Mayfield. She is going to be helping you in the fitting room."

Ann, being her usual affected self, smiled at Emma and then turned her back to her. Emma, seeing Ann in profile, knew she had her work cut out for her.

Over the next five hours, Twink and Emma progressed through the thirty-plus outfits that Twink had secured for Ann. More than once, Emma muffled laughter as Ann emerged from the dressing room in an outfit of wild color and fabrics. When she looked cross-eyed at Twink, Twink simply smiled and took a long drag on her cigarette. Throughout the afternoon, Twink made sure that Ann's glass was filled with Chardonnay.

After six excruciating hours, the outfits had been boxed, shoes had been matched and Twink presented the invoice to Ann. Emma would send all packages via courier to Ann's house the next day. Ann didn't even flinch at the $125,000 total bill and tossed her black American Express card for Emma to run. Emma was blown away at how the day unfolded and how clueless Ann seemed to be. What Twink and Emma didn't know was that Ann had lifted two bottles of the pink pills that were sitting on the worktable across from the dressing room when they weren't watching her. Before getting a serious buzz on, she was lucid enough to understand the positive effects of the weight loss pills they were talking about when she was listening in. Ann had tried numerous diets over the years to lose her extra weight but never realized that it was the Chardonnay that was the main culprit. When she saw the dozens of bottles of pink pills sitting on the worktable, she quickly put a couple into her purse, which was hanging in her dressing room. No one would notice that two had been absconded.

Twink called a taxi for Ann, given her condition, and the women parted ways at the front door of the boutique. Emma plopped herself in a chair and put her aching feet up on an ottoman from nearby. Twink lit a Virginia Slim, sat down, and began laughing out loud.

"That was Ann Franklin, one of the richest and most clueless women in all Clanford! She is also our most lucrative client."

Emma smiled back at Twink and wondered if she was going to be paid a commission for the large purchase.

Twink must have been reading her mind because she immediately said, 'Emma, bring me the corporate checkbook so I can write you a check for your commission."

Emma smiled and thanked Twink for her continued kindness.

Twink nodded as she exhaled a large plume of smoke.

***

Thursday morning, Ann cradled the five pink pills in her palm as she stood in her bathroom after brushing her teeth. She thought she might start by taking one pill and quickly swallowed it down. She was about to put the remaining four pills in the bottle and impulsively took a second without much thought. She waited a few moments, anticipating some type of effect, but felt nothing. She was lingering longer than usual and didn't want to be late to work. She looked at the remaining pills in her hand, put her head back, and finished off the three with a large gulp of water. On her way out the door, she told Pussy to have a nice day.

Ann returned home at her usual 6:45 p.m. She entered the living room, gave Pussy a kiss, and moved immediately to the wine cooler and extracted a bottle of Rombauer, her favorite evening aperitif. A country club pour close to the brim brought a huge smile to her face as she took a large gulp to make the glass more manageable.

Ann walked over to her bird and started to stroke its back, "My beautiful Pussy!I love you so much! I love you, my beautiful Pussy!"

The bird parroted her phrases back to her, making Ann laugh. Ann took another large gulp, which took the remaining remnants down to half a swallow. She moved back to the wine bar and refilled to the brim. Ann had an oversized chair that perfectly fit her oversized ass next to the bird stand. She was making her way over to the chair when she felt a hot flash move across her entire body.

"Oh, my! Oh, my! Pussy, I'm feeling really hot, way hot, Pussy!"

She was getting closer to the chair when her right knee buckled.

She quickly lost her grip on her glass, and it crashed to the floor.

"Oh, Pussy! Pussy! Something is happening to me! Pussy, my beautiful Pussy!"

Within seconds, Ann was overcome with the exponential side effects of taking such a large dose earlier in the day. She regained her composure but was feeling the heat rising in her body. Like the others, her knees locked, and she began undulating forward and backward from the waist up.

"Pussy! Pussy! Oh, my beautiful Pussy! Something is happening to me!"

The full impact of the orgasm was rising in her body, something she had never experienced before in her lifetime. She was helpless to the torrent of emotions as her hands flew up, her fingers splayed, and her head flew back.

"Ha, ha, ha, ha, ha, ha! PUSSY! PUSSY! PUSSY! MY BEAUTIFUL-LLLL PUSSY!"

As she started into her PJ, her body stiffened, and she fell backward hard. Unfortunately, she was a bit too close to the marble hearth of the oversized fireplace in the room and banged her head on the sharp corner. The blow to the head was immediately fatal.

The good sister's catechism at SBH had taught all of their students that every human is born with a soul roughly the size of their heart. As you grow and mature, good deeds, kindness, and love expand the size of your soul to fill one's larger body. Likewise, people who are unkind, mean, and unloving have their souls shrivel over their lives. Poor Ann Franklin's tiny, shriveled soul at the time of her death exited her body through her anus as a small, chardonnay-infused, buttery fart that exploded near the beak of Pussy as it wafted upward.

"Holy shit—what the fuck was that?" cried the stunned bird as it attempted to move away from the putrid remnants of its former owner. In death, as in life, Ann was defined as nothing more than a buttery fart.

***

After two days of not showing up for work, a wellness check was requested of the Clanford police by Ann's executive assistant. After breaking into the home, they found Ann on the floor of the living room, dried blood on her head and a still liquid puddle of urine by her crotch. The bird was sitting on its perch and began screaming as the officers entered the room.

"Oh, Pussy! My beautiful Pussy! I love you so much! Oh Pussy! Pussy! Pussy!"

The officers looked at each other and began to chuckle. The bird continued, "Oh Pussy! My Pussy! Something is happening to me! I'm feeling hot, my Pussy! I'm really hot!"

The first officer looked at the other and spoke.

"Whoa—are you hearing what I'm hearing? The bird must be parroting this old bag before she died. Looks like she hit her head, but it sounds like she was having some weird type of sexual thing going on! Ickkkkk! I don't even want to think about it."

The second officer was laughing pretty hard now as the bird continued, "Look, he said, take a few pictures of her head showing where she hit the corner. Cause of death is an accidental fall with a resultant head injury."

The bird wouldn't stop, "Oh, my Pussy, my beautiful Pussy! I love you Pussy!"

Both officers were now in hysterics as they called for an ambulance to remove the body.

They also called the animal warden to come and grab the bird. Unbeknownst to them at the time, Ann's will left everything to her beautiful Pussy, which secured living accommodations in the mansion for the remainder of Pussy's pampered life. Not living in the wild, cockatiels have a life expectancy of over thirty years.

Number Two

Thaddeus Brancovic, Jr. was the adult son of Thaddeus and Ana Brankovic, who had emigrated to Clanford from Serbia twenty years prior. In order to Americanize their names, they shortened Brancovic to "Brank," and Thaddeus senior went by Ted. Ted was a cab driver, and Ana worked in the admissions department at St. Gerard's Hospital. Together, they created a comfortable life for themselves and their son. Although as a child, Thaddeus, Jr. was called Teddy, as an adult he liked Tad better and required others to call him that.

"Tad" was openly gay and had lived as such since his sophomore year in high school. Although his parents loved him dearly, his flamboyant dress and mannerisms put a strain on the parent/child relationship. Tad chose not to go to college and remained living at home after high school graduation. To say that Tad was a weird duck was an understatement, not because of his sexual orientation, but because of the idiosyncrasies of his daily life. With the help of his parents and money saved from childhood jobs, Tad purchased a 1968 Cutlass Supreme Convertible for his sixteenth birthday. The car was bright orange with a white leather interior and a white rag top. Tad loved cruising in the car with the top down and music blaring regardless of the weather or season. He dressed in bright clothing and trained his thick, dark, black hair into an upward swooping pompadour. Tad was six foot four inches tall and weighed all of one hundred and sixty pounds. He was Ichabod Crane-like in stature, very strange at best. For better or worse, everyone in town knew Tad Brank.

Tad took a job out of high school as an attendant in the locker rooms at the Butternut Club.He was offered the position by the head of golf operations, who was secretly gay after an encounter at a gay bar in Waukegan. Bill, the head of golf, ran the locker rooms with military precision. The only black spot on his record was a complaint from the high school golf team that Bill had been a little too helpful with towels when they were showering after practice. After that event, Bill kept a much lower profile away from Clanford.

As locker room attendant, Tad was responsible for keeping both locker rooms clean (the women's after hours) as well as cleaning and shining the golfer's shoes after play. The women's locker room was set up with a v-shaped drop bin where they placed their shoes that opened into a small room behind the locker room where Tad would collect and clean them. Again, after hours, they were placed back into the women's individual lockers.

Another strange idiosyncrasy of Tad's was that he was a shoe sniffer. Yes, women's shoes! Each afternoon, as he collected the sweaty shoes of the golfers, he would hold them up to his face and take a long and hard inhalation of the foot stench. The stronger, the better. The smell of the shoes was like an energy drink for Tad, as his whole body would become electrified with each hard sniff. Since the inside of the shoes held the golfer's name and locker number, he created a notebook of his favorite dogs and categorized them each night based on the strength of the bouquet. Without fail, Ann

Franklin's was at the top of the list. Her size eleven shoes, strangely worn on the outsides of the shoes, he thought, could be recognized in the bin before he even saw them. They were always the sweatiest and the stinkiest of all the shoes, and Tad went crazy for them. Even the cedar shoe trees that Ann required to be replaced after cleaning did not dull the amount of stench that radiated from her colorful Foot Joys.

Tad became so obsessed with her shoes that he decided he needed to concoct a chance encounter with Ann so he could meet her in person. He knew that she was a regular Thursday afternoon women's nine-holer participant. Early one Thursday, he removed her shoes from her locker and placed them in the cleaning room. He left a note asking Ann to call his cell phone so he could discuss an urgent issue with her shoes. Needless to say, Ann was less than happy with not having her shoes ready for play. She called Tad's cell and screamed at him to return the shoes at once. Tad told her he would meet her immediately outside the women's locker room entrance. When she arrived, she was furious and demanded he hand over her shoes. Tad, with a stiffened backbone, explained to her that her shoes were wearing excessively on the outside of the shoes and suggested an alternative shoe from the pro shop that had a better insole structure to improve her comfort and, more than likely, her play. Ann, thought for a minute and then inquired as to what shoe he had in mind. Tad was ready with an alternative size eleven and presented them to her. Not one to be appreciative of kindness, Ann grabbed them from him and muffled a hardly audible thank you. Tad told her he would dispose of the older shoes and quickly left.

Tad couldn't believe his good fortune. Not only had he met the best shoe stench extraordinaire in person, but he also secured for himself a pair of "take-home" shoes for later enjoyment. He began to ask around about Ann to some of the other club staff. Who was she? Where did she live? What was her story? What he found out blew him away. Single, really, really, rich, and a huge bitch. Tad immediately thought he should figure out some way to be a handyman or errand guy for her. He now knew who she was, and he just needed another reason to connect with her. Later that afternoon, Tad made a point to be near the ninth hole as the ladies worked their way back to the clubhouse. When he saw Ann, she was walking by herself, dragging a pull cart with her clubs. He quickly ran up to try and help her.

"Ms. Franklin! Let me help you with your clubs."

In full character, she replied, "Who the hell are you?"

"I'm Tad Brank, the locker room attendant. I helped you with your shoes before your round of golf. How did they work out?"

Annoyed by someone of such a low status even addressing her, she stopped and gave Tad a withering stare, "Mr. Brank, I do not believe it is in your job description to be providing shoes or requesting a follow-up report on those shoes from a club member. Please remember your station!"

Tad was undeterred, "Ms. Franklin, I apologize if you think I'm being too bold. I've heard such great things about you. I wanted to be helpful, and I wanted to let you know that I do errands and small jobs for several members who have busy schedules."

Tad's compliments caught Ann off guard. She continued to glare at him but thought he actually may be helpful to her.

"Mr. Brank, please leave your contact information in my locker after you have completed your duties for the day. If I need an errand boy in the future, I may call you."

With that, she pushed the cart to Tad and duck-walked to the Nineteenth Hole Bar. Tad again couldn't believe his luck. She had agreed to take his contact information and potentially hire him for side work.

"What a day!" he told himself he needed to buy a lottery ticket on the way home.

Two days after their brief encounter, Ann reached out to Tad to hire him for lunchtime bird visits. This was early April, right after the golf course re-opened. Tad's responsibilities included visiting Pussy each weekday during his lunch break to give her fresh water and a couple of pieces of fresh fruit and stroke her feathers and talk to her. The pay was $50 per day. Tad accessed the home via a garage code and a specific alarm code that identified when he arrived and when he left, which Ann monitored daily. Since there were no internal cameras in the house, Tad took the liberty of "exploring" the huge home and all its amenities.

Upon arriving each day, Tad changed out the bird's water and grabbed some fruit from the fridge. No way in hell was he going to be stroking the bird, but he did realize pretty quickly that the bird was smart enough to repeat what was said around it. Tad would say pretty bird a few times and then ignore the bird so he could explore.

His first stop was always the master closet, where Ann kept a museum-sized, separate shoe room. It was enormous and made Tad quiver the first time he set eyes on the hundreds of pairs of shoes all arrayed on shelves in perfect order. He couldn't contain himself and raced over to grab shoes and sniff them. Unfortunately for Tad, some of the shoes had never been worn and proved to be duds for his newly found fetish. This, however, presented Tad with a challenge. Each day, he would attack a different area of the closet to "sniff out" the shoes that Ann had worn. Most days, he was rewarded with a well- sweated shoe to indulge his olfactory senses.

Tad was careful to make sure anything he touched was replaced exactly as it was found. He was also extremely careful to arrive and leave at exactly the same time each day so as not to raise any concerns on Ann's part. Tad was extremely pleased with his new responsibilities and loved the extra $250 in cash he was paid each week, plus the free reign of her shoe closet.

On the afternoon of the day Ann expired, Tad was making his way out of the master bedroom through the master bath when he noticed two unmarked prescription bottles on the bathroom sink counter. He walked over to examine them a little more. He immediately saw one was empty and the other had five small pink pills in it. He thought to himself, that old bag was a pill popper. Although he couldn't figure out from the unmarked pills exactly what they were, he was convinced they were some type of hallucinogenic. He certainly had his share of out-of-body experiences from pills that looked pretty much like these. He wanted to take a couple but knew when she came home, she would see them missing. His devious mind concocted a plot right away. He took the full bottle of pills and put four of them in his pocket. He then placed the bottle on its side in the sink, with the fifth pill sitting dangerously close to the drain. When Ann returned, he surmised, she would think that she had knocked the pills over in the morning and all but one had escaped into the drain pipes. He congratulated himself on his genius plan and couldn't wait to pop a few after work. He said goodbye to pussy, locked the door, and returned to the club to finish out his shift.

A little after 8 p.m., Tad pulled out of the club parking lot and headed to a local watering hole that he frequented regularly where they served cold beer and great burgers. Tad was in a particularly good mood this evening because he had saved almost all of Ann's pay over the past seven weeks and was getting a daily fix of shoe sniffs. He sat at the bar and ordered a draft beer and smash burger. He looked at his phone because he was completely uninterested in the MLB game on the bar's television. Just before he left, he took the four pills from his pocket and threw them down his throat with the last gulp of beer. He drove over to the park by the Clanford River, reclined his front seat, and, with the top down on the car, stared up at the star-filled sky, awaiting the imminent buzz from the pills.

After about thirty minutes, Tad grew anxious wondering what the hell happened to his buzz. Maybe the pills were some sort of woman thing and weren't really what he thought they were. He put his seat back into its regular position and decided to drive slowly along the parkway beside the river. Given it was well after sunset, there were no other cars on the narrow street. Tad knew the path well because it was a place as a teenager he would retreat to when the bullying at school became too intense.

Around the half-mile mark of the five-mile parkway, Tad began to feel a strong, heat-like electricity move across his body. He slowed down for a second as the feeling passed through him. Wow, he thought, that was pretty wild. Was it the pills or that smash burger, he wondered. A little further along, a more intense similar feeling struck him unexpectedly, and he cried out in surprise, "What the fuck?"

Before that passed, a second round came on even stronger. This caused him to press on the accelerator pedal, and the car lurched forward. Tad caught himself and immediately braked the car to a full stop. Without any warning, the mother of all full-body orgasms was upon him. His whole body was quivering, and he became frightened at the loss of control in his arms. To gain some level of control, he forced himself to grab the steering wheel with both hands. The continued rise of elation in his body locked his grip on the wheel and tightened all the muscles in his lower extremities. As the PJ approached, his head flew back, he began to laugh, and his legs straightened out, forcing his foot onto the accelerator again. This time, he had no ability to control the car as the 5.7-liter V8 engine exploded with power, pushing the car over the curb, through the guard rail, where it became airborne, arching up toward the middle of the Clanford River.

Tad laughed loudly and screamed,

"I'm COOOMMMIIINNNGGG," as he entered the water, where the momentum pushed the car into the muddy depths of the fast-flowing river.

Without any ability to release his grip on the wheel and try to swim upward, poor Tad drowned with a smile on his face and a load in his briefs. His one-hundred-and-sixty-pound frame was just not robust enough to handle a quadruple dose of the man-up pills.

An early morning runner on the parkway alerted police to the damaged guardrail and tire tracks leading to the river. A dive team was dispatched, and Tad's pride and joy car, as well as his body, were recovered from the river floor. The coroner would find nothing strange about the condition of Tad's body other than rigor mortis had already set in with the stiff legs and hands gripping the wheel. The toxicology report would come back negative, leading the cause of death to be listed as accidental drowning due to a vehicular accident.

Number Three

For the first time in her life, Marguerite Ford Smythe bore more envy than disinterest for her daughter Fluffy. Since her childhood, Fluffy had fought being overweight, which always allowed Marguerite to stay in the spotlight ahead of her daughter. Fluffy never posed a threat to Marguerite as a younger and more beautiful version. Although Fluffy was obviously younger, Marguerite had prided herself throughout her life on being more svelte and stylish, even into advanced middle age. That all changed with the pink pills, and Marguerite did not like it at all.

Even though Fluffy was still trying to contain the social damage of her "medical emergency" at the Butternut opening luncheon, she was gaining attention and praise for her new, more stylish figure. When she dined with her mother at the club, it was Fluffy, not Marguerite, who was getting the attention and compliments on her outfits. When they shopped together in town, the attention again was focused on Fluffy. Her weight loss was truly transformational.

Although Fluffy had kept her pill-popping secret from Marguerite, her mother had been asking around to some senior club members in the know. Rather than confront Fluffy, she went to Twink to find out more about the noticeable slimming down of many of the Butternut auxiliary. Twink was a dear friend of Marguerite but still felt that she could not disclose the business she and the Mayfields were running out of her boutique. When they met for lunch at Butternut, Twink was intentionally evasive, only divulging that she had heard the women were taking some new diet pill that was being sold through some sort of black-market system. She added that there was pressure on whoever was distributing them to back away before the Clanford police were involved. Twink felt that this may dilute Marguerite's interest in the matter. It did not.

No one in Clanford had a better pulse on the politics of the social stratum than Marguerite Smythe. As the long-term leader of the Butternut auxiliary, she understood who was and who wanted to be, a higher status. Fluffy was clearly on the bubble when it came to retaining her leadership role, and Marguerite was not above using that fact to get the information she wanted. Fluffy's two ladies-in-waiting had been reduced to one after the Mother's Day extravaganza meltdown of Melinda Walsh. Clare Johnson was now heir apparent if Fluffy was requested to relinquish her spot. Marguerite placed a call to Clare and asked her to join her for lunch the following afternoon in a private dining room at Butternut. Clare graciously accepted, but her antennae were up to any possible subterfuge from Fluffy's mother.

When Clare arrived ten minutes early, Marguerite was already sitting with a glass of wine in the private dining room.

"Clare, darling, how wonderful to see you! How is that charming husband of yours and those delicious children?"

Clare immediately thought the adjective delicious was more than appropriate, given Marguerite's history of eating people alive.

"Why, Mrs. Smythe, you are so kind to ask. They are all doing wonderfully."

"Clare, please call me Marguerite." "Thank you, ma'am."

Clare took her seat at the table and immediately joined her host in a tall glass of white wine. She wanted to stay focused but also knew she had a bad habit of letting her nervousness show.

"Clare, I wanted to see if you could help me gather some information on all of the goings on with some of the Auxiliary membership."

"Absolutely, Marguerite. What exactly are you referring to?"

Marguerite jumped right in, "There seems to be a black market diet pill that some of the women have been taking that is giving them rapid and sustainable weight loss." Clare took a large pull of her wine, afraid of where this might be going. Marguerite continued, "I'm impressed with the focus on healthy living and weight loss, but I am concerned about the content of the pill given that it is being attained through a black-market source. I think the prudent thing to do is to have several of these pills analyzed by an accredited lab to make sure they do not contain any dangerous ingredients."

(Clare thought to herself, holy shit, if you only knew!)

"I think that is an incredibly smart idea, Marguerite. How do you plan to get hold of some of their pills?"

"Clare, darling. That's why I've reached out to you. I'm sure your network of ladies in Butternut can provide you with several so I can quietly get them tested."

Clare was now in full lying mode, "Marguerite, I don't think I know anyone who is actually taking them."

The sweat beads were mounting on her brow, and several were about to repel down her face.

"Clare, allow me to be blunt. I want you to have a bottle of those pills at my house before 5 p.m. this evening without mentioning this to anyone, especially Fluffy. OR ELSE!"

The cascade of sweat was now streaking Clare's foundation, and Marguerite smiled at the intended effect. There was no reason to ask what "or else" meant. It was fully understood.

"Clare, darling, I do have to run to another engagement. Feel free to stay and have a salad. I've booked the lunch under your club number."

Game, set, match!

After Marguerite exited the room, Clare ordered another white wine and slumped into her chair. She kept thinking it could have been worse. She would call Emma immediately and tell her that her weekly bottle of pills had been accidentally disposed of by her housekeeper, Consuelo.

Clare arrived at 4:45 p.m. with a bottle of five pills. Marguerite's housekeeper accepted the package and assured her that the chain of custody would end with Mrs. Smythe. Clare stressed that she needed to have them in hand before 5 p.m. The housekeeper, sensing the fear in Clare's mannerisms, assured her that she would personally take them directly to Marguerite immediately. As she closed the door, the housekeeper thought to herself that Marguerite's reign of terror clearly had a larger range than just the Smythe household.

***

Marguerite had dinner by herself in the dining room, given her husband was off shooting some helpless animal at an exotic location that was much too difficult to pronounce. In fact, the only shooting he was doing was Viagra induced with his latest girlfriend on a friend's yacht in St. Barth's. Marguerite retired to her bedroom, and while she was getting ready for bed, she stood in front of the full-length mirror in her dressing room to take inventory of her sixty-plus-year-old figure.

She certainly had a figure that was envied by many women her age, but there clearly were places, in her personal opinion, that needed to be reduced and or tightened. Most women would make a quick trip to Dr. Buttman (his real name), the most prodigious plastic surgeon in Clanford. Marguerite had taken great pride in the fact that the only work she would let him do was above her neck. She toyed with the idea of taking a few of the pink pills to see if they would take care of her "issues." She opened the bottle and put two in her hand. She thought better of it and returned the pills to the bottle.

As she laid in bed watching the latest episode of The Bachelor, she began scrutinizing the figures of the six remaining contestants. Sure, they were twenty-somethings, but she envied their looks and their athleticism. She once had a body like theirs and, for her age, was still in great shape. She watched the conclusion and turned off the lights. Unable to sleep, given her obsession with the women on the show, she returned to the bathroom, opened the bottle, and downed three pills.

"What the hell? They seem to be working for Fluffy!"

She returned to bed and fell asleep immediately. She rang her call button in the morning for her coffee, croissant, and daily paper. She lingered until 9 a.m. and then made her way to the bathroom for her morning shower. At 9:45 a.m. promptly, her daily blowout would be administered by her staff hair stylist.

She entered the shower and began washing her way down from her head to her feet. She loved the rain shower that allowed her to engulf her body in warm, pulsating water fully. Many mornings, she just stood under the strong pressure of rainfall to clear her mind of any concerns. This morning, she was standing under the shower thinking about the pills she had taken the night before. How many days should she wait to check her numbers on the scale? She usually weighed herself every morning to ensure it didn't deviate more than an ounce or two.

Maybe it was her age or possibly her "mature' circulatory system that drove the effects of the pills so violently through her body. All the usual incrementally stepped symptoms experienced by the younger women compiled into one large wash of an orgasmic tornado that struck her so hard she couldn't even enjoy the sensation that hadn't revealed itself in many years. Before she even reached her PJ, she collapsed backward, hitting her head on the gold-plated towel hook in the oversized shower. The blow itself was not fatal, but as she fell, her body covered about ninety percent of the drain. With the powerful rain shower pounding down, it only took a few minutes for the water level in the shower to cover her unconscious head. She died peacefully from drowning.

When she didn't answer her bedroom door at 9:45 a.m., the hair stylist alerted the house manager. They opened the bedroom door and were met with a wave of water coming from the master bathroom. The house manager and stylist both screamed when they saw Marguerite's lifeless body at the bottom of the flooded shower. 911 was called, and resuscitation efforts were applied, but to no avail. Marguerite Ford Smythe had passed on to what she firmly believed would be the next universal level of status and wealth. Oh, would she be surprised!

***

Fluffy was at the driving range when she received word that her mother had taken ill and was being taken to the emergency room at St. Gerard's. She took a few minutes to finish her bucket of balls before heading to the hospital. She quietly was hoping that this could all be resolved quickly so she would not have to cancel her lunch with her three golf partners.

When she arrived at the ER, she was met by her mother's personal assistant and the hospital chaplain. She was ushered into a side room and given the news of her mother's fall and drowning. Her immediate thought was whether she would look insensitive if she went back and had lunch with her girlfriends, but she quashed that idea. In reality, Fluffy had very little emotional attachment to her mother who pretty much abandoned her to nannies at a very young age. She was trying hard to force some tears, but it just wasn't happening. She looked at the two others in the room and said good riddance and left.

Marguerite had left specific instructions for an elaborate wake and funeral to be held at both the Grand Hall at Butternut (visitation) and the Catholic Cathedral (funeral) in town. (Her directives included the same gold casket as Michael Jackson, a change of clothing between wake and funeral like Aretha Franklin, and placing most of her jewelry on her body and in her casket for burial like Whitney Houston). When her dad returned from his St. Barth's frolic, he and Fluffy would have nothing of it. They went to the local funeral home, had her cremated, and held a luncheon at Butternut the next day. There was no pageantry, long eulogies, or rooms full of flower tributes that Marguerite had ordered and expected. Instead, Fluffy negotiated the cheapest buffet for the lunch and had a cash bar, which ensured the event wouldn't last more than an hour.

Fluffy had no choice but to let the many personal assistants go but gave each a $100,000 severance check to ease the transition and thank them for putting up with her mother for so many years. The house staff would stay on until her father put the house on the market. He had his sights set on a villa high above Gouverneur's Beach in St. Barth's. Fluffy had a safe cracker open her mother's jewelry vault since she trusted no one with the combination. Fluffy would sell all of it and donate the proceeds to charity. Her final act of daughterly devotion would be to take Marguerite's ashes and scatter them at a homeless encampment in Waukegan.

Done and dusted!

Chapter Twenty-Two

Befuddled and Bedazzled!

The membership at Butternut was reeling from the news they received from the club manager in an early morning email following what appeared to be some very busy days for the Grim Reaper. Over the most recent thirty-six hours, two of its most prominent members and one employee had all died in what was being referred to as "freak accidents." Many of the members rushed to the club to demand more details of what happened. Some believed there was a conspiracy out to rid Clanford of some of its most prominent citizens. Others just wanted the dirt on two of the most reviled members of the club. William had received some details, but nothing near the level that the membership was requesting. He explained that Ann had fallen and cracked her head, probably in a drunken stupor (now that's the kind of details they were after). Marguerite likewise had collapsed and drowned because of her advancing age (oooh, advancing age!), and poor Tad was most likely just high and not paying attention (as twenty-something idiot men tend to do.)

Clare was one of the members who raced over to the club when she heard the news. She was going to show everyone her leadership abilities in this trying time to try and cement her position as true heir apparent for Auxiliary board president. In her mind, Clare couldn't help but wonder if the diet pills had had something to do with Marguerite's death. Did Marguerite lie to her when she said she was concerned about safety and had planned to get them analyzed? Could she possibly have tried one, two, or maybe all five? Even if the pills had something to do with her death, Marguerite had demanded she bring them to her. Then Clare began to wonder about a possible police inquiry. Her fingerprints, for certain, were on the bottle. Would she be linked back to this? If she was, she would immediately throw Twink, Emma, and her husband, what's his name, under the bus without regret or delay. That's it. She was just delivering the pills for Twink and Emma. She had no idea what they were or why Marguerite wanted them. That was her story, and she was sticking to it. She walked into the bar and demanded the bartender ignore the 11 a.m. first pour rule and hand over a glass and a full bottle of Fumé Blanc.

***

As a member of Butternut, Twink had received William's email in the morning as well. For the second time in a little more than a month, she arrived unannounced at Emma's house. She climbed the stairs, cigarette in hand, and rang the doorbell. As usual, both Emma and Craig were at home. She entered the home, went straight to the dining room table, and sat at the head. Emma and Craig quickly followed.

She started in immediately.

"I received an email this morning from William, the club manager at Butternut. Two women members, Ann Franklin and Marguerite Smythe, as well as one of the male locker room attendants, have all died suddenly over the last three days, all freak accidents! I also spoke to William, who gave me a few more details about Ann and Marguerite, specifically that Ann was most likely drunk, and Marguerite may have just slipped and fallen in the shower."

Emma and Craig looked quizzically at each other, and Craig spoke first, "Soooooo, what do you think that has to do with us? Were the two women on our customer list?"

"No, of course not! They were both in their sixties and would have no reason to be taking the pills."

Emma interjected, "Is that the same Ann Franklin who was in our store this week?"

"Twink, becoming annoyed, snapped, "Of course it was! Do you think there is more than one Ann Franklin in all Clanford?"

Emma continued, "Twink, I hadn't said anything before this, but I noticed that two bottles of the pills have gone missing since the last pick-up. Clare Johnson called me the day before yesterday and said her housekeeper had accidentally tossed her weekly allotment of pills while cleaning. I met her at your shop at 4:30 p.m. and gave her a new supply. She seemed a little nervous, paid me, and left quickly. When I returned to the worktable, I recounted the bottles and noticed that we were down three, including the one I gave to Clare from my weekly inventory report."

Twink, pondering this news, said, "Do you think Ann took two of the bottles from the table, Emma?"

"I don't know, it just seems strange that there were two bottles missing after she was in the shop for her fittings. I keep meticulous inventory reports because each bottle is worth $5,000."

Craig, seeing the possibility of another pushback from Twink about continuing the business, jumped in, "First of all, even if she took the bottles, there is zero proof that they had anything to do with her death. Didn't you say she fell and hit her head? You also said William had heard she was drunk. Is she known at Butternut for being a big drinker?"

Twink acknowledged that, "Yes, that was what William said and yes, she was known to be a heavy drinker at the club."

Craig continued, "Okay, so she drinks too much and falls down. That's standard operating practice for millions of people. I don't think you can draw anywhere near a straight line from our pills to her death, end of story!"

Both Twink and Emma remained silent as they processed Craig's words. Then Twink replied, "Okay, maybe we can't draw a straight line, but I am becoming increasingly concerned about safety. We need to do something to wean these women off the pills and close the operation."

Craig became indignant, "Twink, with all due respect, there is no FUCKING way we are going to close down this business. These women are clamoring for the pills. This business is a cash-fucking- cow! We aren't forcing these pills down anyone's throats. They are grown women who can make choices for themselves. If you are concerned about safety, then come up with a safety idea because we are NOT closing down the business."

Twink, unaccustomed to such frank talk, glared at Craig but kept quiet.

Emma chimed in, "Helmets."

Craig looked at her and replied, "What the fuck do you mean by helmets?"

"We sell bike helmets at the boutique as a safety precaution for women who seize and fall down. If they protect their heads, then they protect their brains, and ultimately, they are protecting their lives."

Twink smiled broadly and took another long drag on her now third cigarette since arriving, "That is a brilliant idea, Emma. We will order bike helmets from an accessories supplier I have in Shanghai in the colors from this year's fashion color wheel. We will also have them bedazzled so that each woman who wears them has a unique fashion statement to make. It's genius!"

Craig was dumbfounded, but Emma got it and replied, "If we position these as the latest fashion accessories, the women will eat it up. We can also make wearing them a requirement, like the vitamins, to receive their ongoing supply of pills."

Craig clearly didn't get it but kept quiet since the topic had quickly moved away from shutting down the business.

Twink stood up abruptly and told Emma to meet her at the boutique in thirty minutes. They would look at the color wheel together and determine what the order would look like before calling her supplier. Emma agreed, and Twink left.

When Emma arrived at the boutique as directed, Twink had the color wheel as well as numerous current outfits from the shop, placed on the largest worktable. She suggested they order one hundred to start and showed Emma her thoughts on color selection. Emma made a few suggestions, and they both moved to Twink's desk where they dialed up the Chinese supplier on the speaker phone.

As the phone began ringing, Twink told Emma his name was Mr. Pey Mi Naw.

"Miss Twink, my favorite customer, what do you need from me?" "Oh, Mr. Naw, I'm sure everyone is your favorite customer." "Please call me Pey Mi. What you want to buy?"

"I need adult women's bike helmets in my own custom colors, and I need you to place colored rhinestones on them to make them fashionable."

"Twink, Twink, Twink, you crazy lady! No one wants to buy something like that."

"Pey Mi, please. I know what I want, and I know you can get me them. I need them here in Illinois in one week."

"You crazy, crazy, crazy! How I make and ship in one week?"

"Pey Mi, I know you can do anything; it always comes down to price."

"Cost you big, big money! You got big money?"

"You know I always pay my bills right away. Like I said, I need one hundred in the colors that I will email at the end of this call in my boutique in one week. Send me the invoice by the end of the day, and I will wire the money."

"You crazy, Miss Twink. This be very expensive, very expensive. I will do it as a special favor for my best customer! Don't forget my name, Pey Mi Naw!"

Twink acknowledged his name and ended the call. She asked Emma to email him the colors immediately. Emma was curious.

"Twink, is that his real name?"

Twink laughed out loud, "I have no idea, but it certainly aligns directly with his payment terms!"

They both got a good laugh out of that. Emma chuckled to herself the rest of the day every time she thought about the telephone call.

***

As expected, the helmets arrived in exactly one week. The price of each turned out to be just shy of $75, clearly not "big money" to the Clanford crowd. Being the good businesswoman that she was, Twink would mark them up to $500 per helmet for her "special" customers. As the pill poppers arrived for their weekly supply, the helmets were waiting on two large tables set up in the main sales room. Some were solid-colored, some multi-colored, and some hombre. All had geometric patterns of either matching or contrasting rhinestones across the helmet. No two were the same, which was important to these fashion-conscious women. Twink explained to each of them as they arrived that they would be required to purchase and wear one of the helmets as a safety precaution if they wished to continue to receive the pink pills. What went unsaid was the acknowledgment that these pills were causing medical havoc amongst these women, and Twink was clearly trying to defuse any possible liability risk. The women excitedly picked out their new head gear and left wearing them.

Over the next several days, across Clanford, bedazzled bike helmets became the latest craze in fashion accessories. Since the first group of women wearing them were notably the upper-class members of Butternut, the "regulars" in town became envious of this latest fashion trend. Word spread that Twink's Boutique was the place to buy them. Even at the exorbitant price of $500, women were clamoring for the helmets. Twink was adamant that all pill poppers receive at least one helmet (several had purchased more than one to coordinate with multiple outfits) before she allowed other interested women to buy.

Twink instructed Emma to place a new order with Mr. Pey Mi Naw for an additional 250 helmets. He responded to her email with his usual "you crazy lady" but delivered the goods as contracted. Twink moved the helmet operations to the alley door with a new sign so as not to disrupt her usual clientele in the boutique. Rumor had it that several women from Chicago had arrived to purchase helmets after seeing the new craze on social media. That migration would continue to increase over the subsequent weeks. The last piece of the puzzle was a visit by Twink to William at Butternut in order to pay him a little "skiff" to ignore, for the near future, the no-hat rule for the clubhouse.

Chapter Twenty-Three

Chaos! Chaos! Chaos!

Unexpected consequences would be an understatement to describe the chain of events that the tiny pink pills brought to the sleepy town of Clanford, IL. Over the course of three short months, Clanford residents had been exposed to wildly seizing women screaming and peeing in every imaginable public venue, the sudden and unexpected deaths of two longtime and prominent members of the community as well as a significant number of the town's women parading around in gaudy bike helmets when not even riding bikes! What had started out as a simple plan to help Twink sell her small-sized inventory had blossomed into a cult-like movement of weight-obsessed women who refused to give up their pharmaceutical du jour regardless of the serious side effects?

The chaos seemed to touch every aspect of daily life. Shelly, at Piggly Wiggly, had put in place some serious restrictions as well as high-priced fines for any medical episodes on and by the fancies. Although she could not completely discriminate against young moms, she put a no-bike helmet rule in place after seeing the new trend explode in town and in her store. This required women to doff their bedazzles and literally run through the store to complete their shopping, silently praying they did not fall prey to an unexpected episode. If, perchance, they did, there would be a thirty-day ban from the store as well as a $1,000 fine. Since The Pig was the main shopping venue in Clanford, a ban of any sort would require an almost one-hour-long roundtrip to Waukegan to get groceries. Shelly was quite pleased with herself because the frequency of emergencies had greatly decreased. Unfortunately, she received word from headquarters that her weekly volumes had been declining, except, of course, wine sales. Shelly was seriously thinking about calling it quits!

The postmaster at the main Clanford Post Office was seventy-five-year-old Dick Maynard. He had been a postal employee since age sixteen and a postmaster for twenty-three years. Although he was well past retirement eligibility, the district postmaster allowed him to skirt the retirement rules and stay on as long as he was able. Dick was a fixture in town. The first few episodes occurring in the post office lobby really rattled Dick, as well as the other postal employees. His first solution was to escort women, one by one, to the customer service desk after having every one form a line outside. This seemed to work for about a week, but after several had full PJs at the counter, he closed the lobby until further notice. Anyone needing in-person assistance was required to access a makeshift customer service window on the side of the building. Because only one postal employee was needed at the window, Dick was forced to lay off four seasoned peers temporarily. Needless to say, there was a growing resentment building for the wealthy women.

After repeated episodes across all religious denomination services, the respective pastors, priests, and rabbis met secretly to discuss a solution. Every one of them was well aware of the drop in collection basket giving during the COVID lockdown and didn't want to impose a similar moratorium on attendance. Many, if not all of the religious structures, churches and synagogues had been built at a time when "crying rooms" had been part of the architectural design. These rooms historically were sound proofed so unruly children could be seen and not heard when they decided to act up. Fr. O'Flannery from St. Thomas Aquinas Parish suggested that the ladies "at risk" should be required to take their seats in the crying rooms during services. Special mention was made that the collection baskets would be passed in those rooms as well.

The Shell Station across from the town square was the first to re-instate full-service gas pumping for any and all women customers. This service would require a mandatory twenty-dollar surcharge to the price of the customer's gas. This new service was the result of a very dangerous episode that occurred during the first weeks of the "medical emergencies." Mary Sullivan, a long-time Butternut member, was pumping high-octane gas into her Mercedes SL 500 convertible. A master at multi-tasking, she was talking on her phone with one hand while clutching the fuel nozzle as it rested in the car's fuel tank opening with her other. As her "episode" hit she dropped her phone but continued to have a tight grip on the gas nozzle. Her crescendo move of arms rising above her head did not include the signature splaying of fingers, which might have allowed her to drop the nozzle which had an automatic shut-off when the handle was not compressed. Instead, Ms. Sullivan held tight to the nozzle as she raised her arms, and the gas shot out in all directions as she seized right and left, backward and forwards. The spray of fuel covered the nearby cars, the front window and door of the mini-mart, and the two young boys filling bike tires at the air pump. As she finally hit the pinnacle of her orgasm, she screamed and dropped to the ground, finally letting loose the fuel handle. By this time some twenty gallons of gas had drenched herself as well as everything within twenty feet of the gas pump. As the staff rushed to help her as she laid covered in fuel, a small rainbow of liquid was seen streaming from between her legs as the fuel pooled above her pee-grenade. The station was closed for two full days as a special hazmat team was dispatched to remediate the fuel spill. Other gas station owners, upon hearing the news, imposed similar female customer rules. Costco took the added precaution of shutting down gas sales until further notice. All in all, the simple task of filling one's car with fuel was now much more expensive and time-consuming.

The Uber/Lyft industry was also hugely impacted by the women's episodes. Not unlike the houses of worship, the ride-share business was finally coming back after almost two years of COVID restrictions. Many of the drivers were from outside of Clanford and were driving as second jobs to supplement their hourly employment in the service industries. Many of the drivers intentionally hung out in close proximity to the Butternut Club in the evenings, counting on drunk members needing rides home to their affluent neighborhoods. It was steady work with usually healthy tips. What they hadn't bargained for were the orgasmic seizures that were occurring in the backseats of their Toyotas and Hyundais. The distractions that occurred from the episodes had caused several to crash their cars into parked cars and some trees. Luckily, there had been no injuries.

In cases where the driver was able to keep control of their automobiles, the backseat clean-up effort took them off the road for at least a full day. Many tried to refuse rides to and from the club, but their personal ratings were being negatively impacted. This resulted in many of the drivers just completely pulling out of the Clanford market. New drivers coming in from Waukegan soon learned why the market was so open and abandoned the town. The resultant ride-share desert in Clanford negatively impacted everyone, not just the Butternut crowd.

The local Chamber of Commerce scheduled an emergency small business owners meeting to hear for itself the complaints that were bubbling up from the local entrepreneurs. The Pine Tree Shoppe, a thirty-year pillar of the local business community, had lost over $10,000 of inventory when a woman seized directly in front of the Simon Pearce Glassware display of vases and tableware. She was made whole by the interloper, but re-ordering would take weeks, if not months. Callie's Candies had to trash a whole batch of saltwater taffy after a pee bomb ricocheted from the floor up the wall into the automatic taffy-pulling machine. Aside from the inventory loss, many children in the store were so traumatized Callie figured they would be adults before they entered the store again. Myron, the butcher, had limited business disruption because the glass on his refrigerated case was thick, and the traditional sawdust on the floor absorbed the urine of his seizing customer. Missy's Fabulous Florals moved her flowers onto the sidewalk in rubber buckets after a customer earlier in the week took out her whole wall display of glass vases and knick-knacks. The managers of The Gap and J Crew posted scan codes on their front doors, encouraging women to shop online. It wasn't that any of the shop owners feared not getting paid for their damaged goods. All the embarrassed culprits literally threw cash and credit cards at them to make everything right. Rather, they were most concerned that foot traffic would be permanently reduced by regular customers to avoid being witnesses to these upsetting sights. Something had to be done, the group demanded, to the head of the Chamber. The shop owners could not be transacting business in an environment where they feared for their own physical well-being and that of their regular customer base. Although Twink did not attend the meeting, the head of the Chamber was an old and dear friend of hers and relayed the sentiment of her fellow business owners. Twink feigned any knowledge of the events but had more than a few heart palpitations as she listened to him speak.

It was quite a conundrum for the town leaders, especially the mayor. Since the town had officially "re-opened," business was strong, people were out enjoying the public spaces, and money was flowing back into the town coffers through sales and restaurant taxes. Historically, it was the wealthy residents that fueled the economic activity in Clanford. Mayor Fray had no intention of insulting the Butternut crowd in any way that would negatively impact the renewed economic health of the city. It was a balancing act that was becoming more difficult by the day. She decided she would meet with the president of Butternut to discuss the delicate situation to find a mutually agreeable solution.

Interestingly enough, the current president of Butternut, Charles Martinson, was completely unaware of any of the goings on with the women members. Charles was seventy-eight years old and had been widowed from his longtime wife for more than five years. His position was mostly ceremonial because the real work of the club, budgets, operations, personnel, etc., were handled by the governing board of six members. Each year, two members were put up for re-election, thereby giving them each a three-year stint on the board.

Mayor Fray met with Charles at Butternut for lunch in a private dining room. She had asked that the meeting be low key and discreet. Charles didn't even know Clanford had a woman mayor until she appeared at the dining room door.

Charles spoke first, "Can I help you with something?" "Mr. Martinson, I'm Colleen Fray, mayor of Clanford."

"Wait, what the hell? We have a woman mayor? Nobody ever told me that!"

Colleen Fray was a little caught off guard by his aggressive remarks but didn't let them intimidate her.

"Yes, Mr. Martinson, I am a woman, and I am the mayor.

Probably a direct result of women getting the right to vote!"

The humor went right over his head, "Okay, Mrs. Mayor (Colleen was unmarried), what can I do for you today?"

Colleen took a seat and started in, "Mr. Martinson, I wanted to speak to you about a delicate situation going on with many of the women members of Butternut."

Given his age and the fact that he was born into the club, Charles had never been a fan of women having any membership positions in the club.

"What were these women doing now to screw things up," he thought to himself.

"To be honest, Mrs. Mayor, I don't think I like the thought of discussing a delicate issue about women. That's not something men of my generation do," Charles replied.

"I understand Mr. Martinson, but we really do need to have a discussion about some noticeable behavior of these club members that is negatively impacting the community as a whole."

"Okay, let me talk to the board about kicking them all out. I will get back to you as soon as I can."

Charles rose from the table, extended his hand for a farewell shake, and abruptly left. Mayor Flay was speechless as he left the dining room. She clearly had misjudged who she thought the decision maker, at least a lucid decision maker, was in the club. She would have to try another approach. She badly wanted a glass of wine but thought better of it and left. The chaos from these pills had literally impacted almost every aspect of Clanford's daily life. Things were certainly going to come to a head soon, very soon.

Chapter Twenty-Four

Every single woman in the pink pill poppers club at one time or another had experienced the full body orgasm and accompanying physical side effects. Many had very frequent episodes, and some women claimed daily eruptions. Although no one was keeping copious notes on the subject, talk amongst the Butternut crowd confirmed it was never a one-and-done event. In fact, there seemed to be a direct correlation between the amount of weight loss and the frequency of the orgasms. What seemed to be occurring was a self-perpetuating cycle within the women's group. The more weight they lost, the more orgasms occurred, which drove them to try and lose even more weight. The orgasms they experienced were fast becoming the most intense and pleasurable that they had ever had in their lives.

One of the young members of the group had created a Facebook page, by invitation only and very private, for the women who were taking the pills. The young mother who set up and monitored the forum was confident she had almost 100% participation. Many of the women were mere voyeurs, watching to see what the others were posting. Some were very descriptive of each "event," giving before, during, and after blow-by-blow details. As time went on, one of the most common threads amongst the posters was that they were quickly becoming addicted to the pleasure from the random and often overpowering episodes. In reality, they were so addicted that they were finding sex with their husbands to pale in comparison. (Could this also be the reason why so many vibrators had been secretly spirited away from the women's homes to the Thrift Store along with their "fat" clothes).

Although many of the women embraced their new sexual autonomy, not all were pleased with this unexpected development. Interestingly, the level of concern with this issue seemed to coalesce around age. For example, the younger women in their thirties and forties, tended to look for ways to suppress the strong reactions to continue strong relationships with their husbands. They were more concerned with the total connections they had in their relationships than just the hypersonic orgasms from the pills. Many of them posted possible solutions they were exploring that would limit the episodes, all the while maintaining the weight loss. On the other end of the age spectrum were the fifty-plus women. These women were much more engaged in embracing this newfound pleasure and were less concerned with the impact on marital relations. Many of them were either empty nesters or soon-to-be empty nesters who had fallen into a pattern of less inspired sex. They openly posted about the frequency, intensity, and after effects of their episodes. They seemed to revel in the details and were almost competitive in their descriptions compared to the other posters. The young women read these posts with amusement and some amazement. One of the younger women who was a regular on the forum nicknamed the mature group the "bangers." She joked that these women were reliving the intense banging experiences of their younger years as well as getting banged up with bumps and bruises from the physical demands of their repeated episodes. Some of the bangers embraced the nickname, while others were greatly insulted. One of the women, who was not at all enamored with the epithet, snapped back with a rebuttal badge for the younger women of "prudes." The battle lines were drawn, the bangers versus the prudes! The prudes posted suggestions for rekindling the romance with their spouses and pledging to minimize, if not eliminate, any future episodes. The bangers, on the other hand, bragged about gleefully cutting off their boorish husbands who only cared about golf, gin rummy, and drinking in the men's locker room at Butternut. They had no need, sexually, for them anymore.

Over the course of the spring and into summer, a growing number of the "prudes" were posting "home remedies" for how to thwart the episodes but remained on the pills. A small minority of the women were trying to figure out ways to stop or at least lessen the frequency of the attacks. With young children and houses to manage, they didn't have the time or patience for these distractions any longer. One woman did some internet research on homeopathic remedies for seizures, believing that the episodes were basically one version of what were many presentations of seizure symptoms. She read that some forms of childhood epilepsy were treated with high-calorie doses of heavy whipping cream. She was convinced a pint of the thick and sweet goop every morning was suppressing her own symptoms. Another woman claimed that the broccoli cheddar soup from Panera Bread was giving her the same relief. Could the high lactose/calorie content of the soup provide the same benefits as the whipping cream? This revelation seemed to pique the interest of many of the "enough is enough" crowd.

Panera Bread was a daily staple for a number of young moms in Clanford, including the Butternut women. They opened early and had great coffee and pastries as well as quick dinner options for their tightly scheduled children. The soup and sandwich menu was the go-to for many of these moms. Although the broccoli cheddar soup was the least healthy on the menu, it was a guilty pleasure for many. Jane Sandley was one of the prudes who had decided the pink pills had caused too much havoc for herself and her family. She had lost the impossibly stubborn twenty-five pounds of post-pregnancy weight in two months from the pills. She was now happy with her weight and had no interest in the orgasmic time bombs any longer. She was the one who posted about the Panera soup after experiencing firsthand, its redemptive qualities. She went into the local restaurant promptly at 11:30 a.m. each morning for a single order of soup. She often ate at one of the tables while perusing her social media feeds.

One particular morning, two other members of the Butternut crowd also came in for the soup. They were newbies to the soup solution and chose to dine in. They both acknowledged Jane with a smile as they passed by her on their way to a booth in the back. Jane continued to eat her soup and look at her phone. Within minutes, the restaurant went from the muted buzz of the lunch hour to dead silence as one of the two women began the familiar pattern of orgasmic surrender in the booth. Both had only taken a spoonful or two of the soup when the eruption began. Being seated in the booth had stifled a good portion of the physical gyrations but not the vocal. The seizing woman's lunch mate quickly exited her side of the booth and made her way to her friend to try and help mitigate the event. As the one woman seized, the other held her head back and literally poured the soup down her throat to try and end the event. This only served to exacerbate the situation as the now choking woman projectile puked the cheesy sludge across two tables of patrons as well as the ceiling and wall across the room. When she finally finished, she laid across the bench seat covered in her own vomit and soaked with pee. One of the stunned onlookers did notice that she had a huge smile on her face and was speaking some gibberish about coming or going or something to that effect.

The manager of the restaurant was livid. He came rushing out of the kitchen as the events unfolded. This had been the second such event at his restaurant in the past week, and he knew any continuation of this nonsense would definitely start impacting his business. He had an associate make a sign that was posted on the front door. "ABSOLUTELY NO DINING ROOM CONSUMPTION OF BROCCOLI CHEDDAR SOUP!" He ushered Jane and several other women out of the dining room and pointed to the recently placed sign to ensure they were aware of the newly posted rules.

Jane and many of the other prudes were undeterred. They decided that they would use the drive-thru window for future soup purchases. The very next day, the line grew long well before noon as it wrapped its way through the parking lot and out into the street. A Clanford police officer driving by moved his car to the outer lane and put his lights on to alert oncoming traffic to the full curbside lane. Many of the women in line, like the two the previous day, were new to the cheddar/broccoli remedy. Many thinking they would be getting several meals worth of calories in the single serving of soup, refrained from a morning meal. Probably not the best idea. As they approached the window to place their orders, several were anxious over the possibility of a "mobile" episode. Most women, after receiving their soup, quickly moved to a parking space to consume the healing broth. Although most ate and moved on without incident, several were not so lucky. The manager, now aware of the line and the high number of b/c soup orders, was closely watching the ladies make their way through the drive-thru window. Several of the prudes, who also parked in the lot, began eating the soup at the same time the eruptions began occurring. Not unlike the booth episode the day before, much of the recently consumed soup was violently expelled onto the interior of the windshield as the seatbelts held the victims secure. At least five high-priced cars (all with white leather inside of course) had the matching interior windshield adornment by the time the soup had sold out for the day. If the women had chosen tomato soup instead of cheddar, the resulting messes would have looked like a mass execution scene out of the Godfather movies.

While the prudes made great strides in detaching themselves from the whole shit show, the bangers continued to ramp up their activities. A small group became competitive against one another and were working hard to one-up their fellow seizers. What started out as a pretty innocent post by one of the bangers as to how many nights she had rebuffed her husband's amorous overtures quickly turned into the latest competition amongst the over-fifty crowd. Several had already talked jokingly amongst themselves about the level of frustration they were causing their husbands. The recent post, however, shouted "Game-On!" to the rest. What resulted was the inverse of a hunger-type strike whereby the bangers were depriving their husbands of all forms of sexual sustenance. Each day, the number of competitors in this dark game grew as they gleefully posted about another "dry" night for the hubbies.

Out of the one-hundred-plus Butternut women taking the pills, about sixty-five were confirmed bangers, which made sense because the total under fifty-year-old members in the club represented about thirty percent. The women in the minority, the prudes, were aghast at the newly posted competition. None of them would ever consider cutting off sex with their husbands because the pink pills produced a more powerful panty-pulsating pinnacle. They began posting the frequency of sex they were having to counter the banger's braggadocio. Who would ever have thought this would be the latest competition going (or not going) on in the bedrooms of Clanford's elite? The chaos that was playing out daily in public had now taken the bedrooms of the Butternut members hostage. The question became not if but when the pendulum would begin swinging back in the opposite direction as well as the velocity of that swing.

Chapter Twenty-Five

EVERY ACTION HAS AN EQUAL AND (OR WORSE!) OPPOSITE
REACTION

There were two things Butternut men never spoke about in the company of other men: how much money they had and how often they were having sex. Both topics paled in importance to golf handicaps and college alma mater football rankings. Unfortunately, recent events made the topic of sex one that needed to be discussed.

Mary Sullivan's husband, Wiggins Gilmore Sullivan III, "Wiggy" to friends, was the first to drop a casual non sequitur over gin rummy at Butternut when one of the players called last hand.

"Whoa, why last hand? Why so early? It's only 8:45 p.m."

The player who called out replied, "Wiggy, you know we never play past 8:00 p.m. What do you mean by why so early?"

Wiggy forged on, "Well, I can't go home this early. Mary is wearing me out in the boudoir, if you know what I mean. I need to take a break at some point."

Mary was the one who posted first about the sex drought she was imposing on poor Wiggy. Wiggy would stay wiggy instead of taking shape anytime soon. What Wiggy was trying to do, in a roundabout way, was see if others were also suffering from the same sexual snub. It worked.

Mike D'Mato, another septuagenarian who used multiple prescriptions and other devices to attain manly status, spoke first, "Good for you, Wiggy. Betty, for some reason, has cut me off completely. I don't think it's another guy; no one else would be stupid enough to pay the credit card bills she racks up every month."

Bob Murphy, another player, chimed in, "My wife is doing the same thing! It's been over a month, and she keeps telling me she has a headache. The woman has lost a ton of weight and looks as good as she did twenty years ago. For some reason, she just ain't interested anymore!"

The rest of the players at Wiggy's table, as well as others at nearby tables and at the bar who were listening in on the conversation, were gathering around Wiggy and complaining of the same droughts.

Wiggy's plan had worked. He finally confessed that he too, had been put out to pasture but wanted to figure out if it was just him. Several men who were in the locker room heard the rise of voices in the bar and walked in to investigate. More than twenty men in total were in the locker room bar now, all complaining of the same thing. Wiggy took a leadership role immediately.

"Something is going on here. These damn women must be in cahoots. I suggest we reach out to others in our circles and find out if there are any more guys being cut off. Get the word out. Any other men in our club who are suffering this same fate need to meet here tomorrow night to discuss some possible remedies. I will alert Charles Martinson about the meeting and ask him to join."

By 7 p.m. the next evening, the men's locker room bar was filled with more than fifty men. Charles Martinson had been briefed on the problem, and he spoke first, "Fellow distinguished members of Butternut, it seems some type of pox has been afflicted upon us by our significant others. As you all know, my dear wife has been gone for over five years, but I feel your pain and frustration. When Wiggy first spoke to me about this, I found it very interesting, given that I had an unexpected meeting with that woman Mayor, what's her name...earlier in the week. By the way, how many of you knew we had a goddam woman for a mayor in this town?"

The men all chuckled at the last remark. Charles continued, "She told me she needed to speak to me about a delicate situation that had arisen in town that somehow had something to do with Butternut women."

Another longtime member spoke next, "Charles, what the hell was the delicate situation? Are they cutting other men in town off from sex, too?"

This received a loud outburst of laughter from the men. Several one-off comments were shouted over the laughter that seemed to imply no one else would want to be having sex with their wives. Charles elaborated.

"We were supposed to have a nice lunch. Then this woman mayor starts right in on the "delicate" situation bullshit. I cut her off right away. I didn't want to know about any women's issues or situations, then or ever. I told her I'd talk to the board about kicking them all out. I remember years ago when women were only allowed in the dining rooms and bar if and only if they were with their husbands. Then, all hell broke loose when they got to play golf and tennis, and some even were allowed in as members. Members! At Butternut! Now they run around here like they own the place!"

Charles, who had been standing, took his seat.

Wiggy stood and responded, "Charles, I wished we knew what the delicate situation was that she wanted to talk about. Are you okay if I make a call to her to get more information? There must be some type of linkage between what they are doing in town and what they are doing to all of us."

Charles nodded his approval.

Wiggy continued, "You may have hit on something, Charles, when you told the mayor you might kick them all out. That's an interesting thought. My wife Mary would die a thousand deaths if she was cut off from the club and all her lady friends here. She practically lives here. If they put bunks in the women's locker room, we'd never see any of them."

One other member shouted out, "Would we get conjugal visits?"

Again, the room erupted in laughter. Wiggy went on, "I will call over to the mayor's office in the morning and set up a meeting. I need one of you gentlemen to figure out which women are actually members as opposed to being a member's spouse. I know there are some, but I think it's only a few. Do you all agree with the plan to restrict the club to all spouses if they continue with this game?"

Again, the room erupted with several replies, "Hell, yes!"

"Of course!"

"In a nano-second!" "Fight fire with fire!"

"Would save us all a ton of dough between club expenses and clothes!"

The D.S.B. (deadly semen backup) afflicted crowd was united in their conviction to cut off club access if the spouses didn't end the embargo.

They would meet again the next evening to hear the outcome of Wiggy's meeting with Mayor Fray and plot the next steps.

***

Mayor Fray's assistant directed Wiggy into the anterior office explaining the mayor was just finishing up a phone call. Wiggy, as usual, was dressed in a suit and tie. After about fifteen minutes of cooling his heels, he was ushered into the sprawling mayor's office adorned with portraits of past city leaders.

"Mr. Sullivan, what a pleasant surprise. I'm so happy you came over to meet with me. I'm assuming Charles asked you to reach out."

Wiggy replied, "Mayor Fray, please call me Wiggy." The good mayor suppressed a smile. "Yes, in fact Charles did ask me to follow up after your earlier lunch meeting. He said there was potentially some unfinished business that needed to be discussed."

In a little over a week, Colleen Fray was sitting across from a second, seventy-plus-year-old club rat, having to explain that some of his club members were wreaking havoc across her usually staid city. She debated in her head how exactly she should address the matter since using a "delicate situation" in her previous meeting sent Charles running for the door.

She began, "Mr. Sullivan..." She knew if she called him Wiggy, she wouldn't be able to contain her laughter. "Before I begin, by any chance are you on heart medication?"

Wiggy found this both amusing and potentially disturbing but answered quickly, "Not at all, fit as a fiddle as they say."

Colleen continued, "That's great. You look like quite a healthy man. The reason I reached out to Charles as President of Butternut is because it has been brought to my attention that several of your women members have been involved in, let's just say, some distressing episodes in numerous venues across the city."

Wiggy chimed in, "First, mayor, there are only a few women members, three actually in the whole club."

Colleen thought this quite misogynistic but continued her thoughts, "Thank you for that clarification..."

Wiggy interrupted, "Have the damn women been caught shoplifting or something like that?"

"No, Mr. Sullivan, the women have not been shoplifting, at least to my knowledge. It seems that more than a few women over the last two months, all apparently connected to your club, have been having, let's call them, medical emergencies in public."

Wiggy was confused, "What the hell kind of medical emergencies? No one has said anything about women from the club having medical emergencies! And why the hell would that be considered a problem if they need medical attention?"

Colleen was aware of the challenges she faced in trying to explain this to an older gentleman, but she dove in fully, "Mr. Sullivan, the medical emergencies are a little unorthodox."

Wiggy's face expressed his utter confusion as Colleen pressed on, "The women are seizing, screaming, and soiling themselves, all the while yelling to anyone that would listen that they are having a huge orgasm before dropping to the ground."

Colleen couldn't believe she had done it. She used the "O" word to a man who was old enough to be her father. Wiggy's face went pale, and Colleen was glad she had inquired about any heart issues. At first he sat in stoned silence, a noticeable bead of sweat gathering across his forehead. He cleared his throat as if to say something but remained silent. Colleen broke the uncomfortable moment.

"Mr. Sullivan, I'm sorry I had to be so descriptive, but you need to know the full extent of the problem. This has been happening multiple times a day for months and has literally caused businesses to change operating procedures. It has also put a huge strain on our Emergency Medical Services."

Wiggy was still processing the word orgasm. He hadn't heard it since the sex education portion of health class his freshman year of high school and it was uttered by a priest, not even the basketball coach who taught the rest of the health curriculum. Colleen grew worried as Wiggy remained silent.

"Mr. Sullivan, are you still with me? There seems to be something these women are doing or taking that is causing these episodes. When asked by the ER doctors, they remain silent. I'm concerned for their well-being as well as that of the rest of our citizens. Do you understand? Can you hear me? Would you like a glass of water?"

Wiggy hadn't heard a word, she said. He was still focusing on the word orgasm. What a weird but descriptive word. He knew what it meant for a guy to "orgasm," he was shooting his load, draining his snake, or just good old cumming. He never heard about a woman having an orgasm. How the hell did that even happen?

"Mr. Sullivan, are you okay? Can you hear me?"

Wiggy finally snapped back, "My dear, Mayor, you have given me some vital information that I will take back to Butternut leadership. I appreciate your candor and your concern for our women as well as the town's citizens. You were most kind to accept my meeting. Good day."

With that, Wiggy stood up and made his way toward the door. His legs were shaky, and he felt his shirt cling to his back from sweating. He nodded to the mayor's assistant and left the building. He sat in his car for more than thirty minutes, trying to regain his composure and process what the mayor had told him. Was Mary part of this crowd? Was she taking something, or had she become part of some weird orgy-like thing? Mary?? He thought about confronting her first but decided he would report back to the Butternut men that evening as planned.

***

By 6:30 p.m., the locker room bar was packed once again with the guys who were being cheated out of their manly rights. The room was buzzing in anticipation of Wiggy's report from his meeting with the mayor. Wiggy was sitting at the same table as Charles as well as several of the club board members. When he rose to speak, the room went silent.

"Gentlemen, this has been a trying but instructive day. As you all know, I met with Mayor Colleen Fray this morning to see what she was so desperate to make Charles aware of last week. She did not hesitate to give me a very descriptive outline of what some of our Butternut women have been accused of doing in public. It appears that some, not all, have been afflicted in public with some type of medical emergency that results in screaming, soiling themselves, and falling over, which all result in the "O" word."

The men looked at each other, and one called out, "Do you mean obnoxious?"

Another query, "Oppressive?" Yet another, "Overbearing?"

"No!" Wiggy yelled out. "The real "O" word!"

The men were still clueless. What was Wiggy talking about? "No, you idiots, orgasm, the "O" word, orgasm!!"

Stunned silence and then a giggle from the back of the room.

Wiggy continued, "The women are claiming they are having huge orgasms in public, in PUBLIC! Can you imagine this?"

One older gentleman spoke up, "Since when did women start having orgasms?"

Another guy chimed in immediately, "Since men started taking longer than three minutes to finish!"

This brought the house down, and another yelled out, "Three minutes, shoot, my best time is under two!"

Again, an eruption of laughter that wouldn't die down. Charles sat in stunned silence. Finally, Wiggy pounded his fist on the table, looking for order., "Gentlemen, please! This is a serious matter. Some of the women associated with our club, our wives, are besmirching the reputation of this esteemed institution. In public! This must come to an end immediately. Clearly, although I am fearful to inquire fully, there is a connection between these episodes and the Heisman our wives are giving to all of us. I suggest we all have a discussion with our wives TONIGHT and find out what is going on. If they refuse to give us full information, as they have apparently been doing to the ER doctor, then they get cut off immediately from club access and activities. Full expulsion!"

With Charles being present, the governing board members at the meeting had sufficient support of a quorum to approve the new measure. Any member whose wife was holding back on sex AND refused to give answers to the questions surrounding the public episodes would be banned from Butternut. An unprecedented but necessary action. The meeting adjourned with the reports from the members due back by noon the following day.

Without exception, every woman who was queried by their member husbands refused to give any details about the episodes and feigned complete ignorance on the matter. The names were tallied and given to Charles. He alerted William of the list without divulging any details and informed him of the newly imposed banishment. William was more than a little shocked but moved forward to execute the necessary steps. The total number of women was sixty-three.

***

It didn't take long for the full brunt of the banishment to be acknowledged. Women used the Butternut Club app daily to book tee times, court times, spa appointments, and lunches. It was the most frequented app on most of the women's phones. When the app failed to load, the frantic women started calling the club to speak with William. Being the coward that he was, he refused the phone calls, allowing them all to go to voicemail. Since several women were not getting any relief on the issue, they raced over to the club to try and figure out what was going on. Unfortunately for them, the transponders on their windshields that opened the gated entrance had been disabled as well. Within an hour, dozens of cars were blocking the entrance with the angry women still trying to reach William. When he finally appeared at the gate, he notified the women they were no longer welcome at the club and if they didn't clear the way for members, he would have no choice but to call the police to remove them. He also told them if they had any questions, they should speak to their husbands.

The women stood stunned. What the fuck was going on? How could they be refused entry to their beloved Butternut? Their pitiful lives revolved around the high society set at the club. They were the club! Some of the women upon realizing what this meant, started to cry. Others became angry and vowed revenge. One screamed out as William ascended the driveway back to the clubhouse.

"William, you candy-ass freak! I'm going to find you, and I'm going to murder you!"

Other women joined in on the chant, "Hey, hey, ho, ho, we'll kill William, blow by blow!"

Upon hearing this, William hurried into the clubhouse, worried he might need a police escort to leave work later in the day. The phone calls would not stop. Several women went home and grabbed their husbands' cars, thinking they could at least get past the gate to make a case for themselves, although they still hadn't figured out the reasons for the banishment. Two women made it through with this scheme but were "perp walked" back to the gate by the two large security men. Again, they were told to speak with their husbands.

When they were forced to leave the club, the women agreed to meet up at Starbucks immediately. As they filled the smallish cafe side of the coffee shop, they all ordered and commandeered the unoccupied tables and chairs into a grouping. The last thing these women needed was caffeine. As they sat together, Angela O'Brien took the leadership role. She was the one who started the threats against William, and she was fuming mad.

"I want to start out by asking if anyone thinks they might do harm themselves." Everyone looked at each other, and when no one spoke up, she continued, "Okay, good. Last night, my husband Bob asked me at dinner about all the public episodes, and I told him that I didn't know what he was talking about. Did anyone else have a similar conversation last night?"

To a tee, they each raised their hands. Angela continued, "Okay, so we have a common thread here. Our mother fucking husbands are behind all of this! What do they think they are going to accomplish with this? Who the fuck do they think they are?"

From the back of the room came a small voice, "The members, they not only think, but they also know they are the members. We are just the arm candy. We have no rights to the club unless they give them to us. We are screwed!"

Another voice from the back of the room added, "Look, ladies, we may have brought this on ourselves. I know most of you, like me, have been denying these guys any pussy. Trust me, I get it. They just don't come close to what I get from those heavenly pills! But maybe our little competition pushed them a little too hard, no pun intended. Maybe we all go home, open a nice bottle of wine, and show them some lovin'. Then, by tomorrow, we will be back in the club."

Mary Sullivan, who had sat quietly, stood up and started to scream, "Are you fucking kidding me? Do you want to give them some sex so we get back into the club? Are you crazy? Who in the hell would trade sex for things?"

The whole group burst out laughing, which annoyed Mary to no end.

Another woman spoke up, "Where the hell have you been, Mary? This is our world, and welcome to it. Although we think we are better than all the people on the other side of the Butternut gate, we aren't. We were just smart enough or lucky enough, or maybe both, to marry our way in.

I don't think there are more than a few women members in the entire membership, and they are all long-time legacies. We pushed too hard, thinking we had the upper hand, and we got pushed back. You all can do what you want, but I know what I'm doing. I will see you girls later!"

With that, she exited Starbucks. Several other women began to leave as well, and the crowd quickly thinned out. Mary drove home but found the house empty. Wiggy, for sure, was either on the golf course or in the locker room playing cards. She would wait. Oh boy, would she wait for him to come home. At a little after 8:30 p.m., Wiggy directed his slightly buzzed body through the door and into his favorite chair in the family room. Mary was lying in wait.

"You big asshole!" she started in. "Who the fuck do you and your buddies think you are for cutting all of your wives off from the club?"

Wiggy was caught off guard but not too drunk to focus on the aggressive query, "Who the fuck do you and your girl buddies think you are to cut your husbands all off from sex? Do you think that was some kind of game? Did you all do not think we would put two and two together?"

Mary was disarmed by his anger and his points. When she tried to respond, he shouted over her.

"I had to sit in Mayor Colleen Fray's office this week and hear about how all of you Butternut women were pissing yourselves in public and screaming about having orgasms. What the fuck is that all about? How the fuck are you having an orgasm in public? Not one of you was honest enough to tell us, when we directly asked, what was going on while the whole reputation of the club was getting sucked into the sewer!"

Mary was really on her back foot now after hearing that the mayor was aware of and questioning all the episodes. Maybe things had gotten out of hand. Maybe the silly competition and the disregard for their husbands and the wider Clanford community was really a game gone badly wrong.

Wiggy stood and pointed his finger aggressively at Mary, "Here's the deal! Until you and all the other women come clean on what is going on, there will be no more days for any of you at the club. If you think holding out on me was a game, think again. I moved my things into the guest room. Trust me, I won't come looking for any loving from you anytime soon!"

Wiggy stood up and went upstairs to his new bedtime accommodations. Mary plopped down onto the sofa and tried to make sense of what had just unfolded. The bangers, who thought they had the upper hand, had essentially just banged themselves. Mary in particular, not only firebombed her daily existence, but she also firebombed her marriage. The little pink pill made her lose more than just her wide ass.

Chapter Twenty-Six

All Roads Lead to Twink

Like many successful women, Twink was a creature of habit and schedule. She rose at the same time every day, had her cigarettes and coffees at roughly the same intervals, and kept a tight calendar for both personal and business appointments. There was little, if any, variation in her planned activities on any given day.

This day would, unfortunately, be different. Twink usually arrived promptly at 9:40 a.m., twenty minutes ahead of opening time at her boutique. She started the water kettle for her instant coffee, lit a Virginia Slim, and turned on all the lights. Next, she opened her laptop computer to her calendar to see who she would be expecting and at what time. The schedule looked busier than usual. Several Chicago women who had made their way to Clanford for the bedazzled helmets had peeked their heads into the boutique and liked what they saw.

They reached out to Twink afterward and set up morning appointments to visit her shop. There were five women in total, which were more bodies than Twink typically saw at any one time. She alerted Emma that she would need her to work the entire day.

At exactly 10 a.m., the electronic buzzer that announced customers into the boutique sounded as the door opened. Twink, believing it was the

Chicago crowd arriving early (they were scheduled from 10:30 a.m. until 1 p.m.), was a little shocked when an unknown man entered her realm. Few men ever, especially unaccompanied by a wife or girlfriend, entered her boutique. Twink tried hard to identify him but was at a complete loss. Possibly a local husband looking for a gift.

She welcomed him in, "Good morning! Welcome to Twink's High Fashion Boutique. How may I help you?"

The gentleman smiled and spoke, "I'm looking for Ms. Buston-Ford."

Twink responded graciously, "I'm she, but please call me Twink."

The gentleman smiled again and introduced himself, "I'm Dr. Lovejoy, the head of emergency medicine at St. Gerard's. I hope I'm not imposing coming in without an appointment, but I needed a few minutes of your time to discuss a pressing matter."

Twink immediately tightened her grip on her cup of Néscafe but otherwise did not reveal the sense of panic that was rising within her. No doubt his arrival was directly related to the weight loss pills. She would be polite but try and lose him as quickly as possible.

"Dr. Lovejoy, it is a pleasure to meet you. I hear nothing but great things about you from my position on the St. Gerard's Foundation Board. Your emergency room is a true model for others throughout the country. Unfortunately, sir, I have a heavily scheduled morning and afternoon, so it would be impossible to spend time with you, especially coming in unannounced."

Dr. Lovejoy was undeterred. "I apologize again for not calling ahead, but I was hoping just to get a few minutes of your time. As I mentioned earlier, it is a very pressing matter, one that I believe is impacting a great number of your clients. It will only take a minute, and it looks like no one else requires your attention at this moment."

Twink tried to remain gracious but was being backed into a corner. Any attempt to push him away, she thought, would reveal a concerted effort to avoid him. She smiled again and welcomed him to sit down.

"Dr. Lovejoy, I can only promise you five, maybe ten minutes at most. Please have a seat and tell me what this VERY PRESSING matter is all about."

Lovejoy took a seat and started right in, "Twink, over the last several months, more than thirty women have presented themselves at the ER with the same odd symptoms of seizures, incontinence, and screaming, all occurring in very public venues. Most of these women have suffered serious falls from these events, and some even concussions. Oddly, when we have pressed them about any change in their medical or physical conditions prior to these episodes, they have all been extremely evasive. Once they are examined, they all have signed themselves out against the recommendation of myself as well as the other attending physicians. After some investigation, I confirmed that all the women, given their home addresses in affluent neighborhoods, appear to be members of Butternut Country Club. When I approached the general manager there to have a discussion, I was immediately turned away. That place is run like Fort Knox. I went back to the drawing board and looked more closely at all of their files, trying to discern any type of pattern for these women ahead of their medical emergencies. I could find nothing. One evening when the ER was fairly quiet, I was sharing my frustration of the dead-end research with several of the other staff members. One of my most seasoned and senior nurses told me that I was missing the obvious. She, like me, had been present when many of these women had arrived, especially the day so many came in from the Piggly Wiggly. She was an astute and curious medical professional. What was most interesting to her, was the fact that all the women that arrived had been well dressed, in very expensive outfits. Notably expensive, in fact. As a man, I clearly did not pick up on that fact, but she and the other nurses all confirmed it was true. That is why I am here this morning. When I've asked around about where the wealthy women of Clanford buy their expensive clothing, I was directed to you."

Twink interrupted him, "Good doctor, that is all well and good and a very interesting detective story, but I don't understand what I have to do with any of this. Even if I sold them their outfits, do you think there is some direct cause-and-effect relationship here? I struggle to see why you are even bothering me with this."

Lovejoy continued, "I'm not saying the outfits caused the medical episodes. I'm trying to determine a common relationship between these women and their seizures. I have a duty in my position to alert the community to potential medical threats. All these episodes have been extremely disruptive and potentially harmful to innocent bystanders. I need to know what is behind all of this. The affected women not talking makes me even more suspect that some type of illicit pharmaceutical is being used. Do you have any knowledge of such a thing?"

Twink worked hard to keep her composure and took a long drag on her second cigarette of the meeting.

As she blew the smoke upward, she replied, "Dr. Lovejoy, I am flattered that you think I have the investigative know-how to help you solve your mystery, but unfortunately, I have nothing to add. My clients are discreet, wealthy women whom I treat with respect. I do not ask, nor am I told, about their medical conditions, love lives, or any other personal matter. I was not raised in such a manner, and I do not delve into others' personal lives. I dress women with the latest and most fashionable outfits. That's what I do. Staying out of personal lives has allowed me to be a trusted proprietor to Clanford's wealthiest."

At just that point in time, Emma emerged from the workroom after coming in through the alley door. Twink used her arrival as the perfect time to cut off any further discussions.

"Dr. Lovejoy, as I said, I have a very busy schedule today. I wish I could be more helpful, but unfortunately, I don't have any information for you. Good day."

Lovejoy rose from his chair and followed Twink to the front door, which she was holding open for him. He put out his hand and thanked her for her time. As he walked away, he wasn't completely sure if she was being truthful or not. Unfortunately, another dead end for him.

Emma was just about to ask Twink what the early morning meeting with the man was all about when the Chicago crowd arrived at the door. Emma noticed Twink was a little unsteady when the gentleman left but quickly regained her composure for the new potential clients. A little internet search on the women's names who had scheduled the appointments revealed addresses in the wealthiest neighborhoods of Winnetka and Kenilworth. Twink would give them her full attention.

***

Emma was cleaning up the demitasse cups and small plates from the coffee and finger sandwiches Twink had hurriedly ordered when she realized her Chicago clients were real buyers. She and Twink spent over three hours with them, and their combined purchases totaled over $30,000. An unexpected but delightful day's haul. Just as Twink was about to fill Emma in on her meeting with Dr. Lovejoy, the door chimed again, and another unexpected guest was entering the boutique. This time, it was Mayor Coleen Fray. Twink looked up and immediately felt a pang of regret embrace her. Colleen Fray had never been a client of Twink's, although they knew each other from several boards. Despite this she greeted her in her usual friendly manner.

"Mayor Fray, what an unexpected surprise to see you. Do come in."

"Twink, you know it's Colleen, not Mayor Fray." They both smiled and shook hands.

Twink continued, "Colleen, have you met one of my protégés, Emma Mayfield? Emma has been working with me since early February."

Colleen moved toward Emma and shook her hand as well, "Emma, the pleasure is all mine. Twink, dear, is there somewhere where we could talk privately for just a few minutes?"

Twink's anxiety level was raised a notch as she turned toward Emma.

"Emma, could you please run to the UPS store and purchase several of the larger shipping boxes please? We need to send the Winnetka women their purchases by the end of the day."

Emma smiled and left on her errand. Twink returned her attention to Colleen, "Colleen, now that Emma has gone, we can speak freely here, although I must warn you, I have an appointment in fifteen minutes, so you will have to be brief."

In reality, there was no appointment on Twink's calendar. Twink was trying to minimize time with Colleen because she felt in her bones that the topic would revolve around the pink pills. Colleen wasted no time in revealing the reasons for her call.

"Twink, I don't know if you are aware of it or not, but over the last several months, there have been some strange episodes in Clanford where more than a few women have been having seizures in public. To be specific, they are wild seizures with full body gyrations, screaming, moaning, and eventually collapsing and soiling themselves. These have not been isolated instances. This scene has been replayed over thirty times in public, and I don't even know if I'm aware of them all."

Twink interrupted, "Colleen, I have heard a few rumblings about these things, but I am curious as to why you are here to discuss them with me."

Colleen continued, "Twink, I'm talking to you because it appears that all these women are part of the Butternut Country Club community. To a one, I believe they are also all clients of your boutique. I was hoping you might be aware of something that is going on with them that is causing all these emergency medical issues. When I spoke to Dr. Lovejoy at St. Gerard's ER, he told me that they were all evasive when asked about any changes in their diet or physical activity. It just doesn't make sense why they won't be more forthcoming. I tried to have a discussion with two of the senior gentlemen from the club, but that seems to be going nowhere. In my own mind, I believe there is some type of drug that these wealthy women are taking recreationally, and it's screwing with their systems."

Twink was hearing for the second time in a little over five hours from senior members of the Clanford community that they believed the women's strange behavior was the result of some type of drug use. The fact that they were questioning her meant that they both believed she had at least some knowledge, if not some level of involvement in this supposed illicit drug trafficking. She could hardly believe what was going on. She knew she couldn't show any outward concern or, heaven forbid, guilt, so she refocused and responded, replaying the speech she had given Dr. Lovejoy hours earlier, "Colleen, I'm not sure why you've come to me with this. I would assume if any of this were true, it would be considered a personal issue for these women. As you know, I cater to a very wealthy clientele where discretion is an important aspect of gaining and retaining these women's trust and business. I have never, in almost forty years of business in this boutique, ever engaged in, solicited, or repeated any private information, gossip, or innuendo. I am slightly insulted that you would come to me with your concerns."

Twink decided mid-sentence to move to the role of victim to deflect any further interrogation. It seems to have worked.

"Twink, please don't take this the wrong way. I would never imply that you were a party to any of this. I was just hoping that maybe you had heard something from your clients that would be useful to me in trying to put an end to all this nonsense. I would never expect you to reveal something said in confidence or even imply you had been given personal information from your clients. Maybe I didn't handle this in the best way. I will let you get back to work. I can see myself out."

With that, Colleen Fray left the boutique and headed back to her office. Twink grabbed her cigarette case immediately and pulled out her elongated nicotine fix. She sat for what seemed like a long time until Emma's return prompted her to refocus on the problem at hand.

"Emma, we need to talk. There seems to be..."

Before she could finish, the door chime alerted them both that another customer was entering the boutique. Twink and Emma looked quickly toward the door and saw Mary Sullivan and two other pill clients rush in. All three appeared completely out of sorts unkempt, and each was wearing mismatched (gasp!) sweatshirts and pants. Twink almost didn't recognize them. Mary approached Twink immediately and grabbed both of her hands.

"Twink, dearest Twink, the unthinkable has happened! Catastrophe has struck! I have a hard time even uttering the words!"

Twink shook loose of her sweaty grasp and told Mary to pull herself together.

"Mary, what the hell is going on?" Twink was clearly agitated and still reeling from the two earlier meetings because she never swore in public. She continued, "What has happened that is so catastrophic? Has someone died? Has someone been seriously injured or diagnosed with a dreadful disease?"

Mary shook her head, holding back tears. "Twink, much worse than any of those things. I can hardly speak the words...TWINK!!! We have been banned from Butternut!!! We aren't allowed to go back to the club, EVER!!!! YOU MUST HELP US !!!!"

With that, the onslaught of tears and shaking ensued. Mary was a mess, and her two companions were inconsolable as well. The compilation of the day's events caused Twink to finally lose her temper.

"Ladies!! Pull yourselves together! I need to know what is going on! I can't help you if I don't know why you've been banned by the club!"

Mary began to speak in a halting, childlike cadence, "Some...of...us..."

Twink finally exploded, "For god's sake, Mary, pull your shit together or leave immediately. I cannot suffer this nonsense one minute longer!"

Mary got the message and started to calm down, "Some of us thought it would be funny to have a contest of how long we could cut our husbands off from sex..."

Twink was enraged, "What exactly do you mean by that???"

Mary waved both hands to get Twink to listen to the whole story, "The pills were giving us these awesome orgasms, Twink. We found them much better than the sex with our husbands. You know how competitive some of the ladies at the club are. So, we started a contest to see who could keep their husbands out of the bedroom the longest and…"

Mary suddenly realized as she said the words how twisted everything sounded. She was bracing herself for another verbal blow from Twink, but surprisingly, it didn't come.

Twink calmly said, "So, the husbands compared notes and figured out what was going on. To be honest with you ladies, I don't blame them one bit for taking the club away from you. What you did is unforgivable. You put yourselves ahead of your husbands, and you did it all in the name of competition. It's pathetic. I suggest you all go home and show your husbands a little more love and a lot more respect. Maybe they will then lift the ban."

Mary felt ashamed but knew she had to tell Twink the whole story, "Twink, there is something else. Apparently, the mayor reached out to Charles Martinson at Butternut about all of the public episodes that we have all had as a result of the pills. He couldn't handle the news, and my husband, Wiggy, ended up having to meet with her. She told him very frankly that the Butternut women's episodes were disrupting daily life for everyone in Clanford and that he needed to figure out how to put an end to it. William at Butternut was told that until they were told why these episodes were only occurring to the Butternut ladies, no one would be readmitted. They are expecting us to tell them we've been taking the crazy pills."

Twink's blood pressure began to rise again, "Absolutely not! You cannot tell anyone about these pills! I've denied any knowledge of them twice today to both Dr. Lovejoy and Mayor Fray. I will not be caught in a mistruth to help you get your butts back in good graces at Butternut. You can and should explain your competition to your husbands. That's the right thing to do. I will reach out to Charles and William and have my own discussion with them. Until then, NOT A WORD ABOUT THE PILLS TO ANYONE! DO YOU UNDERSTAND??"

All three women sheepishly agreed. Twink opened the front door as a signal for them to leave. On the way out, Mary thanked Twink and told her she would be indebted to her forever. Once they were gone, Twink immediately looked for her cigarette case. She sat at her desk chair, lit up, and pushed herself back into a reclining position. Emma watched from nearby, half afraid to speak after having watched the unfolding of events. Twink took down half the cigarette in less than a minute.

Once nicotine revived, she called out to Emma, "Emma, darling, please phone your wonderful husband and have him meet us here immediately. There are several pressing issues that the three of us must discuss. You do understand what immediately means, correct?"

The sarcasm was not lost on Emma, who "immediately" phoned Craig and told him his presence was required "immediately" at the boutique. Emma made herself busy in the showroom while awaiting his arrival.

***

When Craig walked in, he knew immediately a serious discussion was about to take place. Emma gave a halfhearted smile, and Twink sat at the desk looking intently at nothing in particular on the wall in front of her.

Twink spoke first, "Craig and Emma, let's all sit at the round table in the showroom where we can see each other clearly."

"Whoa," thought Craig. "Why does she need to be seeing us clearly? Is she sizing up how difficult it will be to dispose of the bodies?"

The three moved to the table and sat down.

Twink continued, "During the course of this day, I have been visited by two individuals separately and a group of three women. All these unplanned meetings had to do with events revolving around our little subscription business..."

Craig tried to interrupt but immediately thought better of it after Twink shouted at him, "SILENCE! You will keep your mouth closed until I am finished."

Both Emma and Craig knew now that something serious was going down.

"The two individuals I met with were Dr. Lovejoy, who runs St. Gerard's ER, and Mayor, yes Mayor, Colleen Fray. Both were looking to me to provide them some level of information as to why a group of Butternut women were having violent, sexually driven episodes across the city of Clanford. For some reason, they felt that I could provide some insight. For some reason, they thought I might be able to help eradicate the problem. For some reason, they are linking me, Twink Buston-Ford, a long-time pillar of the Clanford community, with all these events. The third group that called on me today were some of the pill poppers who have been banned from Butternut for bad behavior, also seeking my help. IT'S OVER!! IT'S OVER!! Starting here and now, we stop this madness and put our little business OUT OF BUSINESS!!"

Twink paused to take another long drag of her cigarette. Craig and Emma smartly remained silent.

Twink continued, "I don't want to risk any further medical issues by making the women go cold turkey. Instead, Emma, you will reduce next week's allotment to three pills from the usual four the following week to one pill, and then we will be done. I don't care, Craig, if we are leaving money on the table! You have made millions, and enough is enough. Emma, I want you to send out an email telling the women that we can no longer obtain the pills from our supplier. Explain the weaning process and then destroy the email list and chain. Any and all linkages of the three of us to the business must be destroyed."

Craig wanted to ask if the lower dose allotments would still be priced the same, but he knew better. Emma understood her marching orders and immediately pulled out her laptop to get started on the email. She would portion out the pills for the next two weeks and have everything ready by the end of the day. Then, she would destroy all records of the clients. The next step after receiving the final payment from the ladies would be to record the final revenues, tally all expenses, and file a final tax return for OMG! The last step would be to dissolve the corporation.

***

The Butternut piece of the puzzle was Charles Martinson, and Twink would handle that. Twink called Charles on his cell phone. Prior to her death, Charles' wife was a dear friend to Twink. After her passing, Charles and Twink stayed in contact as a means of helping each other through the grieving process. Charles always picked up Twink's calls. He agreed to meet her at her home for a cocktail at 7 p.m. If any day's end required a cocktail, it was this day.

Twink and Charles sat on the bluestone patio at the back of Twink's home. With martinis in hand, they both spoke about the perennial gardens that graced Twink's large and well-manicured yard. Both, unbeknownst to the other, were closet gardeners who had a great admiration for the beauty of flowers. Once Charles seemed fully at ease, Twink began to "delicately" describe the "situations" that had occurred regarding some of the Butternut women. She told him that during the COVID lockdowns, many of the women had not felt as healthy as before because of the limitations placed on everyone. Some of them decided to take a new "vitamin" that was offered by what they thought was a reputable source but later found was not. Some, although not all the women, had some uncomfortable side effects that caused them to become slightly ill in public. Once these events were shared with others taking the vitamins, they all agreed to stop. The vitamins would work their way through the women's systems in short order, and all would be resolved. This was just an unfortunate set of events that occurred to the women who wanted to make themselves healthier for their husbands and, most importantly, their children. As usual, no good deed went unpunished for these selfless wives and mothers!

Twink further explained to Charles that she was aware of the restrictions placed on some of the women at Butternut because of these minor inconveniences. She was further aware that two conditions had to be met for them to grace the grounds once again happily at the club. Although she wasn't aware of any details regarding the condition these women's husbands had imposed (untruth), she was aware that the other condition was that William would be made comfortable that the public issues with the women had been addressed and resolved. Twink would be happy to meet with William the following morning, on Charles' approval of course, to alert him that condition number two had been met. A second martini convinced Charles that he no longer had the need to worry and that he would not expect any repeat visits from the goddam woman mayor. Twink promised!

Chapter Twenty-Seven

The last week of July found Clanford in a much more serene condition than the last week of June. Peace had been made in the bedrooms of almost all of the bangers (with the exception of Mary and Wiggy, who were in the throes of a divorce), and the repentant women were once again allowed the privileges of the club. Once consumption of the pink pills ended, the women ceased the orgasmic eruptions and found great pleasure in regular marital relations. Most of the women were able to retain the weight lost on the pills after the first month and were hopeful they would continue to do so. All of those banished from the club quickly forgot the fine line between being on the inside versus the outside and looked down, once again, on everyone they considered to be of a lower social ranking. Fluffy retained her position as Women's Auxiliary Board President and iced out Clare Johnson for good.

Twink spent much of the month traveling to Europe and New York to fill her boutique with fall and winter fashions. She was able to spend less time on this effort, given she no longer needed to search out the wacky and flamboyant outfits for Ann Franklin. Twink was now sixty-five and beginning to feel the challenge of such a heavy and constant workload. She decided that after Emma's baby was born in August, she would offer her a full partnership in her business. Over the next five years she would train Emma in the finer points of running a premier haute couture operation. When Emma's baby reached kindergarten age, Twink would be seventy years old. She would then begin to dial back her work schedule and slowly transition the business to the only woman she felt capable of upholding her high standards. She also decided to begin distribution of her vast wealth to several charitable trusts and organizations, at the top of the list was the SBH convent.

The Mayfields were once again enjoying the benefits of a stable, loving, and debt-free household. After all tax payments, Craig and Emma owned their home and cars outright and had current bank balances in excess of six million dollars. Craig was becoming stir-crazy but agreed to postpone any job search until the following January so he could help Emma with the boys after the new baby's arrival. Their new level of wealth had been shared with both sets of their parents, allowing them all to retire. Craig was trying to coax his parents to move to Clanford with the promise of a new home for them so they could be closer to their growing gaggle of grandchildren. With just two weeks to her due date, Emma was more relaxed and happier than she had been in many years.

William replaced Tad with a young but less olfactory-focused locker room attendant. Ted and Ana Brank received word from William that they would receive a $100,000 life insurance payment from a policy Tad had put in place through the Butternut Human Resources office before his death. Shelly at Piggly Wiggly had decided not to retire and was still terrorizing the small children of the fancies whenever possible. After some severe bouts of coughing, Pussy's legal guardian took her to the Clanford Veterinarian Clinic for observation. Sadly, Pussy was diagnosed with a malignant and terminal lung tumor that was most likely the result of inhaling Ann's final putrid soul explosion. Pussy would direct that her vast wealth be donated to the Wild Birds Unlimited Foundation upon her death. Charles decided it was about time to put himself back into the dating world and thought he might invite that goddam woman mayor to dinner at Butternut. Speaking of the mayor, Colleen Fray was indicted by a grand jury on six counts of corruption of an elected official stemming from her reopening edict. Most likely political payback from the butt-hurt governor. After watching one of his lifelong personal heroes, Bruce Jenner, transition to a woman, Dr. Lovejoy decided he would follow in his/her footsteps and become a Sisters of the Blessed Humility novitiate. Now in her mid-eighties (and after multiple back surgeries), the former Sister Mary Tits was still riding Harleys with her fourth husband in Camden, New Jersey. Sadly, she and Twink would never meet each other despite their mother/daughter relationship.

All is calm. All is bright!

Chapter Twenty-Eight
The Wizard of Oz!

During his "paternity leave," Craig had been investigating different areas in the finance world to direct his job search in early January. Commercial real estate was immediately taken off the list, given his past experiences as well as the changing work dynamic post- COVID. Healthcare always seemed like a strong area, given the aging population and the longer expected life spans of most people. Within healthcare, he had paid considerable attention to the weight loss arena. Obviously, his recent experience had shown that the weight loss industry was almost completely price inelastic. Proven effective weight loss plans and supplements could charge just about any price.

At the same time, Craig had also taken notice of the growing importance of tele-health companies. Because of the COVID lockdowns, most insurance companies had approved tele-health visits as reimbursable expenses. This was truly going to change the face of how health care would be delivered in the future. Was there a way to combine weight loss and tele-health? If so, Craig figured it would be an investment home run.

One day, while searching the internet for new weight loss companies and schemes, he came across an article about a Diabetic drug that had shown, as its main side effect, considerable weight loss in the patients who were using it. The drug was called Ozempic and was produced by a pharmaceutical company named Novo Nordisk. What if he could create a tele-health company with doctors on staff (much like the company's pitching Viagra online) that could discreetly provide patients with this drug to be used solely for weight loss? Everything could be covered by insurance and sent to the patients via the mail. Genius!

What if he could build a national, on second thought, an international business that would bring this drug to fatties everywhere? This would be a low-capital investment, low-risk and high-return business. He quickly realized, however, that he would have to be one of the first to market because others would be able to copy his idea fairly easily. Unlike the man-up pills, he would make billions rather than just millions of dollars. He patted himself on the back as he sketched out the rough outline of a business plan. He dubbed his plan "The Wizard of Oz." Fat shots for everyone!

What could possibly go wrong??